Martin Shannon was born in Paisley in 1965, the youngest of three brothers.
He studied Philosophy at Glasgow University before beginning a career in journalism.
He lives in Aberdeen.

The Tin Man

The Tin Man
Martin Shannon

First published by

119

303a The Pentagon Centre
36 Washington Street
GLASGOW
G3 8AZ
Tel: 0141-204-1109
Fax: 0141-221-5363
E-mail: info@nwp.sol.co.uk
http://www.11-9.co.uk

© Martin Shannon, 2000

A catalogue record for this book is available from the British Library.

THE SCOTTISH **ARTS** COUNCIL
National Lottery Fund

11:9 is funded by the Scottish Arts Council National Lottery Fund.

Efforts have been made to contact copyright holders of the material in this book. If any copyright has been overlooked, holders are invited to contact the publishers.

ISBN 1-903238-11-0
Typeset in Utopia
Designed by Mark Blackadder
Printed by WS Bookwell, Finland

For Julia and Rosie

What's best for Georgie?

It's neither night nor morning but the lowest ebb, when the patched-up crises of the daytime weep easily into emergency. I'm scrabbling for her mother's words, once tender now estranged, preserved in a large manilla envelope. I know where to look. The envelope has a presence of its own. I'm aware of it sometimes when I'm cooking or watching tv. Lying in the dark at the bottom of a cardboard box full of old junk in a corner of the wardrobe. Waiting for me. Mocking me with my own history.

I empty the box onto the bed and the personal debris from 33 years' selfish drag on the earth's finite resources scatters over the duvet. Bureaucratic litter – Social Security, Abbey National, Bank of Scotland, Institute of Business and Entrepreneurship, and the like – is carelessly filed here among the ticket stubs and match programmes; small change in francs and pesetas; a couple of early school jotters; Elastoplasts; condoms; buttons; plectrums; paper clips; dried out felt tips; a blood donor card; a key ring; half-completed courses of prescribed placebos for hypochondria; expired guarantees; fabric fluff and accumulated dust. The ripped and ragged manilla envelope itself, bursting with mawkish sentiment which didn't seem mawkish then, spilling its guts onto the bed: love letters; love notes; love tokens, too late to cash in. All from the girl I married and no one else. Souvenirs of the only previous significant romance had long since been dumped and discarded in a demonstration of monogamous commitment. I'd have read her letters again, looking for cryptic clues on what could have gone wrong but I'm diverted, sifting through the wreckage, by a lock of baby's black, black hair in a clear plastic money bag; the master copy of our wedding video like a black box flight recorder; and – unearthed by happy accident at this opportune moment – my survival kit.

• • • • • • • • • • • • • • • • •

Aberdeen is freezing already and it's only September. I mean *really* freezing. The wind-chill factor alone would keep me indoors all weekend but I've established a Saturday routine I feel compelled to fulfil, that at least takes me away from the tv for a couple of hours. I walk down George Street, through the Bon Accord Centre, through the St Nicholas Centre and way up Union Street past the Music Hall to where the bookshops face each other on either side of the road, and all the way back again. I try to vary this and go into different shops now and again. Y'know, maybe one week HMV, Dillons, Tesco; the next week Virgin, Waterstone's, Somerfield; that sort of thing. Keeps it interesting. I worry people from the Aberdeen Institute of Business and Entrepreneurship might see me and realize this is all I do when I'm not there trying to look busy, writing obscure press releases in front of a computer screen. They might pity me and that's the last thing I want right now, thank you very much. I don't want people feeling sorry for me, for God's sake. It would be so embarrassing. I don't want people even to notice me living here in relationship limbo. Anyway, there's something almost heroic in abject isolation, isn't there? It's like being a castaway on a desert island but still managing to get by, building a fire, building a shelter, building a kind of life. Just getting by, getting on with things. Subsistence living. Surviving.

It's been a year since Georgie, aged four then, first asked her mum, 'Where's Daddy gone?' and Helen told her hopelessly: 'He's gone away.' Should've explained to the kid that love, marriage, they're just like every other consumable consumers consume. They're not built to last. They're built to fall apart. That's what keeps the motor of the market economy running, isn't it? Products are designed to fail so we have to buy new ones. Cars rust, businesses go bust, why should love last?

I got a transfer from the Perth Institute of Business and Entrepreneurship to its Aberdeen equivalent. A fresh start, I thought, in a city I'd never even visited before. You know, like Americans do in road movies and in real life, probably, when they shoot off to Nevada or Nebraska and leave their troubles behind in Pennsylvania. Scotland's small-scale in comparison, I know, but the differences are huge if you look at the minutiae. Others might have noticed how the granite buildings sparkle with low-level radioactivity when the sun shines and wash a dull, dull grey when it rains, but me, I was struck how people in Aberdeen all talk like Smurfs. Smurfs in Smurfland. Cold Smurfs in a cold land that don't much take to unfamiliar human beings. These Smurfs seemed colder to me than the weather. I didn't recognizse myself in them. They were strangers. I was a stranger to them. I felt like a shy, retiring, warm-blooded mammal lost in the reptile house.

My top floor flat – found at short notice from a small ad in the *Evening Express* – is five flights of stairs above George Street near a pub called The Butchers Arms. From the tiny kitchen, I look down on the roofs opposite and I can see big, ugly herring gulls – gangsters in white tuxedos – beside the chimney stacks tending their big, ugly young. From the living room I look over the red brick boilerhouse chimney at Richard's textile factory and, close by, a big, ugly concrete tower that makes me feel like a prisoner in an American penitentiary watched by guards with telescopic lenses on their automatic rifles.

There's signs of fire damage in the close, which doesn't inspire great confidence in me, as the tenement stairs – as they often seem to be in Aberdeen – are tinderbox wooden. It's not a happy place, my flat. A lot of tears cried here, I reckon. I'm not being melodramatic: it's the absolute truth. It's got that special transient feel like it's never really felt like home to anyone. People passing through. These are waiting rooms. I feel like I've been here before. Where the carpets are coated so deeply with shedded human skin no vacuum can remove it. And the walls are peeling papered, peppered with experimental holes in the plaster. The grimy single mattress on the bed has a history I don't want to know, both sides.

Worst of all is the smell. A smell that clings to your clothes. The stale odour of other people and their personal habits, people whose main concern, like mine, is moving on, finding a place to call home away from this bus station waiting room. Living here's like eating, sleeping and watching television in a public place. Everywhere and everything is dirty, so deep and ingrained there's no point disturbing it by trying to clean it up.

This is another waiting room on a journey somewhere else. Maybe this time it will be my last stay at the Great Eastern Hotels of my life. I mean you can put up with it when you're young or a student or just starting out 'cause you hope it's only temporary but it's nowhere to be at my age after where I've been. I tell myself it's good, in a way, 'cause, as my Mum would often say, people who've never experienced life in the wilderness will never appreciate The Ritz. I'm just passing through, I hope, but there's plenty that get trapped here.

I wander from room to room and back again like the demented polar bear I once saw at a zoo. Let's face it, the vast expanses of an Arctic wilderness and the ridiculous confines of a rock no bigger than a single-decker bus are poles apart. The poor beast would crawl to one end of the rock and turn and walk to the other – endlessly, like a madman banging his head against a brick wall. My flat, small and smelly, always exactly how I left it when I get back from work, nothing changes, another pause I'd like to fast-forward.

There's an old Expelair fan in the bathroom which sounds like the phone ringing in the other room. Some cruel trick of acoustics means it only happens when the bath is full, I'm in it and topping it up. It sounds far-fetched, I know, but it gets me every time. I hear my phone ringing, get out the bath, grab a towel and drip through to the living room where the ringing abruptly stops. I dial 1471 to double check: 'There are no calls stored,' she says. Not even cold-calling double glazing or kitchen unit telesales. Sometimes I think I can hear someone calling up to my window from the street below, 'Joe! Jo-ey!', and I go to the window, pull back the curtain but there's nobody there. Or I'm walking along the street and I think I can see Helen and Georgie and my heart does a back flip, triple salchow and I just know they're here to find me and take me home. Couldn't make it without me. Should I be gracious? Should I play hard to get? I catch up, I'm just about to speak and I realize it's not them at all. It's someone else's wife and daughter wearing my family's clothes.

I can spend entire weekends without talking to anyone except to say 'Thanks' when a till operator hands me my change. Today, though, I talked to a traffic warden, nothing special, just a passing reference to the freezing weather but the thing was the sound of my own voice surprised me. It sounded so well-adjusted, so rational. Like I was just a regular guy on my way home to my wife and family who I love very much and who love me right back. I didn't sound at all hysterical. I didn't sound at all like someone who'd seen a vision of his future in the evening paper's headline: BODY LAY UNDISCOVERED FOR SIX MONTHS. Thing was, I acted all just-another-day-ish when inside I was screaming. I was trying not to let on that I'd like to ask this old guy if he wants a drink in the pub and maybe we could be pals and hang out together, me and him, round some of the clubs. Have a blether, laugh at him up on the dance floor still in his uniform with some hip clubland chick. I didn't want to let him go – my new best friend. I wanted to show him a photo of my little girl when she was a baby and hear about his family, the places he'd been, his hopes and dreams, just have a laugh for God's sake, talk some football. But, in fact, the conversation was already over. I'd given him a cheery wave and hurried along as if to say, 'Well, can't stop here gabbing all day, things to do, people to meet, and all that,' when in actual fact I *could've* gabbed all day, had *nothing* to do, *no one* to meet.

Before – when I had a life – I used to notice how old people would chat to you at a bus stop, or in a queue at the Post Office, with a kind of desperation. A real thirst for human contact. Just for the simple things, like comparing notes on the news that day or the weather or whatever. Stuff the rest of us take for granted. But today an old woman asked me the way to a solicitor's office in Golden Square. She showed me the address on a letterhead she was carrying. She only wanted to be pointed in the right direction and be told, 'Yeah, see the second set of traffic lights? Turn right at the Music Hall and you're in Golden Square.' But no, she'd evidently recognised in me, quite rightly, a person you could rely on in times of trouble and she was now officially my newest new best friend, and I would not let her down. She also had the misfortune to remind me of my gran so that was the clincher. I took her gently but purposefully by the arm and led her down the road, nice and slow, partly because she had a walking stick but more because it gave me an opportunity to exercise my vocal chords and stop them from seizing up altogether from neglect. By the time we'd reached the address she was after, I'd charmed her onto first-name terms but as we were pausing outside to enjoy, I thought, some pleasant chit-chat on the pros and cons of a new roundabout system, she turned quite bolshy, saying, 'Look I don't mean to be rude, son, but I do need to get on, thanks for your help', looking really quite sprightly for an old girl as she all but skipped into the solicitors.

The weekends seem to last longer than the weekdays. I don't look forward to holidays – I don't know how I'll kill the time. I go to work on a Monday and tell my colleagues about my wild weekend with some old school friends from my home town who came up for a drinking session. Then I'll forget how the anecdote went and I'll have to invent more lies to cover up the first one. But it's still better than telling the truth, that I walked up Union Street and back again and endlessly cruised the tv channels looking for women in states of undress. Television isn't necessarily a passive activity at all.

I had been counting on my libido hibernating – I heard that it happens to explorers lost in the jungle with neither sight nor sound of women for months on end. It would be nice to think about something else for a while. It really would. I'm interested in all sorts, me: art, cinema, literature, vacuuming the car – a regular Renaissance man, I am – but it's hard to hibernate when Eva Herzigova's breasts, blown up to measure twenty feet across on giant billboards, constantly remind me of my obligations for the continuation of the species. 'Hello, Joe!' she says, so coy, but she wants me! Why else would she be parading around in her underwear?

I can't even buy a newspaper right now without the top shelf whispering seductively down to me: 'Hey, Big Boy! Looking for some company? I'm all yours tonight, every night, any time, any way you want!' and I wanna shout back and say, 'Look just fuck off, will you? I'm not a big boy, as you well know, I'm average height, average intelligence and I daresay, though I've never actually researched the matter, I've got an average-sized ... ' I pause. Other people in John Menzies can't read my thoughts, can they? She just won't let up. Tries a different tack: 'Mmn, Baby, I feel so hot and wet! Reach up here and touch me, Baby, take me!' she coos. 'Look, I'm not your baby!' I tell her, 'why, I don't even know you. And will you please stop talking to me in that nauseating, albeit ridiculously effective, whisper. I'm not stupid, y'know. Underneath all that make-up, without the flattering lighting, you're just a plain Jane – too short for the catwalk and too busty to be a fashion model. I don't even fancy blondes.' Suddenly her pout looks fragile. I've hit a soft spot. 'Look, I'm sorry if I offended you. I know you're just making a living and you were secretly hoping glamour photography would be a stepping stone into movies. I apologize. And okay, okay, you *do* look strangely, primevally, alluring in stockings.'

Actually, I do myself an injustice. I did recently experience a threesome. It's the most intimate contact I've had with another human being for a year. Two pairs of surgical gloves stretched open my mouth so wide I thought my lips were going to split and my chest was mistaken for a table. But visiting the dentist is not – and never will be – a sex substitute.

It's a morose routine I've fallen into. Work, tv, sleep, work, tv, sleep during the weekdays then sleep, tv, sleep, tv at the weekends. I couldn't tell you for sure if ITV and BBC have saved my life or are stealing it away from me. All I know is, when the lights are out and I can't tell the colour of the carpet or the wallpaper or the furniture and I'm watching the clean, blue brilliance of the *Nine O'Clock News* with some reassuringly familiar newsreader I could be anywhere. And I like that. I could be back with Helen in our flat in Perth like a proper family. I could even be a kid again, back when my brothers still lived at home, and we were a proper family.

It's addictive. I go to bed late and get up in the middle of the night to watch some more tv in case I've missed something. The long hours of the night are the worst. I try to read till I'm so tired I'll have to sleep. But it doesn't work. My body is fatigued but my mind is spinning and spinning like the squeaky wheel of a hamster's cage. Running and re-running the film of my life. Not those moments when I did something good, made someone laugh or happy, but those horrible moments of misunderstanding when I hurt someone I loved by being thoughtless or selfish, or by saying something out of turn, or when I stood up in front of a business conference to do a presentation and saw all those faces looking at me with all their false expectations of who I am, what I do, judging me within ten seconds by my choice of tie and the cut of my suit and I forgot all my practised lines, fell apart, couldn't carry it off, the faking, the phoneyness, made an utter fool of myself. I want to go back in time and sort out all the confusions. I want to live my life again with the benefit of hindsight. To live a different way. To see it coming and step out of the way. Iron out the mistakes before they happen. Make different choices. Fall in love with different people.

Maybe, about four or five am – the luminous hands of the alarm clock have been marking time with me – I'll finally fall asleep where Georgie's, often as not, waiting to haunt my dreams. I'll tuck her up, lean over the bars of the cot, make sure she's comfortable, check her in the night, is she too hot, too cold? I wake up. Hold my breath and listen for changes in hers. I can't hear her at all. Why's Georgie's night-light not on? Where's the bedside lamp? Where's the bookcase? Where's Helen? The orange glow of the street light is on the wrong wall. The window's where the wardrobe should be. This isn't home. I remember through the fog of half-sleep where I am. My bed is cold. When I pull the duvet round my shoulders my feet stick out the bottom. To wrap the duvet round all of me I sleep in a quasi-foetal position. But it's a living death, more accurately. Alone in a bed, as cold as a grave, high above the rooftops in a living city of 214,382 Smurfs.

• • • • • • • • • • • • • • • • • •

Georgie gurgled contently and stretched out her fat little arms as she eyed the kitchen scissors in her mother's hand with fearless curiosity. Helen snipped two curls of lush black hair off the baby's head, placing one in a clear plastic bank bag and the other in a pink paper envelope on a page of a Baby's First Year book.

We were in the grip of Georgiamania – had been from day one when Georgie's whole, tiny hand first clasped her mother's ring finger. We maintained a loving topography in the Year Book, detailing every little birthmark and landmark of progress in her tiny world. Baby's first jag (diphtheria); first tooth (lower front left, giving her the most economical of cheeky grins); first pair of shoes (purple moccasins, actually from a market, but I told Helen they were treble the price from Lewis's or else she wouldn't have allowed them near Georgie's soft feet); first words (Da-da); first fears (being left alone, even for a few seconds, spiders, the intercom buzzer). All her firsts were firsts for us too.

Helen handed me the bag with Georgie's hair. My own keepsake. Now we've all got some hair: Mum in her Year Book, me with a bagful and Georgie on her head. Plenty more where that came from. I study the specimen. Georgie's black hair held the code if you could read it. I wanted to take it for DNA analysis. Find the key to the lock. Not just for some glorified chemical barcode or cosmic National Insurance number. Because Georgie's not just another number. She's special. She's mine. I wanted to know her entire genetic inheritance. I wanted a computer read-out of her family tree from roots to fruit, from the first ever seed from the first ever caveman and more ... I wanted to be her guardian angel. If I could read her DNA like a palmist reads a hand then maybe I could work out where to stand to catch her before she even falls.

• • • • • • • • • • • • • • • • • •

Georgie Street, I'm walking down Georgie Street on my way to work. Other towns might have a George Street but only Aberdeen's got Georgie Street. Ironic, huh? Where I should wash up, I mean, after sharing a door plate for so long. So long, Helen! It's a sign. A sign, all right, that I'm so lost, I'll call any tired old coincidence a sign. Give it special meaning. I'm looking at the signs above the buses as they go past. Trying to work out how to get to the Institute. Wouldn't do to be late on my first day. I know I should've sorted this out before now, obviously, but what with one thing and another I never got round to it. I could ask someone, couldn't I? I could flag down a bus, that one for instance, going to ... Faulds Gate? I could ask the driver 'D'you go down Holburn Street?' and he'll look at me like I'm mad, the whole bus will stare. 'Can't you read, son? This bus is going to Faulds Gate.' Yeah, yeah, I know that. But where the hell is Faulds Gate? What I'll do, right, is keep walking and keep an eye out for a likely looking bus. Like that one ... Auchinyell? Where the hell is Auchinyell? Just keep walking, Joey, you'll get there in the end. A journey of a thousand miles begins with a single step – Mao, I believe, but don't quote me on that. The Institute would love that, me quoting Mao, I mean. No way the Chairman would've shook my hand after the job interview if I'd done that! No, no, no! (Even though that's all the Mao I know.) I told them what they wanted to hear. Told them what the Institute is all about. Cash Converters! Look at that in the window! A foot spa! Who's ever going to buy a second-hand, old foot spa? Who'd want something that's been so intimate with someone else? I hate Helen's boss. I hate how she'd slump in her joggers on the sofa at home but was always made up, showered and smiling for work. Like it wasn't really work at all for her. Like it was hard work coming home. That's pretty sordid, isn't it? That's dirty, that is. Last night, right, I was trying to wash myself with this diagonal bar of soap my mum had packed with washing-up liquid and washing powder, a few Brillo pads and some tins and a jar of my favourite coffee in a cardboard box like a Red Cross parcel for a prisoner of war. She's worried about me. Thinks I'm incapable of looking after myself. So anyway, there I was in the bath, trying to get a lather out of this white soap she'd given me. It was rubbish, though, and, in the end, I just gave up on it. Then, this morning, I'm getting the coffee out the box and the packaging for the soap falls out. 'Vanish', it said. For your clothes! So, first of all I'm thinking I'm going to die of skin poisoning, man! Then ... hold on, hold on, I made it through the night, I'm still here, aren't I? I feel all right. People vanish but they don't die from it, do they? So that should be okay. Then I'm thinking, I'm going to work, right, meeting a whole lot of new people, and I'm not actually very clean. But then, I figured, it was more likely the other way round, I was probably very, very clean – starchy clean, in fact – and at least there'd be no chance of any collar or cuff grime on my shirts this week. Vanish, huh? I'm walking to work and no one can see me. I'm the invisible man! There's a girl who's used to attention, I'll bet. Coming towards me, outside of the pavement. Probably on her way to the college. Only stupid guys stare, I reckon. D'you want to be the beholder or the beholden? Stare and she'll look away, it stands to reason. Ignore her and she'll be chasing you down the street Benny Hill-style like you're catnip or something. Now watch me, a master at work. Observe how I completely ignore her. See how she walks right past me with not so much as a second glance, never mind a second thought. Bad example. She's the exception which proves the rule. It hasn't worked this morning, obviously, 'cause she's late for class or she's a lesbian or something. It hasn't actually ever worked, if the truth be told – not even with Helen – but it's another pet theory I'm loathe to let go. Helen would like this. Georgie too. Laura Ashley stencilling on the pavements under the trees. The leaves have decomposed on the concrete and left a pattern so clear you could name the different trees they've fallen from. Even after they've long been swept away they've left an indelible mark. Georgie'd go: 'Is that why they're called "leaves", Daddy, is it? 'Cause they leave marks?' I can hear her say it. See opposite the Marischal College? That seventies concrete area round the City Council's tower block and the tourist office? Skateboarders and rollerbladers must go there a lot. I saw them last night. Doing jumps and stunts off the steps and along the low wall of the concrete flower beds. Thing is, you wouldn't believe it, but they've actually worn off the sharp edges of the concrete with their wheels. How about that? Sharp, ugly edges smoothed off by a few daft wee kids. I like that. Walking onto Union Street now. This is the best thing about Aberdeen so far, by far, this street. Better than Sauchiehall Street or Princes Street, I reckon. I've given up on the buses now, I'll walk it this once. The Music Hall steps are wet – scrubbed clean with Bon Accord civic pride – while the rest of the street is dry. It looks as if it's only rained under those Doric columns. There's a poster at the box office for a show at a planetarium. Georgie'd like that. Mad keen on her school space project, she was. 'My Very Easy Method Just Speeds Up Naming Planets,' she said proudly, 'Miss Robertson learned us that.' She could reach for the sky – know all the planets in our solar system off by heart – but she still needed a footstool to reach the bathroom sink. 'My-Mercury, Very-Venus, Easy-Earth, Method-Mars ...' she recited at the table, Helen and I only half-listening as we ate and talked about more earthly, grown up concerns, 'Just-Jupiter ...' Georgie persisted in the background, 'Speeds-Saturn ...' and then, in a momentary lull in the conversation, 'Up-Uranus!' And that was just about the last laugh we had as a family – Georgie joining in, happy to make us laugh, not getting the joke – before I was turfed out on my arse. 'You've got no ambition. No goals. You'll never achieve anything. You need a rocket up your bum to do anything.' Charming, eh? 'You don't have enough get-up-and-go.' So here I am, got up and gone. Bye, bye, Helen Here I am turning the corner into Holburn Street, the invisible man at the Institute.

•   •   •   •   •   •   •   •   •   •   •   •   •   •   •   •   •

Recognition is immediate. The small tobacco tin as familiar to me now as when I first sealed it. I'm not the sentimental type. Well, I try to fight it. I've only kept the manilla envelope because I might one day want Georgie to know her mother loved me once and, *ta-ra*, here's the proof. Otherwise it'd be out. Clutter makes me claustrophobic. Cling to the past and it clogs up your present. Course it does. Throw away old diaries. Get next year's early. Keep moving forward. But, yeah, all right, I kept the tin. It was the exception that proved the rule – surviving periodic purges because it was neat, tidy, functional. Its clutter was minimal and contained. Each tiny piece of survival equipment confined to rattle in its box like I might rattle my brains for ideas (despite the cotton wool stuffed inside to minimise the noise). I'd see it now and again, when moving flat or looking for something else, and I'd just ignore it, leave the decision for another day. No action taken. Not opened. Not thrown away.

Tonight, though, I'm seeing it afresh. I sit on the floor with my back against the wall and study the tin closely. It's a nice size. As tactile as a pack of cards or a cigarette packet (never mind the nicotine, I think people get hooked on packaging), heavier though, with all that's inside and the weight of my expectations. I recognise my own childish script on the label I'd stuck on the lid. I must have written 'SURVIVAL KIT' with some dedication, as each letter is embellished with neat serifs. Pre-pubescent self-assurance and optimism writ large but now blurred, like the ink, with age. I'd sealed the tin with remarkable efficiency for an eight year-old. Sellotape, I suppose, would have made it air-tight for a while but any kid could do that. From the tool box under the stairs, I got extra strong and sticky electrician's insulation tape which, wrapped around the lip of the lid two or three times, made the box reliably air-tight and waterproof. Tamper-proof too, against casual curiosity. So much so that on odd occasions over the years when I've been tempted to remind myself of its contents I've always decided it wasn't worth the effort. It would take too long to peel off the rubber-backed tape, it would be sticky and, anyway, what the hell, I thought I could remember everything I'd put in it as if it were yesterday.

Then a funny thing happened. The longer I kept the tin the more I was loathe to either open it or throw it away. Lying almost lost, doing nothing for years, it gradually assumed accidental status as a time-capsule and talisman. I'd captured and hermetically sealed an eight year-old's world of absolutes and certainties against unforeseen, future emergencies. As long as I had my survival kit no ill would befall me. I would get by. Worked too. None of the desperate, life-threatening survival situations I'd anticipated and planned ahead for ever actually happened to me. I'd never been shot down in flames over enemy territory, lost at sea, or washed up on a deserted island. Well, until now. Until the Institute. Until Aberdeen.

I'm going to fetch a sharp knife from the kitchen, slit open the pocket museum and breathe a tinful of 1973.

•   •   •   •   •   •   •   •   •   •   •   •   •   •   •   •   •   •   •

The peace pamphlet my big brother gave me when I was eight made me lie awake at night with worry. James – not Jim or Jamie or Jimmy but definitely *James* to all those in the family – had read *A-Bomb Apocalypse* and reckoned it was kidstuff. 'Nobody's gonna survive The Bomb by putting masking tape on their windows and hiding under the mattress. It's garbage!' he told me. 'The Government's got secret bunkers hundreds of feet deep made of reinforced concrete. They've got more food down there than the Co-op. It's like a fancy five-star hotel but it's not for the likes of us. There'll be bouncers on the door so we won't get in. Don't have a reservation? Don't have a ticket? Don't have an old school tie? We don't even know the address! It's members only, man! It's private. Exclusively for the Royal Family. The aristocracy. The courtiers. The cabinet. All the army's top brass'll run there when the balloon goes up, I'm telling you, they've all got beds waiting for them. The sewer rats! But say *you* found out where it was. *You* go there, chapping on the door, gasping for breath 'cause everywhere above ground's radioactive, what d'you think they'll say, eh? Over the intercom, eh?'

The Bomb comes down! The balloon goes up! Aristocrats and sewer rats! I was too enthralled by my brother's magnificent moral indignation to answer what turned out to be a rhetorical question anyway as James affected the voice of doorman to the Queen's own nuclear bunker.

' "I'm *terribly* sorry, Mr Copeland, your name doesn't appear to be on our list of the chosen few so no, I'm afraid you *can't* come in. I think you'll find you're supposed to congregate on the Underground. That's why we put maps at the back of your diaries – so you'll know where to go for your *Waterloo Sunset*. Haven't you read the instructions for the working classes? Haven't you built your shelter at the bottom of your allotment?" So simple, so stylish! Just a trench with a couple of sheets of corrugated iron above it. All this build a shelter shite! It's propaganda to lull us into a false sense of security. Like we've got control of our destiny in our own hands. It ain't so, Joe. Don't be fooled. If Nixon gives Brezhnev the finger and pushes the button no amount of masking tape on the windows'll save us. The only things that'll survive The Bomb are a few cockroaches and a whole lot of horsey, chinless wonders.'

I gazed at my brother in abject admiration. If he said it was so, it was so. If he said it was not so, it was not so, Joe. As far as I was concerned, James spoke the gospel. He was nearly ten years older than me. He cut an impressive figure, especially to one so impressionable as I was. He had shoulder-length red hair and inflammable eyes which, I imagined, had seen the injustice of it all and were not best happy.

James lived his life like The Bomb was going to drop tomorrow. He stole cars – albeit in a very small-town 1970s sort of way – not hi-jacking them, ram-raiding and burning them out, as is *de rigueur* in today's urban jungles but 'borrowing' them from friends' parents without their knowledge or permission and bringing them back with a mysterious extra 100 miles on the clock and a faint, musky mix of aftershave and perfume emanating from the back seat.

Girls pursued James, he didn't have to chase them. They'd rearrange the seating in the class and fight over who sat near him. They'd manufacture all kinds of lame excuses to ring our doorbell and ask to see him. I imagined this was normal and commonplace. It was obviously how the dating game worked: girls queued, boys chose, that sort of thing. Imagine my disappointment and disillusionment to discover much later that, although we were brothers, I'd inexplicably missed out on the gene that gave James such magnetism. Girls believed he was the rightful heir to the tortured soul of James Dean and they all craved the excitement of being close to danger – which, of course, is a different thing altogether from craving the excitement of actually being *in* danger. They were the kind of girls who might like to stand close to Niagara Falls – sense its power, enjoy the spectacle – but wouldn't contemplate going over in a barrel and risk chipping their nail varnish or getting their hair wet.

Sometimes, if James had travelled far in his carefully selected car for the evening (though, I admit, Canada would be stretching credulity), he'd thoughtfully refill it with syphoned petrol from another vehicle in the same street or even – if he'd driven up some muddy off-the-beaten track for a love tryst – take it through the early morning garage carwash before neatly parking back exactly where he'd found it. Owners would wake up for work and wonder why their cars were still warm.

Such was his unshakeable self-belief – insouciance, if you were sympathetic, arrogance, if you were not – James secured a holiday job behind the counter and the wheel of an ice cream van scheduled to start the day after he was to sit his driving test. He passed, of course, 'cause life was a breeze that summer. I got free strawberry 99s every day for a fortnight before he was fired. James was a strong advocate for the redistribution of wealth and to his eternal credit put his principles into practice. Like a latter-day Che, he believed in direct action and dished out free ice creams and bottles of American Cream Soda to some of the poorer children on the estates. Word got round and queues of kids – most, it has to be said, with plenty pocket money jangling – posed as penniless street urchins whenever they heard the Pied Piper's tinny music. Even I could see, as I sat a couple of times in the coveted passenger seat, that it couldn't go on but James was oblivious – told me it was good marketing for Corbone's. Every cul-de-sac held an ambush of whooping little savages, some running back for seconds, and although he'd return the van to the shop with the last scoopful scraped from every tub the till remained strangely empty. Corbone twigged. Called my brother a flake. Free 99s no more.

By the time his peach-fluff moustache had finally grown in, James had become something of a legend among the kids at Pitlochry High School. It carried kudos to be his brother. Bullies picked on other kids and left me alone. I happily fed the myth-making, telling my pals James had been offered trials for Celtic and Man United but had turned them down. Older kids would scoff but admire my gall, while peers thought this was entirely plausible. My brother, they understood, would actually be too cool to break sweat in public.

I started to believe my own stories. I began to think the black and red poster in James' bedroom was a brooding self-portrait with star and beret. But my father, Physics teacher at James' secondary school and elder of the kirk, had no such trouble distinguishing the two. He had reasoned answers for all my brother's unfocused rants on international brotherhood: 'I don't know why you want him for a hero, Son,' he said, nodding in the direction of Che Guevara on the wall. 'Jesus was a revolutionary too 'cept He didn't need a gun.'

I read *A-Bomb Apocalypse* and the sequel *H-Bomb Holocaust* end to end. When we closed our eyes at school assembly to mouth the Lord's Prayer, Soviet-American relations preyed on my mind. I had deduced that we'd be the first to perish in the conflagration because Britain – at the centre of the classroom map – would, inevitably, be caught in the superpower crossfire. At night, lying in my bed, I'd listen out for the tell-tale whistle of The Bombs being dropped and wonder if it might be possible to avoid a direct hit by making a run for it – like in films when the hero escapes from the burning wreckage of a plane just before it blows. He gets flung six metres into the air but walks away with only an attractive battle scar on his chiselled cheekbone, miraculously healed anyway by the very next scene. But when I told James I'd worked out we'd go first when The Bomb dropped and showed him a piece of paper detailing my last will and testament his angry eyes went soft on me like it had all been just a game.

'Aw, c'mon, Joey,' he said as gently as a mother, 'get real, *you're* not going to die, stupid! You're just a kid. Nobody's after you. Nobody wants to hurt children. Where d'you pick up all this doom and gloom? We're not talking politics any more – you take it way too seriously. Whoever heard of an eight year-old making a will? What would I want with your *Commando* comics and your Action Man? Forget all this morbid nonsense! You're only a kid once, let the grown-ups do all the worrying. You should be out playing on your bike, being a kid, doing kiddish things!'

Pretty soon after that though – seeing that my preoccupation with The Bomb wasn't going to die quickly – he gave me an army survival manual to help nurture a less fatalistic attitude. Survival techniques, he said, would come in useful either after The Bomb or during The Revolution – whichever imminent event came first.

The survival manual was my salvation. Here was something positive I could do beyond pulling the duvet over my head. I took it with me everywhere I went and quoted extensively and knowledgeably from it whenever the opportunity arose and often when it didn't. The manual seemed to me to contain absolutely vital, relevant information which my school were inexplicably neglecting to teach me. I now had access to true knowledge and it felt like my duty to share it. My family, however, were dangerously parochial. They didn't seem to grasp the importance of my new studies. I'd read out useful pieces of information to them and they'd treat it as a joke.

'Dad, d'you know the main differences between poisonous tropical plants and edible ones?'

'Tell me Son, it'll be useful if we ever get peckish in the Botanic Gardens.'

'James, if you get a leather belt and cut two tiny crosses for your eyes and tie it round your head you can actually avoid getting snowblindness in Antarctica *and* sunblindness in the Sahara.'

'Yeah? But more importantly, how d'you stop your trousers falling down?'

'Mum, it says here the way to survive a sandstorm is to curl up in a wee ball with your back to the wind and sleep till it's over.'

'Well, that'd suit your father. North Berwick, last summer, remember? Too windy even for the windbreak! But your father would've slept in his deckchair just the same, if we'd let him.'

'Jackie, see if you're caught in an avalanche? Best thing to do is try to swim backwards as the snow is falling on you.'

My middle brother took a sharp intake of breath, made his eyes go big: 'Ouch, 'magine all that snow in your trunks!'

I made a mental note not to gloat or say 'I told you so' when they came running to me for survival advice and guidance in the aftermath of The Bomb.

Preparation, I learned, was the key to survival. So when the book advised adventurers to get an old tobacco tin and fill it with essential survival equipment I followed the instructions to the letter. It wasn't just a matter of life and death in the abstract. It could be *my* life and death on the line. Things had to be done properly. Finding a tobacco tin was my first problem. No one smoked in our house, officially, although James was forever hanging out of his window puffing on contraband Embassy Regals, hopelessly wafting smoke away as it curled behind him into the bedroom, and I didn't know anyone who smoked a pipe. Mum suggested I ask old Mrs Murray next door *nicely* if she could help. And Mrs Murray – for whose allegedly delicate sensibilities we were often told to keep the noise down else she might hear us through the adjoining wall even though you had to shout for her to hear if you met her face to face – took pity on me and gave me one of her late husband's old tobacco tins. It had 'Craven Mixture' on the lid and though empty still smelt sweetly, reassuringly, of tobacco. I tried not to think of Mrs Murray's husband, who'd died the year before, putting his chubby fingers into the tin and building a bird's nest in the bowl of his pipe with tiny twigs of tobacco – I was a bit squeamish about dead people. On the other hand, I admit, it did add to its appeal. I wanted hard-edged authenticity for my survival project and, without doubt – though he modestly never mentioned it ever himself and no one ever knew – Mrs Murray's husband must have been a war hero who'd won medals, Victoria Crosses, probably, for single-handedly knocking out German machine-gun positions, and the like. Soft kids would be settling for survival kits in clean-smelling little Tupperware boxes on loan from their mums but my tobacco tin was the Real McCoy, complete with a glorious military heritage. I went even further, telling pals that not only had the tin been a gift from a bona fide decorated war hero but, what the hell, I'd smoked the tobacco myself.

The survival manual said tobacco tins made ideal mini survival kits because everything could be fitted inside, nothing wasted – even the reflective lid could be used to signal passing ships or aeroplanes. I tried this out a few times but never once got an acknowledgement from the fighter jets from RAF Leuchars which periodically thundered through the glen, reminding me – if I'd been distracted and preoccupied for a few moments with a frivolous game of football – that the Third World War was due to commence any minute, assuming it hadn't already commenced and I hadn't heard yet. Dot, dot, dot. Dash, dash, dash. Dot, dot, dot. I'd signal to the pilots – even though I did worry I might be court martialled for wasting military time if they actually responded. I should worry! By the time I'd located one of the Phantoms (so called, I believed, because they 'hid' way in front of the searing sound of their engines) it would already be disappearing into the distant sky, leaving a trail of vapour and shrinking a whole nation to the size of a stroll to the bottom of the garden.

Once I had procured an authentic war hero's tobacco tin, the next step was to fill it with survival necessities. I wanted these to be as faithful to the survival manual as possible but I had to improvise. The following items would save my life in a survival emergency: matches (coated with melted candle wax to make them waterproof); a tiny magnifying glass for making fire from the rays of the sun; extra strength fishing line (for fishing, obviously, but also handy for mending clothes and any number of tying jobs); candles (made do with old birthday cake ones from the back of the kitchen drawer); paper and pencil stub (to write messages for rescuers, I think, or maybe to compose poetry in lighter survival moments); snare wire (a couple of broken electric guitar strings would have to suffice); needles, thread and safety pins (good for emergency repairs to ripped clothing and could also be used to make fish hooks); barbed fish hooks and little lead weights; water purification tablets (which I had to pass on as we didn't appear to have any in the bathroom cabinet. I put in a few Disprin instead, which wouldn't make water drinkable but might come in handy if I had to perform any amputations); a razor blade (also handy for amputations – we only had double-bladed ones so I layered one side with Sellotape to make a handle); various sized Elastoplasts; and cotton wool to fill in the spaces. My tin was packed – I felt ready for anything. Family, friends, indeed freedom itself would survive The Bomb with me: the tin man. Hey, Brezhnev! Nixon! Come ahead!

• • • • • • • • • • • • • • • • • •

Our Georgie had a survival kit too. A bright little duffle bag with friendly lions, smiling tigers and not-so-deadly cartoon snakes on it. Well, she had to learn – it's a jungle out there. Her mother and me would take the bag everywhere when Georgie was still in Pampers. It had nappies and baby wipes and all things Johnson & Johnson. Georgie couldn't appreciate such functional details but she must've noticed we'd hardly leave the house without the baby kit. She felt much the same for a small, stuffed hippopotamus which, for unfathomable reasons to us, was her special toy. She wouldn't leave home without it. It wore a vulnerable and rather dim-looking expression and gave Georgie uninterrupted quality time, all the time. It needed a lot of looking after. It needed to feel safe, secure and loved.

• • • • • • • • • • • • • • • • • •

There was a wall in our back garden that I knew better than the back of my hand. I'd often walk along the top of it, arms outstretched, like I was Blondin crossing Niagara. (If James had done it crowds of girls would have gathered to watch.) I knew the smooth stones which could be treacherously slippy after rain and the jaggy ones which could hurt your feet even through your trainers and the highly dangerous jutting stumps of iron spikes from railings cut for the war effort. I drew a treasure map of the garden in which the wall was an integral part. I detailed all the potential pitfalls along the way with advice on how to avoid them with the benefit of my years of experience. I could act as daredevil but trusted local guide for my imaginary companions as we made our way along the hazardous Himalayan track. No one noticed. Kids are invisible. No one asked me. But I knew the way.

I only mention this because, I swear to God, that six year-old, right up to about age 11 – when I first began to lose my way – knew more about life and love with more certainties and absolutes than I do now. I had it all mapped out – all this and everything – with a greater clarity, the less I knew. Like those old codgers who thought the world was flat. Lucky them, I say, life was simpler before Columbus. I had a clearer vision and a better, simpler, uncluttered, unfettered idea of who I was and where I fitted in on the almighty plan. When all I knew was that stupid wall, I knew it all.

Then I was blissfully confident I was the rightful heir to success in life and love and everything. A hopeful romantic. I would play for Celtic at 16, Scotland at 18, marry at 20 to a woman who could laugh easily but knew when to be serious. We'd have kids, of course, probably a boy and a girl. I never thought things out too clinically but basically we'd be a little tribe who'd never betray each other. Our sanctuary would always be safe for everyone to be who they wanted to be. To find out who they really were. To let the kids shout, laugh, dance and be happy and not tell them to be quiet too often. The kitchen would smell of baking and coffee. The kids would play and learn and grow up and watch cartoons. I'd kiss my wife and hold her close on the sofa as the light from the tv flickered on our contented faces.

We'd go for a day at the seaside and breeze past all the traffic jams on the other dual carriageway into the city. We'd arrive at the beach, put a travel rug down on the golden sands and the kids would run and play among the rock pools and squeal at tiny crabs and seaweed. We'd eat sandwiches and drink fruit juice. It wouldn't be too hot or too sunny but fresh and warm with only a gentle, cooling breath of wind which wouldn't disturb the sand grains. Then we'd kick a football or fly a kite on the hard sand as the tide went out and we'd all run about getting huge lungfuls of salty sea air. We'd pack up, buy Italian ice creams. Then go and watch a Disney film at the pictures. *Bambi* or something, so the kids would value their mother. I'd glance at my pretty wife in the half-light of the stalls and she'd smile back at me. And the children's faces would be lit up by the big screen, revealing their tiny enthralled expressions. We'd motor home, kids falling asleep in the back. We'd hold hands in the dark across the gear stick as we glided down easy street. We'd get home and lock the door on all the crazies outside. We'd make love, then sleep knowing the next day was Sunday.

Some people want fame and fortune and Littlewoods cash. Mine was a modest dream, was it not? I never for a moment thought this wouldn't be my rightful inheritance. I never for a moment thought the odds against such simple perfection might be longer than the Lottery.

Mum liked *The Waltons*. She'd sit and let it get to her. Willingly giving herself up to the plaintive pathos. We were boys and had to fight it. James, Jackie and me would be in the living room doing other stuff, like reading *Commando* comics or building the Forth Rail Bridge with Meccano, and James'd snort and snigger every time John Boy said something gauche. I'd snort and snigger too, a tell-tale couple of seconds later, raising my eyes to the ceiling in agreement. But by the time those Waltons were hollering their goodnights to each other and the lights in the big white house on Waltons' mountain went out to a high-pitched note on the harmonica, we'd all be choking on the tightness in our throats. We'd have to cough through the final credits, trying to shake off the cloying sentimentality, and we'd wonder how it had managed to sneak up on us unawares.

We were a proper family then – not scattered to opposite ends of the British Isles like now. Mum, in her wing-tipped spectacles, would ask me to set the table and that meant five knives and five forks and that was our family. Same as the Famous Five – that's how I could remember what to take from the cutlery drawer.

Like Mum's vegetable soup, which she blasted in the liquidiser to disguise the carrots I wouldn't eat otherwise, these meal times have blended into each other. Only the most eventful ones stand out, like the infamous 'egg on the tv' incident, when a hot Pyrex plate exploded on the cold mat we'd got free with every four gallons at ESSO. It really spooked me. All the noise and clatter and chatter was silenced by one loud crack. With Dalíesque absurdity tomato ketchup dripped off the wallpaper and a poached egg, oozing yellow yolk, perched bizarrely on top of the black and white television. The silence was broken by Mum stepping back onto a piece of shattered plate, breaking the jigsaw into a further five pieces, and my father roaring with laughter at all our shocked faces. I didn't like the plate doing that. Plates should know their place in the cosmos is a passive, domestic one. Bombs explode, plates keep poached eggs off the table. This is the way. Only our family would have to play host to some maverick terrorist plate trying to lead crockery into violent revolution. Mum did the right thing. She played it low-key, tidied up without a fuss, mustn't let the other plates on the table and those listening in the dark of the cupboard make a martyr out of the broken one.

The meal time I remember best – worst, really – was soon after James' head-on smash with adolescence. Growth spurts must've short-circuited his brain because he kept spinning out of control like a mad, malfunctioning robot.

One lunchtime I was supping my soup, wee legs dangling from the chair, when he exploded into 'wild one' mode. I haven't a clue what sparked him off but once ignited he soon worked himself up into a raging, roaring, redhead fury. James squared up to my father. Staring him out, seeing who was the tallest. My father wore a slightly quizzical expression as if to say 'What monster is this I have created?' but said nothing, just eye-balled James, waiting for him to burn himself out. James threw up his arms in exasperation as he backed down first and made his exit, shouting something hopelessly melodramatic like James 'You're tearing me apart!' Dean in *Rebel Without a Cause,* before extravagantly flinging his chair towards the table in a final grand, show-stopping gesture. Spilt my soup, it did. Froze me in shock for a few moments. My spoon halfway between bowl and mouth. Froze James in shock for a second too, as if he had forgotten his lines and might not complete the scene. He made a lightning quick inventory with a single glance towards me, saw I was unscathed, then he was off, concluding the drama nicely by slamming shut the outside door, which I took as my cue to regain motor neurone movement. But I'd lost my appetite. There was a deep gash in one of the table legs but, to be honest, you'd need to know where to look to find it. I knew, and would regularly examine it for years afterwards as if it was my own leg that had been bruised.

Round about the same time my middle brother Jackie – not Jack like he was grown up, or Jake like he was a hairy Klondyker, but *Jackie*, definitely Jackie to all those in the family because he had a cute, baby face with pinchable cheeks – who was eight years older than me, got into making his own ginger beer. In what seemed like a mystical process to me, he refilled empty T.C. lemonade bottles with water, yeast, sugar, ginger and a dash of lemon juice to make the foul-tasting brew. The glass bottles had to be stored in a cool, dark cupboard to allow their muddy-brown contents to ferment. Every day the mysterious ginger beer plant would divide into two and Jackie would fill ever more bottles in his one-man ginger beer factory where production wildly outstripped demand. Of course, in his boyish enthusiasm, he'd only skim-read the instructions and overlooked the importance of using corks which could expand in the bottles and harmlessly pop out if necessary during the fermentation period, unlike the screwtops he favoured. Every so often one of the bottles would explode and Jackie would gingerly open the cupboard door to find broken glass everywhere and a sticky brown mixture all over the walls and doors. One incendiary exploded as he was checking on its progress and he still carries the scar, a little nick really, through his left eyebrow – which he could show you along with the burn mark on his thumb from hot wax during his candlemaking fad, as well as one on his chin from falling off his bike, and another on his knuckle from early ham-fisted attempts at DIY.

If Jackie is typical of a type, we owe him and all the accident-prone a great debt. Jackie attracted way more than his fair share of cuts and grazes and minor slips and falls, selflessly soaking up a whole lot of accidents waiting to happen, thereby making the world a statistically safer place for me and James. Thanks, Bro'!

James was just like one of Jackie's Molotov cocktails, festering away and liable to explode at any moment without warning and for no apparent reason. I never understood why he was raging and only saw the conflict and unhappiness it caused my mother, who would occasionally surprise us all by loudly shouting that enough was enough and she had to get away from us, go for a walk to clear her head. She'd go out and my father would say: 'Now look what you've done – upset your mother,' and we'd all feel guilty and tidy our rooms, wipe the kitchen surfaces, be as good as choir boys for a couple of days.

I was never afraid of James, though. He was mad, I was sure, but somehow I knew he wasn't mad at me. I was safe from his fury and frustration. There were times I was the only member of the family he would speak to. I was so much younger than him I was perceived as blameless and innocent of all he was rebelling against in true 1970s style.

He indulged me with his time, staying in goals for

hours on end, allowing me to take countless pot-shots from all angles and really develop my kick. He played good finger-picking guitar like Woody Guthrie and I'd sing along and do the harmonies to Beatles numbers which were still fresh then. All the patience he lacked with authority figures was lavished on me. He taught me one of the first phrases I ever learnt to write: 'Keep Hair Long!' which was more a way of life than a fashion statement. We got to vent our free expression and vandal instincts by painting the inside of the garden shed any way we liked. Outside was a sober black creosote but inside, around a tangle of bikes and a push lawnmower, were psychedelic walls covered in flower-power graffiti: 'Power to the People!', 'Ban The Bomb!', 'Make Love Not War', and other slogans from a slogan-happy era.

Windows were broken in the house more often than they were washed (and they were kept pretty clean). Footballs and Frisbees appeared to possess in-built homing devices and would attempt to take the shortest route from the back garden to the bedroom cupboard via the bedroom window. What with Jackie's ginger beer and exploding plates, breaking glass was a familiar childhood sound. James broke a window in the middle of the night with a stone, trying to attract Jackie's attention so he could let him in without waking everybody up. But Jackie would sleep through The Bomb, no problem, and it was me who ran to the crack in the window pane, smiling and waving and happily shouting: 'You're in for it now!' waking up anyone still asleep.

James and Jackie were good to me. They didn't mind me using them as reassuring trump cards when older primary kids got pushy. 'I'll get my big brother on to you' was a useful deterrent I was never actually forced to deploy. Except once, I tell a lie, when like a lot of other kids I was getting grief from a particularly dim-witted bully boy in the class above us. Jackie waited for me at the gates looking older and much, much meaner than bully boy and walked me home like a personal bodyguard.

Why should I ever have imagined that this wonderful brotherly sandwich of affection and protection would ever be taken away from me? It was great to be the youngest, to watch and learn but never have to prove myself. It was easy. My older brothers blazed a trail for me so I got to amble through the bramble unhindered and unfettered, with time to admire the view. It is the baby of the family's privilege to naïvely believe he'll never have to pick up the tab.

•   •   •   •   •   •   •   •   •   •   •   •   •   •   •   •   •   •

Watching *Teletubbies* with Georgie.

(In the domestic politics of our flat in Perth, before the split, it was a political statement to call her 'Georgie'. Drove her mother up the wall. She'd insisted on calling her 'Georgia'. A name heavy with her mother's expectations of class and deportment, she'd chosen, we disagreed on, she put on the birth certificate and I never used. Put me in mind of some spoilt kid with a fat, puckered face like a Pekinese. Fortunately, Georgie confounded our fears for her development daily, growing poised for her mum and well-balanced for me. Shrugging off our petty name-calling, she'd answer equally, without favour, to either Georgie or Georgia, proving herself more mature and well-adjusted than her warring parents. I told her more than once she was 'Georgie' to me 'cause she was the 'Best'. She didn't have a clue what I was on about, of course, and although I had a wee chuckle to myself like it was an oh-so-clever private joke, I stopped saying it because what's so clever about talking over a wee kid's head or comparing her – Girl Utd, all Pears-soap skin and perfect smile – with a lost Ulsterman whose football genius we preserve in the collective memory as he pickles his insides? He's not fit to lace our Georgie's boots, I think.)

I'm imitating *Teletubbies* talk, saying 'E-oh!', going Dipsy, waving my arms and attempting to dance like they do while Georgie, sitting Po-faced on the sofa, her wee legs crossed like she's her mum watching the news, is gesturing to me to get out of the way of the tv, saying: 'I can't see, Daddy! Shh, will you, I'm *trying* to watch this.' Like *I'm* the kid. And I remember my brothers, way too old for *Playschool*, doing much the same thing, leaping about the room pretending they were elephants as the presenter had invited them to do. They were swinging their arms in front of their faces like trunks. Taking the piss, actually. And I'm lying on my tummy, my elbows on the carpet, my hands holding up my chin, trying to pay attention to what the presenter was saying as I was, after all, exactly the target age for the programme and all my nursery-school chums would be watching too. I treated my brothers with the disdain they deserved. What was so amusing about pretending to be elephants, anyway?

'This isn't meant for you. It's for children,' I told them. 'You're not funny, y'know.' I must have said it so seriously they laughed. James and Jackie could be *so* immature.

Watching *The Liver Birds* when I was little I laughed at all the jokes along with the whole family.

'So what, exactly, was funny about what she said just then, Joey?' James would ask cruelly, nodding towards the screen, knowing the mildly risqué gag was beyond me. 'What are you laughing at?'

I was mortified. It was true, I had no idea what was funny about the joke. I couldn't even be sure what the funny line was. All I knew was that everyone else was laughing, everyone was happy. It made me happy too. I just wanted to join in. It really didn't matter much that I didn't get the joke.

Georgie makes me re-live my life all over. We'd be watching some repeat of *Friends* or *Frasier*, she'd have no idea what the joke was – way over her head – but she'd be chuckling away with her mum and me, enjoying the atmosphere, just glad to see us smile for a change. I suppose.

Interactive television.

We always had interactive tv, our family, it's nothing new. My mum, she hates snakes, always has, can't bear them. Not even a picture of one in a book. A real phobia. So whenever a snake came on tv she'd let out a short scream and look away. We'd have to jump up double-quick, run to the set and turn it over.

My father, he's weird, it's like he hasn't quite grasped that people in films are only acting and it's all only make believe. Any kind of drama which bares a reasonable approximation to real life and he can hardly bear to watch. He objected to violence on tv and would rather leave the room than watch another cops-and-robbers show.

Me? I'm the first generation to grow up with tv. Bang, bang, bang, another smokin' gun, big deal. So what? – it all just washes over me. I can't remember the last time I was moved or amazed or surprised by anything on tv. Zap, zap, zap through the channels, mindlessly. People dropping like flies. Wall-to-wall murder and mayhem – big deal, so what, who cares? There'd be a fight scene in some film or a boxing match and my father would come in and say: 'What you watching this rubbish for? There must be something better on.' He'd feign disinterest and pretend to read yesterday's newspaper – second hand after Mrs Murray had finished with it – but I'd hear the pages rustle as he gawped over the top of them, his head imperceptively dodging and weaving, ducking and diving with every punch, getting in a few of his own.

Hollywood car chases and explosions my father deplored, but put on the news? Blanket bombing in Vietnam, typhoon in Pakistan, snipers in Belfast? Real-life murder and mayhem – he'd look grim but wouldn't flinch. He'd watch the news religiously on ITV, then turn over to BBC to watch their version. And, guess what, I do exactly the same now. They reckon men like watching news because it's therapeutic. It puts their own problems into perspective and, unlike the demands of wives and kids and work, no one expects them to come up with solutions. No one's going to ask them how to get the Russian tanks out of Czechoslovakia or how to get the Red Cross airlifts through to Biafra.

Our interactive tv had James and Jackie scrapping all the time over which channel to watch. There was a choice of only three then but they still couldn't agree. (I'd just be spectating, as the best programmes, the ones for younger kids, had finished by then.) Mum would come in: 'Enough! Stop this shouting! Mrs Murray'll think she lives next door to the zoo! If you can't stop fighting this television is going back to the shop, d'you understand?' (Which we assumed was an idle threat, she said it so often.) At this point, she'd usually switch it off altogether and tell them to do something else but she once surprised me by suggesting: 'Joe, you can decide what to watch for a change.'

'Wh ... what Mum?'

She probably thought she was doing me a favour.

'You decide which channel to watch', she smiled. And suddenly I wasn't a detached observer happily chewing on a Bazooka Joe – wondering about how many labels I would need to collect to send off for a harmonica – entertained by my brothers' never-ending feud. Now I was expected to be Henry Kissinger – solve the problem and make the peace. My mother left me to sort it out: all I had to do was state my own particular preference. Simple enough you'd think, but it's hard to find a compromise when *Animal Magic*'s on one side, *Magpie*'s on the other, Coke and sweets are being offered as bribes by the opposing factions, and there's an underlying, unspoken threat of unspecified consequences should I get it wrong. Nevertheless, after a short deliberation I made my solemn verdict be known: '*Animal Magic* ...' I began, before seeing the thunder in James' face which inspired a swift u-turn, ' ... is a *good* programme to watch, maybe, *next* time. But I think we should watch *Magpie*.' Jackie looked disappointed. I tried to make amends: 'I know! We could *play* at *Animal Magic*, Jackie.' He was insulted at the suggestion. He sat sulking, with his back to *Magpie* in protest (wouldn't even acknowledge an item on Airfix models which, I know, he was mad keen on and would've watched any other time). Instead, he started doing the creepy voice off *Captain Scarlet and the Mysterons,* knowing it always made me hide behind the sofa. I couldn't stand the heat, fled to the kitchen and hid in the folds of my mother's skirt as she made the tea.

James and Jackie fought over the channels all the time and even when they agreed on a programme, they'd find something in its content to fight over. Their sibling rivalry simmered gently non-stop – down the street, in the playground, the garden, the house, the kitchen, anywhere – ready to boil over at the mere flick of a switch, but at the time my parents blamed the corrosive, corrupting conversation-killing influence of television. And when James pushed Jackie through the French windows because he wouldn't stop shouting *Crackerjack!* along with an excitable live audience of Brownies and Cub Scouts at BBC Television Centre, enough was enough. The tv had to go. Browncoats from Granada came to take our friend and teacher away. In mourning, the three of us formed an impromptu cortège and followed the men outside as our tv set – flex limply trailing – was gently placed into a box and slid into the back of their van. James was flashing lethal, 'this-is-all-your-fault, you're-gonna-get-it' looks to Jackie. The living-room furniture was rearranged to disguise our loss. But the hearth had been ripped from our home.

James retreated to his room and started spending a lot more time with Jimi Hendrix and David Bowie. Jackie found a new fad for filling fancy liqueur bottles he'd scavenged from the backdoor bins of some hotel with sand, plastering them with Polyfilla, sticking pebbles and shells on them, buying sockets and shades and calling them table lamps.

I studied insectology.

Honey bees went buzzing mad when I caught them in jam jars – buzzing *crazy* if I caught them then spun the jar on the grass. When you're small and defenceless it's a heady power trip to find something even smaller and more defenceless. I'd stare at the creature at my mercy, face pressed against the distorted glass. He looked as if he was breathing hard, puffing at the hot air in the jar, planning his next move, contemplating his imminent demise.

'You'll need to punch some holes in the lid or it'll suffocate,' Jackie told me helpfully in passing, without bothering to tell me what 'suffocate' meant. Sounded very, very nasty indeed, though. Ha, ha, *ha!* I was the evil Dr No with 007 my prisoner.

'How would you like to die, Meester Bond? By drowning? By spinning? By suffikate?'

I was punching some air-holes with a school compass when the lid fell off the jar and, screaming blue murder, 007 stung me on the hand. Turns out he wasn't so defenceless after all.

Like Kamikaze pilots, bumble-bees were as much a danger to themselves as others. They were loaded but to pull the trigger would be suicide. On a run between flower stops, weighed down with sacs of pollen, they looked like little drunk-driven double-decker buses. I wasn't too scared of them. Wasps, on the other hand, were to be treated with the utmost respect. Not for them a long, hot summer wasted nine-to-five honey-making. They seemed to cruise the skies for purely hedonistic pursuits. I reckoned they would sting again and again and again, any time they wanted, without provocation, for the sheer hell of it. Kept clear of wasps, I did.

In the course of my studies, I learned that the paving stone under the washing line was actually a secret gate to the underworld. All kinds of hideous abominations of nature shunned the light to live under there among the yellow grass and white roots. I'd steel myself and lift the stone. They would immediately shrink from the sunlight like

Dracula, knowing their appearance was too grotesque for the full light of day and that they inspired loathing and contempt in all right-thinking men. I wouldn't catch any specimens. Wouldn't dare. I was convinced there were things under that stone unknown to science. I'd generally poke them about a bit with a stick, letting them know who's boss. Making sure they realized, in case they got ideas above their station, that there'd be no welcome for them in the world above the stone, beyond the garden. There would be no welcome, in particular, for any of them, to the vacant and dusty area underneath my bed, though sometimes I would itch in my pyjamas at the mere thought.

While square-eyed kids were watching wholesome, black and white David Attenborough documentaries, I was educating myself, watching a fly on the wall, jam jar and tweezers at the ready.

• • • • • • • • • • • • • • • • • • •

Monday mourning in Aberdeen. The meep, meep, meep of the alarm. Clattering blindly down the wooden stairs (no one pays to light the close) I make the bus to Holburn Street. Five stops to start the day. And I have *arrived*. I've made it. Here, card-swiping through the sliding doors, beyond the imitation marble reception, past the polished smile of the receptionist, there's a lift that takes employees and visitors alike to the top, the very top, of the rat-racing, go-getting, mirrored magnificence of the Institute of Business and Entrepreneurship.

'People in glass houses shouldn't throw stones,' says Prue, like she's reading my mind as I walk into our ground-floor office, but it's only today's motto on her tear-a-page-off-a-day desk calender. Ensconced first, each and every day, she shares these with me as I'm hanging my jacket behind my chair, before I even sit down. It's disconcerting how she makes them sound like they've been written especially for me. 'If you tell the truth you don't have to remember everything,' she'll say. (I feel rumbled.) 'Many an honest man stands in need of help that has not the face to beg it.' (Am I so obvious?) 'Disappointment should always be taken as a stimulant, never as a discouragement.' (She's got to be making these up.) Prue prefixes each aphorism: 'Oh, *this* is good, Joe, listen to this one' or 'Ha! This is *so* true!' or occasionally, 'Mmn, don't get this, do you?' Her favourites by far – she savours and memorises them – are ones like 'Man's work lasts till the set of the sun, woman's work is never done' or 'An usherette is a girl who puts a man in his place' or 'In spite of seeming different, men are all of one pattern'. She hoards these affirmations for ammunition.

Seeing me arrive, Audrey Marshall – our boss, more bony than bonnie – smashes through the smoked-glass partition doors, brusque and big-brooched: 'Morning, morning Joseph!' she says, cheerily enough, but that's the upper-limit maximum of her small talk before it's down to business:

'Now. I've looked at your press release on the video conferencing link to "Export Malaysia". Only one change – you've split the infinitive here.' She's pointing a chipped red fingernail at the offending sentence.

'Well, I figure if they can split the atom ...'

But she's not listening.

'When are you putting this out?'

'Tomorrow, I think, isn't that what we'd agreed?'

'To?'

One of Audrey's little power tools – these one-word questions. Puts you on the defensive, having to work out both the question and the answer. Makes you seem slow and dim-witted.

'Pardon?'

'Who to?'

'Oh, em, all the business journals, the dailies, the evening papers, the freesheets ...'

'Good. Can I bring you up to speed on the Innovation Convention in the Exhibition Centre?' I nod, she thinks aloud: 'I'm in meetings all morning, lunch at the Chamber of Commerce, meetings most of the afternoon, how's 5.40 for you?'

'Em, yep, that should be fine.' I look at my desk diary but I know it's empty then (that's past home time, man!). 'Yes, that's okay for me,' I confirm, scribbling the time down.

'Should only take about an hour, I have a Global Famine Relief dinner at the Marcliffe tonight so I'll need to get away quite sharp. Have you read the e-mail I sent you?'

'No, I'm sorry, not yet, when did you send it?'

'This morning.'

'But I'm only just ...'

'When you *do* get a chance to read it, can you put together a press release?'

'What's it about?'

'Aberdeen is to host the small businessman's conference early next year.'

'That's the height of bad taste, that is.'

'Sorry?'

'A conference for little people.'

'What? Oh, yes, I see. Ha! Better be careful how we word that.' She pauses, thrown for a millisecond, 'What else? Ah, yes, We're still waiting for the "Ideas in Action" pamphlets to be delivered from the printers. Could you find out what the delay is? I've tried to get through to them three times already this morning. Can you chase them up for me?' She sighs. 'Right! Better get off. Meeting with the Chairman. Should be back about 11, Prudence, I'm on the mobile if you need me.'

And she's gone, disappearing in a puff of powder like some pantomime dame.

If I'm lucky, I'll get a couple of minutes now to get my head together, make a coffee, take a quick dip into the Celtic website, before I start work checking the papers for business news cuttings. The curved desks all fit together like pieces in a jigsaw into one square, space-saving unit in the centre of the room. Me, Prudence and Chris all face inwards towards our computers and a tangle of electrical cables pours onto the floor at the epicentre. I sit with my back to the office door, which is bad Feng Shui, Audrey says (she's been a world authority ever since she discovered it in an in-flight magazine) because visitors see me before I see them and this could put me at a psychological disadvantage. Well, that depends, I reckon. Sometimes people come in and I pretend I don't hear them. They see me on the phone or typing away so they don't interrupt. They shuffle their feet impatiently, cough for my attention, then just as they're beginning to feel as if they don't count, I swivel round in my chair and deign to deal with them. (Actually, I only ever do this to the spivs from consultancy who burst in like they own the place, demanding immediate attention. I always try to redress the cosmic balance by giving priority to shy, blushing, kind people like Fay from administration, who Audrey treats like the Institute's doormat. I sincerely hope, when the meek inherit the Earth Fay'll be President.) Furthermore it's bad Feng Shui, Audrey says, to sit near the door because it makes a person more inclined to slip off early for lunch or at 5.30pm. So there. My actions are beyond my control. Hey, why fight it? It's ancient, it's Chinese.

Reliably the last cog to join the wheels of industry each day is Chris, who drives in from Peterhead.

'Morning, chaps! Traffic was *awful* this morning, nose to tail all the way from Ellon,' she says, by way of explanation, though: 'I'm late this morning 'cause I'm late every morning, it's the habit of a lifetime!' would be more accurate.

Prue tilts her head round her computer screen at me and raises her eyes to the ceiling like she's reading my mind. Chris potters about making herself comfortable, making a few urgent calls, once she knows Audrey's not due back till 11.

'Buchanan. Chris. Institute of Business and Entrepreneurship ... put my Hoover in for repair on Thursday, is it ready for collection?'

'Buchanan. Chris. Institute of Business and Entrepreneurship ... I'd like to reserve a table by the fire for Saturday night.'

'Buchanan. Chris. Institute of Business and Entrepreneurship ... can I book tickets for a party of six in the upper circle for the seventeenth, please?'

'Mary? Chris, here,' there's some hesitation at the other end of the line, 'Chris ... *Buchanan!*'

Then Chris' voice goes all peculiar, droning out the side of her mouth in a strange digitally remastered stage whisper that signifies she's a confidante who can be trusted to exercise the utmost discretion. Chris has evidently embarked on another of her frequent Good Samaritan missions. She's never happier than helping friends and family in crisis. She's got a big heart. She's missed her true calling. It's only when her whisper gets louder than her normal voice and I eavesdrop unavoidably, hearing her squeak incredulously ' ... *foetus in a handbag!*', that I just want to shake my head in despair. Prue leans round her screen at me, shaking her head in despair, like she's reading my mind.

The office settles to a sound like teeth chattering as plastic keys are tapped on plastic keyboards. Focus too much on the sound – hearing nothing but colleagues' erratic typing, their spaces between their words, their new paragraphs, their pauses, their backspace-deleting, their sighs, their composing mumbles – and it would be easy to slip into madness. I could get a number for vermin control from the *Yellow Pages*. Call the Pied Piper, ask him to rid this building from a plague of clicking mice! It helps me shut the noise out, imagining all the computer hardware in the building wrenching loose from its sockets and following the minstrel up Union Street – VDUs, keyboards, printers and mice, lots of mice with long tails, pouring out of shops and offices and flats – down Marischal Street, gathering pace and throwing themselves like lemmings off the harbour into the North Sea.

Outside our office window there is a huge horse chestnut tree – they actually built the car park round it – and I've seen it in all seasons now. Seen it blossom. Seen it bloom – its giant green leaves like hands, the tree awash with applause. Seen the life-colour drain from the leaves. Seen them turn yellow and brown and fall. Seen it silenced. My stupid daydreaming tree keeping me off my work.

It would have knocked us out if the thought had ever occurred to us kids. But it never really registered to me or my best friends, Finlay Lorimer and Niall Reid, that the shiny, brown pearls we coveted were actually the seeds of the cloud-skimming horse chestnut trees which dwarfed us. How could we equate the two? One giant, mature tree – with more rings than a branch of H. Samuel – from one small conker? No chance. We blithely thwarted each seed's bid for germination in the name of sport. Kids can be so cruel. But then we were preoccupied – pearlfishers must feel the same sense of anticipation when they twist the knife to prise open an oyster – as we split open prickly green, outer shells which gave no certain clues to what might be inside. The largest – which held such promise that the kids threw sticks to bring them down from the tree early – would sometimes disappoint with twin conkers too small for competition, or large immature conkers. Occasionally, though, the most perfectly round and ready conkers would be discovered tightly wrapped in the white flesh of an unassuming, thin-skinned capsule.

The best and the biggest conkers were invariably found, naturally wind-blown like the first leaves, on the ground. It was a thrill to spy a Malteser-brown chink in casing cracked open by the fall. Sometimes I think that was the real kick with conkers and the real competition – who found the biggest – and the game back at school was an afterthought. It was the trek to the trees. Running and kicking up the leaves, unburdened by the languid limbs of summer or the extra layers of winter. And even with our schoolboy resistance to poetry we couldn't help but admit – quietly, to ourselves, back in the classroom – that John Keats had captured autumn, as we knew and understood it, like he'd pressed smoky, yellowing leaves inside all of our textbooks.

Conkers didn't always inspire the noble spirit in small boys – we knew how to cheat. Stringing them was a nightmare. Skewering them with a knitting needle is the kind of potentially life-threatening operation that makes children's television presenters caution 'get a grown-up to help you', which for us, of course, was unthinkable. Nevertheless, unsubstantiated rumours abounded that Russell Bradley's dad had used a Black and Decker power drill to make perfect holes in all his prize conkers. Performance-enhanced ones – covered with a clear veneer from big sister's nail varnish, or allegedly soaked in vinegar and kept over from last year to harden more like steel bolts than nuts – were smashing all-comers. Ruses which – while not exactly illegal, as none of us had any written rules – did seem to contravene the Corinthian ideals of the competition. I wasn't above trying to improve my chances. I'd heard placing them in an oven, gas mark 5 for 20 minutes, made sure-fired winners (actually it just makes them more brittle). I followed the instructions to the letter except I got side-tracked with a puncture on my bike and was busy with a basin of water, an orange inner tube, some bubbles and the glorified Elastoplasts of my bicycle repair kit, when a warm, pungent, sweet burning smell wafted out to the front steps from the kitchen. A mulch of black, smoking carbon was all that remained.

Once the competition proper got under way at

assorted venues around the playground, in the cloakrooms, even on the school bus – anywhere there was enough room to take a good swing – the appeal of the game became apparent. It wasn't a contest of strength. The school bully who swung viciously at the small kid's conker as often as not found himself with a loose piece of string in his hand and his prize chestnut scattered on the floor. It gave the picked-on, specky kids the chance of sporting glory they'd earned standing unpicked, on the sidelines, the rest of the year.

Growing up, we forget how we roamed through the trees whooping like Apaches. Our close, unconscious, proximity to nature – dirty fingernails, grass stains, a familiarity with the slippery primeval feel of frog spawn. Now, if you put your ear to the ground – where once you'd convinced your pals you could hear the sound of distant buffalo – you'd just hear traffic. People would think you'd lost your marbles. They'd be right – lost your marbles, your catapult, your bubblegum football cards, your conkers too.

The reverie tree outside the office has conkers now and my eyes seek out the best ones on the branches even though I know I'll never actually pick them up. They'll fall fallow on the tarmac between the BMWs and the monster 4x4s – people from the Institute seem to need to negotiate the dirt roads and stray kangaroos from Aboyne to Aberdeen. I can hardly bear the thought of seeing that tree in winter again, looming outside, through the condensation on the window, its bark like elephant skin as sleety snow drips down its trunk. I don't want to witness the whole process again. I'll end up like one of those video cameras in Dixons' shop window filming constantly the humdrum monotony of streetlife outside, as schoolkids pass by and make faces at themselves on the closed circuit television. Display cameras which end up unsaleable because the lens is indelibly marked by the shape of the pavement it's been trained on too long. That's how I'm getting. I can close my eyes, on the bus home, in the supermarket, in bed trying to sleep, and the shape and form of that window, that view, that tree, endures.

• • • • • • • • • • • • • • • • • • •

Jackie lent me *Mr Galliano's Circus* to read when I wasn't much beyond Janet and John. He'd got it from James who'd bought it second-, maybe third-hand from another kid in primary school. He'd long since out-grown it, of course. I liked hand-me-downs. Meant they were tried and tested. Scratchy woollen jumpers were worn down, soft and comfortable by the time my older brothers had finished with them and I got to wear them. Rebellion was too, and by the time it came to me, arguments with our parents had mostly been fought and won or lost. The rough edges had long since been smoothed over by experience and I could pretty much please myself.

Hand-me-downs were fine except at Christmas. Jackie asked Santa for a bike and, strapped for cash, my father acquired a second-hand bike and put hours of secret work into scraping all traces of rust off and painting it up to look (almost) brand new. Jackie got up on Christmas morning and was overjoyed. It was the best bike ever. Santa Claus was the greatest. How did he know he'd wanted a bike? What a guy! Then, after church, in the afternoon, he cycled down the street as fast as he could pedal to show off his pride and joy to all his pals. Guess what? They'd *all* got bikes for Christmas! Only *their* bikes really were split new, with proper metallic paint and everything. Some kids – too young or too spoilt for tact or subtlety – told Jackie bluntly that his 'new' bike was actually only an old second-hand one. Somebody thought the bike looked awful similar to Dr Milne's son's which he'd replaced with a newer, better one. Jackie was heartbroken. Why should Santa decide he was going to be the only kid in the street who wasn't going to get a new bike this year? I couldn't work it out either.

Jackie came home in tears but my father turned it all around, told Jackie this was his lucky day. Not only had

Santa given him a new bike – a new-to-Jackie bike, that is –
but he'd also been given the chance to appreciate The True
Meaning of Christmas. Jackie stopped crying for a minute to
listen. We were all listening, we all wanted to hear. Even
Mum, making the Christmas dinner, was eavesdropping.
But my father went all silent and enigmatic on us, like it was
a truth worth knowing only if you could work it out yourself.
(It was the same way he taught Physics – what good were
answers if you hadn't wrestled with all the variables and
applied the right formulae to prove their absolute truth?)
Jackie sniffed back the tears and said: 'There are children
who don't have anything at all, even at Christmas they don't
get anything. For them, a packet of Smarties would be the
best Christmas ever and they'd be really happy. And then
there's other children who've got too much, all the toys they
could ever want, but because they get toys all the time
Christmas isn't special to them. We're lucky because
Christmas is special.' Correct. V.G. Gold Star for Jackie. Extra
special birthday present planned for him in May.

If my father ever said we should be grateful for what
we had and we were well-off, rich even, in all the important
things, not even James would challenge him. It was hush-
hush but we knew, from the clues Mum let slip, that Dad
spoke from experience, unlike the celebrity fakers and
phoneys you see on tv who wear their mythical deprived
childhoods like badges of valour. Those who really lived it are
almost ashamed to admit it. They know it isn't glorious. It's
not worth celebrating. All that 'We were poor but we were
happy' shite! Liars! The indignity of it. The scars for life. You
could see it in the way my father practically scraped the glaze
off his plate every time he ate. But he was loathe to talk about
it. Never did. How do you explain 'parish shoes' to the
throwaway Pepsi generation? So none of us dared contradict
him when he told us we were lucky. It was just that, we
couldn't help but notice, some kids were even luckier than us.

That's why *Mr Galliano's Circus* was the big top for

me. The kid hero saves the day. Only adults, hung up on political correctness, don't like Enid Blyton. She knew what we wanted: relentless, breathless, thrilling action and adventure and lots of it. There was even a little subversive romance going on the kids could see but the adults couldn't. She made *me* the hero of the book – the unassuming Jimmy Brown. His father was a joiner by trade (like Jesus, though there all comparisons end) but at the beginning their family's got serious money worries 'cause Jimmy's dad's having trouble finding work until the day – *Da-dara-dara-da-da-dara!* – the circus comes to town. Jimmy would love to see the show but can't afford a ticket so he goes along to the park to watch them setting up the main marquee where he makes friends with Lotta, an independently minded and agile young girl, who rides horses bareback in the ring. By the third chapter, Jimmy's not just seen the circus he's joined it, along with his family. His dad's working as a handyman while his mum's busy cleaning the rickety old spare caravan they've been given. Jimmy's got a special way with animals. They love him. A snarling dog or even a ferocious tiger becomes as soppy as a puppy or a kitten at the sound of his low, soft, hypnotic voice. Jimmy's so good with animals, in fact, that he trains his own amazing dog Lucky to do tricks and starts performing in the circus. Jimmy is so popular and makes so much money for Mr Galliano's circus that he's able to buy his parents a brand new, gleaming chrome caravan for the circus parade. As if that wasn't enough, even though Lotta's always making faces at him and pinching him and other girly stuff, you just know that they're really, really in love and when they grow up they'll get married and have lots of little circus kids.

It's expected of kids to like the circus, so I did. But when I was actually taken to see one, at the Kelvin Hall in Glasgow, I didn't get it. We were so high up in the cheap seats that I could hardly see a thing. The clowns did visual jokes with plastic flowers and watering cans which didn't reach us at the back, though people still laughed and clapped dutifully for the Emperor's clothes. Even the elephants looked small from where we were. Every English bank holiday, when all us Scots kids were usually still at school, we'd race home – in the olden days before VCRs – hoping to catch the end of *The Great Escape* when Steve McQueen leaps the perimeter fence on his motorbike. Instead, by the time we made it home, there'd be some circus on and I'd avidly tune in 'cause kids *like* circuses, don't they? Then one day it finally dawned on me: I *don't* like this. This is boring. Elephants rampaging through an African village wreaking havoc on *Daktari* – now that's entertainment. Elephants in sequinned hats squeezing onto a tiny podium – that's a bit, well, embarrassing. And when you've seen one spangly woman spin from a rope with her teeth, well, you've seen 'em all.

Mr Galliano's Circus was way better than Billy Smart's or Chipperfield's or the Moscow State. It was sheer wish-fulfilment. The book's not in print any more (performing animals are no longer in vogue, although it doesn't stop Disney hawking *Dumbo*) but I found a copy in a second-hand bookshop and started reading it to Georgie. I reckoned she was too young and would probably get bored. But the story grabbed her too. I read it in instalments each night to her and she always knew where we were in the story: 'You got to the bit when Jumbo the elephant's ran off and Jimmy's trying to find him,' she'd tell me, settling herself comfy with the pillow ready to listen.

I wanted to be Jimmy Brown when I was a kid. But we didn't have a dog or a cat so it was stretching credulity to believe, as I did, that I possessed 'a special way with animals'. I could improvise, couldn't I? There were gangs of black hooded crows in the field near our house. Maybe I could rear one, an orphan perhaps, incubating its egg wrapped in cotton wool in a Weetabix packet on the storage heater. The chick would hatch out, see me first and think I was mum. I'd feed him a diet of worms supplemented only occasionally with Opal Fruits and teach him to shit on the grass and sit on my shoulder and not the other way round. I'd teach him to speak. Not just parrot-fashion but really speak, converse, tell me jokes, keep me company. And maybe later, when he was old enough to understand, we'd have a good long talk, and I'd break it to him gently that I wasn't, in actual fact, his real mum.

Crows were cool. They flew about in little gangs and none of the other birds would mess with them, they always picked away at dead rabbits on the road until the very last moment when a car was coming then they'd hop to one side till it passed. No fear. No fuss. And they all dressed, head to claw, in black. I'd teach my crow tricks and take it to school where everyone would want to be friends with the boy with the crow, with the 'special way' with animals.

It wasn't so far-fetched. There was a mynah bird in a large cage outside a pub in Pitlochry. Schoolkids would try and goad it into swearing and they'd squeal with delight when it almost always obliged. It was an unremarkable-looking bird, not much different from your common-or-garden blackbird, but this was one startling starling with the ability, I'm sure, to mimic the sweet song of the nightingale but which chose instead to speak in the most authentic drunken growl, saying: 'Awayafuckenbassaya!'

Crow's nests were out of my reach. I never did find an orphaned egg. Pity. Me and my crow would've been famous, we'd have been on telly, and everyone would've loved us. But the main thing is, we'd have been friends.

• • • • • • • • • • • • • • • • • •

The circus never came to Pitlochry but The Shows did. Quite why me and my pals should greet their arrival with such wanton excitement is hard to fathom now but those glorified see-saws and roundabouts, garishly lit with multi-coloured bulbs, set the school ablaze with anticipation. Word got round by osmosis that the troops and the trucks of the carnival were rolling into town and it was hastily arranged to skip school lunches to welcome them like a liberating army.

Me, Finlay and Moses (a.k.a. Niall Reid) made the long trek down to the lochside car park, near the Hydro Electric dam, where the shows were sited annually to coincide with the lucrative weekend of the Highland Games. We watched from higher ground the well-choreographed operation to set up camp. Wiry boy-men with peach fluff moustaches like our James' hauled tarpaulin off trailers and hammered spikes into the soft grass, laughing and shouting but never once letting the cigarettes welded to their lower lips fall to the ground. We studied them – believing them all to be authentic Romany – like anthropologists. We'd later copy some of their mannerisms and macho swagger to the bewilderment of our classmates. We envied them the fresh air, the purposeful manual labour, the ability to smoke without their eyes watering, but most of all we envied the unbelievably easy access they must enjoy to all those prizes. Imagine! All the goldfish, the Celtic or Rangers team pennants, all the Farrah Fawcett posters you could ever want. We pointed to this machine or that ride, bluffing to each other about our expert knowledge of generators and hydraulics. We could only gawp for a few minutes – playing truant wasn't a realistic option in a school so small you'd be missed and a town where everyone knew your father – before running back up the road for the first class of the afternoon, vowing to return that night.

Streets away we could hear piercing girly screams above the grating sound of cheesy chart music. We were all trying hard to act nonchalant but as the noise grew louder and louder the closer we got, the faster we walked and talked, excitement mounting, change jingling in our pockets. The scene from our earlier vantage point had been transformed. Enclosed by a dark wagon-circle of generators, lorries, trailers and chrome caravans pretty with lace curtains, was a carnival of bright technicolour. We walked into the light and the sweet smell of hot dogs, candy floss, wet grass and barely understood possibilities.

'Don't play or go on anything till you've seen what's all here, then you can pick and choose what you like best – makes your money last longer,' said Finlay's mother, who wasn't there but had obviously possessed Finn's body and was using him as a medium. Me and Moses laughed because we were ready to go mad but Finn was right enough. The dodgems were 20 pence and the waltzers were 40 this year. How was I going to spin out the £2.20 in my pocket? Saucy postcard beauties gave us the come on to throw darts with frayed flights at giant, pock-marked playing cards. Medieval harridans leaned over their counters offering us weapons: hoops and bean bags and chained guns. 'Just look straight ahead,' said Finn, moving us along, deconstructing the shows on our behalf, 'there's sand inside the tin cans on the bottom row – you can't knock 'em down with bean bags. The sights on those rifles are squint. See that game? You don't win a prize first time, you just get a token. You need six tokens to win anything decent.' The witches were so insistent as we passed by their stalls we felt spellbound, almost compelled to obey and pay up, but we resisted, shaking our heads, walking on till we'd completed our tour, taken everything in, savoured the atmosphere, picked our priorities, selected our favourites, and carefully weighed up the most likely prize-winning options like the thrifty, sensible, cynical, street-wise kid Finn was.

Catriona Kennedy was there in a denim jacket and jeans with two other girls from our class. Our gang stopped, too briefly, to talk to their gang. We probably all wanted to hang out together but as soon as the first lull in the conversation arose we got self-conscious and looked at our shoes – surprised to find them caked in mud from the field, churned into a quagmire by the showground vehicles and hundreds of pairs of feet – and the easiest thing was for us to go our separate ways. I hadn't taken much notice of Catriona at school. I'd always liked her but not in that way. We made a clear distinction between the girls in our class who were just like us really, 'cept they were quieter, had longer hair and could only kick footballs with the stubs of their toes, and the women on television with their disquieting curves. But something strange was going on tonight. Some kind of witchcraft in the head-spinning glamour of the flashing disco lights, prizes-for-everyone stalls, and Showaddywaddy blasting out full volume from the waltzers. That same strange, unaccountable yearning in the pit of my stomach I first noticed, but didn't understand, watching Olga Korbut in the Olympics four years earlier and recognized again, a little less vaguely, in that year's Olympics, in Nadia Comaneci's girlhood perfection. Balancing on the brink of understanding, yearning for Catriona.

It was time to start spending. There was a kind of medicine ball on the end of a mechanical arm which gauged the strength of your punch – so we all lined up for a shot. Moses gave it his best sledgehammer blow. Thud! The arm swung back with the force, ringing a buzzer and a bell. He rubbed his sore right hand as we watched the red lights race up the gauge, then race back down again, stopping humiliatingly at the 'Mr Puny! Go lift some weights!' level. Me and Finn thought it was hilarious, confident that while the 'Mr Universe!' level might be beyond our reach this year, 'Mr Contender!' status would be wholly respectable. We each gave it our best shot, loosening our right arms from their sockets with the wholehearted impact. It felt like punching a brick wall and we both scored even lower than Moses. We walked away from the apparatus in disgust, hands smarting. Finn gave it a wee fly kick.

'Must be broken,' I said.

'It's fixed,' said Moses.

I wanted a goldfish even more than a football pennant. That'd *really* screw the shows people, that would. Me actually winning a fish. Me actually seeing a ping-pong ball arc from my hand and get accidentally swallowed, against all the odds, by one of tens of empty, mean-lipped goldfish bowls tantalisingly just out of our reach in the centre of the stall. The idea of walking home with a new pet without anyone running a check to see if I'd got sufficient fish food or a suitable tank or if I was on Interpol's register of fishkillers was a sweet, strange freedom. I mean, how were they to know all creatures great and small loved and trusted me like I was Jimmy Brown?

Above the stall, the goldfish watched us watching them, our faces grotesquely distorted by the thin, clear, bulging bags of water. It was all a matter of angles. Each time I threw a ball it would ricochet off a rim and land harmlessly between the jars. Mo fared no better. Bags of water bubbled as fish laughed. Three goes and no luck. So we tried another angle. Me and Mo created a diversion, asking the lady for another shot and taking an age to find the right money, while Finn took his turn behind her back. He stretched over, practically falling into the stall, and neatly dropped a ping pong ball into the nearest bowl. It spun round fast in there as if not quite believing what had happened. Finn got his fish.

Our paths crossed with Catriona's gang again and we told them how our guile, cunning and skill had won the fish but didn't tell them our scores on the boxing machine. Catriona showed me a silly, long-haired purple gonk she'd won with a lucky numbers ticket and offered me a pinch of her candy floss. Her eyes were sparkling with the strobe light from the waltzers. We were having a laugh together, shouting above the noise, talking like we'd never talked before, but her pals dragged her off to queue for the 'Rib-tickler' ride. Finn saved us 50 pence with a detailed deconstruction of the illusion: 'It's not worth it. You just sit in your seats, right? Inside this cylinder thing, which is painted like the inside of a room, y'know? Then they close the door and start turning the big cylinder but the seats don't actually move at all. It's an optical illusion. You feel like you're upside down, sitting on the ceiling.' Far from exploding the magic, so we could all feel smug and superior saving our pennies for something more worthy of our cash, Finn only succeeded in making it sound even more intriguing, especially as it could be *me* in there, sitting on the ceiling, with Catriona.

'Scotland's smallest man', Wee Wullie Winkie, was somewhere inside a big grey tent. I wanted to see him. So did Moses. So did Finn. It'd beef us up after being KO'd by the boxing machine. But it was a whole pound to get in and I didn't have enough money if I wanted a couple of shots on the waltzers as well. Mo said he'd check it out and tell us if it was any good. He was only gone a few minutes and came back out shrugging his shoulders and shaking his head: 'It's just this wee guy in a kilt and a tammy, sitting on a stool smoking, drinking a can of Special Brew, looking *really* bored.' We started walking away but curiosity got the better of me and I slipped round the side of the tent and popped my head under the canvas, pulling up a peg with it. A spotlight shone in my face. I was right behind Wee Wullie Winkie, who towered two feet or so above me. He turned round to see what people were laughing at. He looked exactly like a garden gnome. I'd seen enough and was crawling back out when Wee Wullie leapt from his stool and grabbed me by the hair.

'What d'ye think this is – a *free* fucken freakshow?' he said, with unexpected menace and venom for one so small, pulling my hair tighter, and really hurting me.

I was frightened. He was calling security. I was in trouble. I lashed out, not thinking, throwing a haymaker towards his red beard. He let go of my head and fell to the ground, pole-axed. He looked out cold. I stared in horror for a moment before retreating back under the canvas. Moses and Finn could see something was up.

'I think I've killed him,' I said, 'I think he's dead. C'mon! We've got to get out of here!'

We ran full pelt – Finn's fish in fright at the storm in

a teacupful of water – to the opposite side of the showground and hung about near the exit ready to run at any moment if the police arrived. But all was quiet. There was no commotion. No nothing.

'Did you get him, Joey? Did you? Did you smack him one?' said Finn, getting his breath back.

'What do you mean, did I get him? I think I might have *killed* him.' I was still too panicky to enjoy being a hero. 'Don't you understand? One punch and I've killed the smallest man in Scotland.'

'Nice one, Joey! Ach, don't worry. He's just a wee shite anyway!' said Mo.

'People *saw* me, Mo. They'll be able to identify me. Let's get out of here.'

But they wouldn't budge. The waltzers were waiting. Nothing untoward was happening anyway. There was no posse of roustabouts gunning for me. There was no wailing or gnashing of teeth, no outpouring of grief for the assassination of the country's premier little person. In fact, everything looked so tranquil and unchanged I was eventually persuaded to venture back towards the crime scene.

I was adjusting to my new status as a fugitive from the law when Mo stopped dead. I froze too. There, only a few steps away from us, was Wee Wullie Winkie. Alive and well. He'd changed into a natty pair of children's jeans and a checked shirt from Mothercare. It was him all right. He walked unsteadily, mumbling apologetically to himself, as he climbed some steps into a caravan. Back at his show tent they were cursing him as they cleared away his empties.

Reassured I wasn't public enemy number one, I relaxed. We still had to spend the last of our money. We bumped into Catriona's gang again on the dodgems. She was a passenger in Caroline's car and I was driving Mo. I'd keep steering towards them like I was really going to bump them bad then ease up at the last moment for only a glancing impact and an exchange of big, laughing smiles. I was so preoccupied having a good time, I didn't see Russell Bradley coming at me from behind at high speed. Whack! Whiplash! Our car just about leapt into the air.

'Get 'im!' said Mo.

I spun the wheel and reversed out of the pile-up into some space. Sparks flew wildly from the wire cage above our heads as our car gathered pace along the full length of the circuit. Russell Bradley was lying prone. Stuck in the ruck. *Smash!* Got 'im!

The power died. We stepped out of our Grand Prix cars. Walked to the waltzers. Girl gang and boy gang stood close to each other on the wooden steps waiting for the ride to stop. It was now or never. Winner takes all. People got off. It was no big deal.

'Catriona!' I said, starting promisingly. 'Em, you wanna waltz with me?' (I must've thought you had to pretend to be a jive-talking American to make it with girls.) She followed me into an empty carriage. We handed over our coins, held so tightly they were warmed to 37ºC. We clung to the metal bar and exchanged shy smiles. Alone at last for the first time. There wasn't any chance of conversation as the music blared and the ride cranked up again. Round and round and round we spun, pinned back against the red leather seat by centrifugal force. A spin doctor twirled the back of our chair and sent us spinning even faster, throwing us even closer together. Suddenly, without warning, the seat spun clear off its moorings and crashed up through the roof into the night sky high above the shows. Open-mouthed in amazement, we looked down below us at Mo and Finn, Katherine and Mairi smiling and waving at us, Russell Bradley getting smaller and smaller as we spun higher and higher. All the pretty lights of the fairground were twinkling, surrounded by dark trees and the reflective blackness of Loch Faskally. We were unstoppable, whooshing on up, watching the tiny car lights race along the A9. We saw the orange glow from the streetlights of Perth, Dundee, Glasgow,

Edinburgh, the whole school map of Scotland laid out before us. We flew past satellites and into orbit.

The waltzers stopped. I opened my eyes. Stepped out the chair and held out my hand to help Catriona onto the wooden walkway. She took it! My God! She must feel it too, I thought. (Girls in our class were forever proving they were *entirely* capable of doing things themselves, thank you, as if we didn't know.) So this was a revelation. It could only mean one thing. Our all-too-brief sojourn to a higher high had swept her off her feet. She did look a little unsteady as we walked down the steps. A little pale too as she doubled up and vomited onto the grass, spattering my shoes. Our first kiss would have to wait then, I thought, as we rejoined our respective tribes back on planet Earth.

As we left the shows, the local bikers roared up for their AGM with the roustabouts. We'd have stayed to watch the battle but it was getting late. Finn's tragic fish lasted only till the following day. He returned from the shops with a small pot of fishfood – harbouring ambitious plans to win a female fish, build an aquarium and start a hatchery – only to find it smelly belly up, requiring a Christian burial. There was no going back for more. Our cash was spent. The shows moved out on Sunday. The magic had gone. It was sad. I'd liked to have consulted a fortune teller in one of the lace curtained caravans and asked her if, maybe next year, I'd get to hold Catriona's hand without making her sick.

•　•　•　•　•　•　•　•　•　•　•　•　•　•　•　•　•

Helen has a sales conference in London.

'It's an emergency otherwise I wouldn't call,' she says. It's the first time we've spoken in three months and she's talking in a cold, flat voice. 'My mother's in hospital, nothing serious, but she doesn't get out till Tuesday, Jane's not able to take her and Marcia's working this weekend. I *have* to go, it's *very* important for my work.'

Georgie's to stay with me for the weekend.

It'll be the first time she's come up to Aberdeen. A couple of weeks after the split with Helen I went to her mum's house to see Georgie. Helen wanted nothing to do with me. Although Georgie's gran didn't quite treat me like the enemy I could see she was wary. I arrived on a Sunday afternoon. Walked into the living room. The tv was playing *101 Dalmatians* but Georgie was preoccupied, sitting in a muddle of Barbies and Barbie's clothes and Barbie's Ken and Barbie's little sister, Shelley, deep in conversation, doing all the voices herself. She saw me come in, I could tell, but she didn't run to me with open arms and shout 'Daddy!' She didn't acknowledge me at all but her voices grew more stagey as she put on a show of self-sufficiency. I chatted stiltedly to Helen's mum, waiting for me and Georgie to make the necessary adjustments. The over-heated room was stifling and stuffy. I suggested we go to the park and Georgie reluctantly left her Barbies to come with me for an hour to the place where we'd chased and ran and fed the stupid ducks in the summer sunshine. Now it was raining, everything was wet, the clouds hung low, everything was muted. I took her back to her gran's.

That was the unwritten arrangement – me coming down from Aberdeen for awkward Sunday afternoons with Georgie at Helen's mum's – which lasted too short a while to become a pattern before the visits all but petered out. Helen was putting her life on hold for me, she said. Georgie had new friends, school trips and birthday parties which had to be negotiated against dull Sunday afternoons with Daddy. I stopped it. I established my own routine for the weekend.

'I'm busy too, y'know,' I told Helen, 'I have a life up here now,' slamming the phone down to the utter silence of my flat.

Then last month – I hadn't seen Georgie for weeks – I didn't ask, no one knew, but I motored down to Perth, parked my car round the corner and hung about inside the video shop opposite Georgie's out-of-school club. I should've been a private eye. I took one of the new releases off the shelf and studied the back cover. Then at 5.25pm precisely, as usual, as if nothing had changed, her mother arrived to collect her. I watched her from behind a rack, through the glass, like watching a film, really. She arrived looking flustered, walking with that nervous, skippy gait of hers, not realizing the belt from her expensive long coat was trailing on the ground. A few minutes later, after I'd picked up another video to avoid attracting attention to myself, they appeared at the steps, chattering away to each other, looking really happy. Like nothing was missing at all. Like I'd never been there in the first place. I felt like an actor whose carefully crafted scenes are cut from the final edit so no one believes they really happened. They looked as if they'd just shared a really funny private joke along the lines of 'Who needs a daddy anyway?' I had a nervous, skippy feeling as they got closer, hoping, not hoping, they'd come in to rent a children's video as they sometimes used to. It'd be good, wouldn't it? I'd get to speak to them, hear the joke too. But, thinking about it, it wouldn't be good at all – it would be *very* bad. I could imagine Helen's scorn: 'What're *you* doing here?' I hid behind the horror section, gripped with fear I'd be unmasked as a stalker. I looked out the window again and they were gone. I drove straight back up to Aberdeen. It was much worse than before.

This time, though, I'm going to get it right, do it properly, the good father, the perfect gentleman. Helen is waiting for me, ready to go, looking the business in a new trouser suit. I'm not invited in so I loiter politely by the door. Georgie's over-dressed for her expedition north in a waterproof jacket and matching red hat and gloves. She looks weighed down with her packed rucksack of overnight things as we exchange shy, anxious glances at each other. Helen locks the door and talks about me as if I'm not there as we walk out onto the pavement.

'Now you have a nice time with Daddy, Georgia,

and I'll see you tomorrow night.'

She puts down her travel case and hugs and kisses Georgie in the street. I stand a few paces back. Mr Periphery. Helen depresses her keyring and her car responds to her touch, waking up and winking, like they're in cahoots. I've never had a car like that. She hands me Georgie's booster seat. Georgie knocks on the window for another kiss before her mum leaves. The window slides down, they kiss, she glides off. Georgie waves.

Georgie's excited about the adventure and I am too. But it's a fragile and fraught excitement. If she cries, if she's unhappy, if she's not feeling well, if it all goes wrong we can't just say never mind it'll be better tomorrow. It's all got to be perfect today, right now, because it's all we've got, tomorrow she goes home, with the memory of how unhappy she was with Daddy. She might associate unhappiness with Daddy. And I dread that.

She's sitting in the front seat, swinging her wee legs, fiddling with the radio, chatting away non-stop. She's got me I-spying already and we're not even out of Perth when she spies something outside beginning with 'f'. I don't want to disappoint her. Don't want to ruin everything by saying no. I guess right. We park and walk to the funfair sited on the South Inch in the shadow of the prison.

The fair is half closed and half hearted in the morning grey. I remember returning to The Shows in Pitlochry with my father on the Saturday afternoon after all the excitement of Friday night. In the daytime everything lost its glamour and sheen. The ground rutted with muddy tracks and puddles. The daylight was unforgiving, revealing the paint peeling off the stalls, the true age of the wrinkled postcard beauties, all sense of urgent excitement chased away with the dawn. No crowds. No Catriona. The whole place with a day-after-the-main-event feel. We chased each other forlornly on the dodgems but there was no one else to dodge. I'd persuaded my father to come and see The Shows, they're brilliant, I'd told him, but then they let me down, only confirming his low expectations.

Georgie pleads with me to let her on the waltzers and I don't want to say no.

'You're a bit young for that, Georgie, it's really for older people.'

But she persuades me against my better judgement and I indulge her. She's all excited and chatty as we sit waiting but the moment the ride starts up she's flung on her side with her legs pinned back awkwardly against the seat. She grips my arm in terror and starts screaming and screaming.

'I don't like this! Make it stop!'

Her eyes are tight shut. I signal to the operator but he's ignoring me or he doesn't notice. Everyone screams on the waltzers, I suppose, but I never want to hear Georgie scream like that again. The ride seems to go on interminably and Georgie is quietly sobbing with fright. We're really getting our money's worth – the ride doesn't last as long at night when it's busy. Finally it stops and Georgie's wee face is white with the shock 'cept round her eyes which are red with tears. She's giving me a look as if to say 'You're supposed to be looking after me, you are. How can I trust you?' but what she actually says is: 'I don't think Mummy would have gone on the waltzers, d'you think?'

Even though it's started to rain I buy her a Mr Whippy ice cream and it drips all over her hand and down the front of her jacket. She hooks a plastic duck with a bamboo stick to win any prize and chooses big, plastic, tarty earrings which look funny on her neat little ears and we laugh, beginning to get over the waltzers though she won't even walk near them. She has a go on a kiddies' ride, driving the fire engine and ringing its bell every time she passes me. She wants a shot on the Ghost Train. She's pleading with me.

'Mummy would've let me,' she says, trying it on. I say no. I lose even more face in her big brown eyes when I fail to capture even one single stuffed dinosaur from a glass case full of them, the pincers dropping our Tyrannosaurus Rex on the brim of the winning chute again and 'one more time' again and 'last time' again.

I give her a 20 pence piece to twist into a gumball machine. She lifts the lid for her little gift wrapped in a plastic ball. We leave the funfair. She walks away a winner, head held high, sparkling with a gold necklace and bracelet from the gumball machine and dangly earrings from the duck. The rain's coming on heavy. It's good to be back in the car. It feels more comfortable now we've spent some time together again and we've got something we can talk about.

We're just outside Perth, joining the dual carriageway to Dundee, and she says 'Are we nearly there?' a phrase she repeats at ten-mile intervals up to the turn-off for Stonehaven when she falls asleep.

'Hey, Georgie, wake up!' I say, just past Portlethen, 'we really are nearly there now.'

She stretches and yawns extravagantly and starts watching ahead intently. Round a couple of corners and there it is.

'Hold your nose, it's Aberdeen!'

She doesn't laugh, stretching up to see better out the windscreen. The city spread out before her in the distance.

'Wow!' she says, taking it all in, 'it's *beautiful!*' she says, as if it was Oz at the end of the yellow brick road.

I glance at her to check for sarcasm. But she's five not 15, and she means every word. I look again at the city ahead, wet roofs shining in the early evening sunshine, tower blocks and church spires, the conspicuous communications structure on the hill, shaped like a steeple stripped bare, ugly with random BT satellite dishes and mobile phone transmitters, a totem to all that's now valued highest, and I concede, seeing the lush farmland lapping at the city's edge and sensing the sea beyond the eastern horizon: 'It's all right, I suppose.' I'm even strangely flattered, somehow, by her enthusiam, as if the city was an unwanted Christmas jumper that had shrunk to fit and I was beginning to like.

In George Street I hold Georgie's hand as we walk up the five flights of wooden stairs in the dark. She's bold and confident and tells me not to be afraid. I'm ashamed of my flat. Helen's never seen it. Georgie wouldn't be here if she had. I'm just about to apologize to her and explain that, hopefully, it'll only be temporary, when Georgie starts gushing with enthusiasm, rushing from room to room opening cupboards, bouncing on the bed, peering out of windows saying: '*Cool!* What a *nice* flat, this is! You're so lucky to be right at the top! Daddy! You can see everything up here! *Look!* There's giant seagulls! Look, Daddy! We're higher than the birds!' She bounces up and down on the cigarette-marked sofa and wanders into the kitchen. 'Wow! This kitchen is tiny! Aw, it's sooo cute! It's like Gran's caravan, isn't it?'

It's getting late – kiddie time. She's tired, though she says she isn't. I can see it in her eyes. I put a fresh sheet on the bed and get her into her pyjamas. She's having a drink of Ribena, clutching her hippo and leaning on the back of the sofa staring out the window.

'What's that tower over there?' she asks – pointing to the concrete tower at Richards textiles factory where the trigger-happy, redneck security guards watch my every move through binoculars, waiting for my escape bid – but before I can answer she says: 'I know! It's a lighthouse, isn't it?'

'Yeah,' I laugh, 'it's a lighthouse smack in the centre of town!'

'What a great idea,' she says, 'I *love* Aberdeen!'

I put eczema cream on her itchy wrists and the insides of her elbows and read her a story. She's still protesting that she's not tired as she stifles yawn after yawn. Says she misses her mummy but she's reassured when I say she'll see her very soon – tomorrow night. I tell her I'm just going to make myself a coffee and I'll come back and kiss her goodnight but when I come back she's asleep. I half close the door, leaving the light on in the hall.

In the darkened living room I watch the *Nine O'Clock News* and pretend I'm in a big house with a big garden and my loving wife and child are asleep upstairs. Later, I look out my window at the dark silhouette of the lighthouse with no light.

Georgie's crying. She needs to go to the toilet but she's disorientated with sleep. I find her all but sleepwalking in the hall, trying to open the outside door looking for the bathroom. She looks as blind as a day-old kitten. I wipe away her tears and take her to the toilet. After that, she doesn't want me to leave. I lie down beside her. She gets comfortable and returns to her dreams as easily as returning to the folded-over page where she'd interrupted them. I watch her sleep for a while. My rosy-cheeked cherub. Black curls cushion her head. Her face wrinkles with the gentle perplexities of her dreams. If there was some way I could help I would, to act like some computer game hero slaying all the dragons and monsters on her behalf.

I stare at the ceiling. Yawn. I'll make up a bed on the sofa later. I fall asleep too. I'm woken, maybe hours later, by her tiny hand outstretched on my face, exploring my chin like the bristle was Braille. Reaching out for answers to her unspoken questions: 'Why did you leave us? Why don't you come home? Do you still love me, Daddy?'

I kiss her hand, she knows I do, and illuminated by the streetlights outside, I can see her smile.

• • • • • • • • • • • • • • • • • • •

Sunday morning and I wake up to Georgie softly talking and singing to herself in the other room. I lift my head a little to listen and my neck locks in pain from a night on the sofa. She sounds contented enough though. It sounds like a little poem or a play. She knows all the sounds but not all the words. I can't quite place it, she repeats it over and over, something off the tv, then she sings the jingle and I realize it's some stupid advert that appeals to her, that she likes to comb Barbie's hair to.

> As a model I *have* to look my best,
> But *too much* brushing and styling
> can *really* damage my hair
> Leaving it looking limp,
> Dull and lifeless.
> *New combination L'antigel* – with its advanced protective formula –
> *gently* conditions *deep down,*
> from root to tip,
> leaving my hair
> *shiny* and *healthy.*
> So I can get on with my life.
> *L'antigel!*
> *Gentle*, but *deep down* conditioning
> for beautiful hair!

I hear her jumping off the bed and creeping through the hall. The living-room door opens slowly, she peeks in, sees me smiling at her, and skips over.

'Daddy, Can I watch cartoons? Can I? *Please?*'

'I dunno, what time is it?' I ask myself, looking for my watch, wincing as I turn my head. There's no clock in the room and Georgie hasn't really got the hang of telling the time yet but she answers me anyway with great self-assurance.

'Eight o'clock!', as if she could make it that time by sheer willpower. '*Pil-ease* can I watch cartoons?'

I reach for my jeans over the chair and pull out the watch from one of the pockets.

'Well, you're almost right, Georgie, twenty-five *to* eight. It's a bit early to be watching telly though. There won't be any cartoons on at this time on a Sunday, are there? Can you not go back to bed for a bit?'

'There is *so* cartoons,' she insists, sighing theatrically in a mild show of petulance, as she walks slowly to the door dragging her feet. I feel guilty.

'Aw, c'mere you,' I say, and give her a hug. 'You're cold, girl! Where's your dressing gown? C'mon we'll get the fire on and get you cosy.'

I pad about in my bare feet and boxers, wrapping her up in my duvet on the sofa till only her angel face and black curls are visible at the top of tog mountain.

Fast-talking, wise-cracking, technicoloured cartoon cultural imperialism invades our living room with the flick of a switch and Georgie's transfixed. I go wash, get dressed and make some toast for breakfast. Uncle Sam's still brainwashing my daughter when I come back. Georgie's watching television with such concentration only her head tilts towards me as I hand her some Ribena, saying 'Careful you don't spill it' but her eyes never leave the screen. I watch too for a while, still waking up, cradling my coffee, feet up on the sofa, watching wall-to-wall cartoons. I'm really concentrating but I can't follow the plot of the *X-men*.

'D'you understand this?'

'Mmn-hm,' she nods, looking at me for a moment like I was thick.

'D'you actually *like* this programme?'

'Mmn-hm,' she nods.

Violence, aggression, cruelty and torture. Good guys, bad guys, lasers, phasers, boom, boom, that's entertainment, kids! Georgie's unfazed by it all. And there's me, stupid me, taking tv too literally, more seriously than it deserves, wanting my child nurtured on a varied and balanced diet and not to grow fat on cartoon sweeties, and I realize – with a shock of self-awareness – I am my father's son.

We crunch our toast. Get crumbs on the sofa. (They're clean crumbs though, our crumbs.) She's spilling Ribena on the duvet. We're happy enough.

If my flat was a home, a proper home, we'd stay longer but there's no toys here apart from the ones she brought with her and I can't bear the contrast of her fresh face and the dirt and decay in the fabric of the building. We negotiate the five flights of stairs down in the dark and it's a relief to open the heavy outside door to the sunshine and the fresher air. George Street's nursing a hangover from Saturday night and there's almost no one about.

At Georgie's request, we head for the park. There's a refurbished play area in Westburn Park the council's done up with tree bark on the ground below the roundabout and climbing frames and chutes. It's an improvement on the tarmac we skinned our knees on as kids but there are plenty of hazards and I can't sit down and let her get on with it. I follow her round as she runs from swings to fort, courting danger. She leaps fearlessly from three times her height onto a pole and slides down, not in one swift movement like a fireman in a fire station, but inching her way down, hands squeaking painfully on the steel. On the swings she puts her head right back and swings her legs back and forth to try and get even higher than I've pushed her.

I'm boring her with advice and warnings and concerns. She's no more reckless than any other kid there, no more reckless than I was then, but kids are blind to risks till they hurt themselves. If she fell, sprained or broke something, I'd blame myself. Georgie and her mother would blame me, too. I fear her mother's wrath almost as much as I fear Georgie's pain. Tree bark is not enough, I want a play park made of feathers and cotton wool and tissue paper and marshmallows. It's a weight off my mind once she's had a shot of everything, twice on the swings, and we can run on the open grass playing tig.

We walk back towards the city centre, get a free plastic lunch with our £2.99 toy in a burger bar. It's too early to drive back to Perth and neither of us wants to return to the flat. We dander. She wants to climb the greying lion statue at the war memorial 'To Our Glorious Dead'. 'No, c'mon, George, you're not allowed up there!'

The art gallery is open for the afternoon and we wander in. Georgie rushes to the centrepiece sculpture. It sits in the middle of a white marble, rectangular pond. Fountains spray regurgitated water into the air towards a stupid chunk of Barbara Hepworth bronze. Pissing on art. There's money in it and Georgie wants to throw a coin too but I say no because that pond hasn't got the power. Too artificial. Too contrived. I'd want somewhere wild. Some place fit for my girl's three wishes. Some place that might grant them. Where her coin will never be found, it'll just sink into the silt, lost forever among the chickweed. She puts her finger on one of the fountain sprays, redirecting it onto the floor. She giggles at my raised eyebrows. An attendant looks ready to intervene but I take Georgie's wet hand and we move on.

Into the Memorial Court where the white marble radiates a cool, natural light. Georgie runs to the exact centre of the room, spins round and round, head up staring at the circular skylight high above her in the roof of the dome. Getting dizzy. Making me dizzy just to see her. We're being watched by three plaster busts above us on the balcony. I don't know, or care really, who they are. Life-size classical statues gaze down from their podiums, affecting the serenity of Italian white marble when they're merely hollow imposters. Dark green slabs of polished granite on one wall contrast markedly with the predominant white of the room. *THEY GAVE THEIR LIVES FOR THEIR COUNTRY AND FOR FREEDOM*, it says on the green granite. Two steps below are 'Roll of Honour' books in glass cases, British Legion flags on either side and a wreath of Remembrance Day poppies. Bizarrely, too, there's a seventh-century BC Corinthian helmet placed, without explanation, in a glass box. The noseplate of the armour is still intact but one side of the skull is smashed in. As if we're supposed to reflect, here in the War Memorial Court, that some things never change.

Georgie's discovered a pleasing echo.

'Shhh! Listen to this!' she says, holding her hand up to me as if I'd been making a noise. She stamps her foot. A few dull slaps echo back. She claps her hand once, a short exchange of sniper fire rains from the ceiling. She claps some more. It's like a machine gun. She shouts out again and again at the top of her voice: 'Ooooo-eee! Ooooo-eee!'. The echo cranks up like an air-raid siren in reply. An attendant outside the hall stands at the entrance looking again like he might intervene. He gives me a this-is-not-a-playground look, like I'm letting her run amok. Like she's desecrating the memory of the glorious dead. But I don't tell her to stop. I don't ask her to apologize for the killing fields of Europe. They died for her innocent freedoms, didn't they?

On another wall there is a woven banner of condolence: 'A TRIBUTE FROM THE WORKERS OF AUSTRALIA' for the victims of the Piper Alpha disaster in 1988. Beneath it is a book of condolence with 167 names resting in a glass case. There are two metal stools with grey leather cushions nearby.

Georgie's tired of the echo at last and she goes quiet. We sit close together on a single seat. She senses a solemnity. I haven't coached her.

'It's like a church,' she whispers.

I nod. I want to explain why. I don't want evil or pain to be a terrible shock to her when she grows up because she's been too sheltered. I want her to know life's not all teddy bears and jelly babies. I want her to know there are worse things than stupid people falling out of love. I want to give her a wee jab of poison in her arm so she's immunized against the future. I tell her about oil rigs in the sea and what happened to one of them. She understands. She really does.

'I'm glad you don't work on an oil rig, Daddy.'

'Me too, George.'

She's staring at the woven banner with only an inkling of the full horror of it but still enough to jump when, without warning, the piercing scream of a drowning man fills the hall. I hear it, too. Round and round it echoes like a whirlpool. Georgie grips my arm, we scan the room searching for an explanation. We look up, following the horrible noise as it calls out again. High above us, through the glass of the round skylight, the tail feathers of a herring gull are visible, preening, twitching. It screeches one more time for our verification. We tag it, relieved to have found the source. It flies off before the last echoes die out.

• • • • • • • • • • • • • • • • •

Monday morning in Aberdeen. The meep, meep, meep of the alarm. Clattering blindly down the wooden stairs. Catching the bus to the hothouse. Five stops to start the day. And I have arrived. Up the steps towards the sliding doors, unavoidably facing up to my reflection, I approach the Institute of Business and Entrepreneurship's mirrored glass walls. There, before me, is a self-made man: a Monopoly man making moves on every significant board game in the north east, who probably collects £200 every time he passes water. Not me, obviously: The Chairman. Bursting out the sliding doors and the buttons on his silk shirt. Digesting his breakfast meetings with kowtowing Audrey Marshall in tow (he so fat and she so thin) with not so much as a boilersuit to protect his pin-stripe Savile Row threads as he waddles off to oil the wheels of industry. Audrey's too engrossed in *very important* papers to acknowledge me but The Chairman nods graciously as we pass like entrepreneurships in the night. And I am ever so grateful that a self-made man, such as him – especially when you consider the exclusive school he went to and his father's lucrative pharmaceutical investments in the fifties – still has time for people like me. My God, he *almost* knows my name, bless him. After the particularly successful 'Aberdeen – A Lot More Besides the Seaside' retail investment campaign for the Beach Esplanade area, he actually stopped in the corridor to congratulate me on my work.

'Sterling effort,' he said, 'well done, John!'

Into the heady, air-conditioned atmosphere of the Institute with a swish of my card, through a couple of other doors into our office still heavy with the invisible haar of Audrey's industrial-strength hairspray.

'To be poor without being free is the worst condition into which man can sink,' quotes Prue from her calendar, by way of greeting, as if she's reading my mind.

Prue, the same dark side of 30 as me, has sat in that same seat (well, okay, she got a new one in the office refit but her position's never changed) since she was 20, when she enthusiastically responded to a recruitment ad for the opening of the exciting new Institute (established in the eighties when the free marketeers were riding roughshod over all they ruled with the battle cry of 'All for one!'). Her contract reliably renewed every six months, Prue's seen three bosses come and go, a whole series of public relations officers and an entire refurbishment of the office – even The Chairman is due to retire soon. Naturally, finding herself to be one of the few permanent features in a place in a permanent state of flux, she's come to see it as her office – in truth, her Institute: The Aberdeen Institute of Business, Entrepreneurship and Prudence.

I didn't realize it was her Institute when I first joined and Audrey introduced me to my new colleagues. Prue's handshake twittered like a tiny bird and Chris gave my hand a matey grip and wouldn't let go after the appropriate moment. All the time, Prue was sizing me up with deep suspicion, wondering how long I'd last before I too moved on, leaving her – like all the others did – to the suffocating inertia of her tiny, stagnant domain between the filing cabinets and the stationery cupboard. But is she bitter? You bet. Being passed over every time there's a round of promotions is only part of it – something else is eating her. I don't know what, but why should I care? – all wrapped up in me as I am.

Prue knows her work inside out. In fact, inside out is too easy for her. She knows her work inside out, upside down, back to front, in pillarbox presentation with 3D glasses and Dolby surround. She has her systems. She has her ways. Everything must be done *just so*. Put an indexed cardboard folder back in the wrong place and she'll tut and say with comic fastidiousness: 'That's *not* where we file that!' but only a fool would think she's joking. She means it. And, I guess, so would I if, like Prue, I'd sat and watched every possible elementary mistake repeated again and again with monotonous regularity by every new recruit till I didn't just know every possible mistake, I knew every possible permutation of mistakes.

There is a correct way for everything to be done in Prue's domain. There are proper procedures. Anything else is an aberration. A step off the path to righteousness. It gives her a wicked little kick, I'm sure, to wait and watch for new recruits to fall into the initiation traps she's laid. Any corruption of the rules will not be tolerated. Standards mustn't be allowed to slip. Blue folders must be filed alphabetically, pink ones chronologically, and green ones numerically. Phone messages should be written in full on the special, made-for-the-purpose telephone-message pad, neatly writing the caller's name in the 'caller's name' space provided, the time of call noted in the 'time of call' space provided and the message in full in the large 'message' space provided at the bottom and so on. Ideally, when completed, these should be placed on the desk of the receiver of the message close to the keyboard of their computer so it is brought to their attention at the earliest possible juncture. It is desirable, though not always essential, to fix the telephone pad message with a short piece of Sellotape to avoid the sheet of paper being blown off a desk by a draft from an open window or from a door opening and closing. Yellow stickies can also be used for this purpose, it is true, but they are not specifically *designed* for the taking of telephone messages, as is the telephone-message pad, but for a multitude of messages so they must only be used if another colleague comes into the office and a message must be left in someone's absence. This is the correct procedure, it has always been the correct procedure, and as long as Prue's in charge of the Institute of Prudence it will remain so.

She's a woman who's lost patience with the world. She can be curt with callers on the phone who ask the same old stupid questions she's heard a hundred times before. She gives them the 'oh-not-that-old-chestnut' routine and puts them right in no uncertain terms. She is super-efficient. No time and motion consultants could possibly make her more productive – nor would they dare to try – as any variation to her routine would be sacrilege. Prue fights tiny battles and minuscule wars and wins little victories all day (closing the window each time Chris opens it: 'What's this? Fresh air fortnight?' Asking Audrey how she'd like something done, being told in some detail, then going ahead and doing it her own way after all. Making sure the *Yellow Pages* for the office is kept handy on her desk even though I use it more often) but she's never got the promotion or even the pay rise she politely requested and deserved.

And yet, for all her superhuman efficiency, Prue is a deftly disruptive influence in the office, like a work-to-rule slowing everything down. I'm so wary of her condemnation of my sloppy work practices I'll spend half an hour seeking out the correct stationery to leave a message on her desk rather than use a scrap of paper which I know will be greeted with a remark as sharp and peculiarly painful as a paper cut. She's like a sleeping farmdog on a long chain which everyone tiptoes round. Everyone has their bite-marks and everyone's twice-shy. Even Audrey Marshall treads carefully near Prue, trying not to disturb her. What would happen if she was let off her chain? Would she have something to contribute to the wider world outside her claustrophobic office domain where she is queen of all she files so diligently? Or would she savage someone and have to be put down? What grudge sustains her? Is she like this at home? Does her husband wear asbestos pyjamas?

Office scandal is Prue's only compensation for a stunted career. She treasures every snippet of private and personal news like a diary columnist. Secrets are safe with her only as long as her next conversation. She'll listen sympathetically to friends telling her their tales of woe and practically before the door is closed behind them she'll be on the phone spreading the word. News of the failings of others is bread and butter to her. If another member of her select, coffee-break clique comes into the office Prue will disappear into the walk-in stationery cupboard with them on the pretext of fetching something and all I'll hear will be whisper, whisper, giggle, giggle, gab, gab. She's never happier than when some particularly salacious piece of news has reached her. Then a suppressed smile reveals itself trembling uncontrollably at the very edges of her thin lips. All that useless information in my survival book about how to deal with snakes and tarantulas and hornets but nothing – no advice, no antidote – to counter the venom of Prue.

Chris arrives late, panting like a wet dog, shaking her dripping umbrella onto the carpet.

'Morning chaps! Had to pick up a prescription for my mum across the way there. God, the traffic this morning. Closing that Peterhead-Aberdeen railway was the worst thing they ever did,' she says.

'You'd think you'd be *beginning* to get used to it – that was over 30 years ago, wasn't it?' says Prue, stirring the pot for the first time that day.

'Yes. Yes,' says Chris irritably, 'that's what I'm

saying, worst thing they ever did.'

Prue tilts her head round her computer screen at me and raises her eyes to the ceiling and says, loud enough so's Chris would hear too: 'Snippy as a pair of scissors, is she?'

Chris settles at her desk to make some quick calls:

'Hallo! Yes, *hello!* Buchanan. Chris. Institute of Business and Entrepreneurship ... I'd like to confirm my tee-off time in the Ladies Championship.'

'Buchanan. Chris. Institute of Business and Entrepreneurship ... I'd like to send some flowers to Ward 41a, Aberdeen Royal.'

'Colin? Chris,' she looks around suspicuously before she speaks, as if we might be taking notes, then switches to whisper mode, though occasional snippets are clearly audible: '... three times the limit and *driving* the police car!'

Prue and Chris are the two people I know best in my new life here but I know nothing more about them than their office habits. They know as much about me. I'm cloaked in anonymity, not being local, which suits me fine. Prue, the National Enquirer, doesn't have much on me. Me in Aberdeen. A pigeon on the Bass Rock. I fabricate my weekends. Tell Prue what she wants to hear. I could be anyone I want to be. I've decided to be single and childless.

• • • • • • • • • • • • • • • • • •

'I felt bereaved today,' my father said to me, shaking me awake in my bed. It was early Sunday afternoon. James had long left home for university, then work. Jackie soon after for college and work. Both far away in England. My Mum and Dad were just back from church. I could smell the dinner cooking in the oven downstairs. We'd always gone as a family before – even James, who'd reckoned he could spare an hour of his time once a week to keep the folks happy. Now my father's only remaining son was proving to be a disappointment to him. He shook me awake from my lie-in – almost violently – made sure he had my attention. Then said what he said and walked out.

And I knew what he meant. I should've shown more faith in my father. Should've tried harder in class. Should've listened in church. How could I ever doubt him? We used to go to North Berwick every summer for our holidays. We'd swap houses with a chemistry teacher, my father knew from his teacher-training days, and his family. His kids would break our toys at our house and we'd break theirs. In North Berwick I developed a fixation for the Bass Rock. A real obsession. Like Richard Dreyfuss had for Devil's Mountain in *Close Encounters of the Third Kind* (though I'm not claiming aliens use the Bass Rock for a landing place, it's way too steep). There was no escaping the Bass Rock in North Berwick, it seemed to follow me about with its strange eerie otherness. I'd stare at it in glorious isolation for hours through an antique telescope from the upstairs window of our holiday house on Marine Parade.

Back at school, mid-winter, staring out the window, I'd imagine how cold and wild it must be right now out in the Firth of Forth. I'd try to imagine what it must have been like to be imprisoned on there, on that great lumpen Bass Rock, as men once were, instead of imprisoned in double Maths. When I was old enough to know better, I still liked to imagine the white-washed sea walls of the Bass Rock were quartz or maybe chalk, like the white cliffs of Dover, instead of countless coats of bird shit. Mind you, it was also the constantly animated white plumage of the birds themselves. Thousands upon thousands of gannets swarming like bees round a hive, turning the volcanic plug from black to white. The Jacobites – who held the rock in the name of King James VII in 1691 for three years till they were granted an amnesty – must've survived on eggs, eggs and more eggs.

On occasional hot days in high summer – there were some in North Berwick – the shimmering heat and light magnified the Bass Rock till it looked as if it wouldn't be all that hard to swim out to – maybe, even, *wade* out to – at low tide. But it was a good three miles away. We did other things on holiday but the rock was always lurking in the background.

Me and Jackie had wooden yachts we sailed in the sea water of the boating pond near the harbour. Until one day I slipped and fell in, screaming in horror at the sudden shock of the cold water but more at the thought of the unknown dangers that creeped and crawled beneath the fronds of seaweed, waiting and watching for warm human flesh to descend into their realm. Worse was to come. I was fished out the water by my father and delivered dripping and shivering to my mother on the beach. She told me to strip out of the wet clothes at once before I caught my death of cold. Noting my reluctance, she added: 'Nobody's interested in what you're doing, Joe! Just hurry up and get on with it.' She held a towel around me to save my blushes. She was lying! Every kid on the beach was watching me. I'd attracted a lot of attention with my screaming and the great stupid splash I made when I fell in the water. Hurrying to get out of wet clothes as fast and unobtrusively as possible, I managed to roll down my pants and trousers till they were ropes around my ankles which I couldn't get off my feet. Finally my humiliation was complete as my father carried me – nearly naked, for God's sake – wrapped only in a towel, through the streets of North Berwick back to our holiday house.

Other days we flew our kite. It flew to the end of its tether easily, tugging at our hands to be let off the leash, to fly higher. Jackie bought a roll of twine from the newsagents and tied it to the end of the kite's string so it could soar even higher in the strong wind. Higher than any kid's kite has ever flown before. Our blue cotton kite was just a dot in the sky, way above the gulls. I worried it'd get scorched by the sun. We were congratulating ourselves on our record-breaking achievement and Jackie was joking about ringing the airport to warn low-flying aircraft in the vicinity of our exploits when the string snapped and fell loose in his hand. The blue cotton dot blew over the town and out of sight. A couple of days later my father took me and Jackie to the police station to see if our kite had been handed in as lost property, though we didn't hold out much hope. The constable said not one but *two* kites had been handed in to lost property and he asked for a description, which we gave him: it's a blue and white kite-shaped kite. He listened to the details and we thought things were looking good when he went to a locker in the office to fetch the two recovered kites. But as soon as he put them on the counter, which my eyes were level with, I could see neither of them was ours. One was a fancy orange and red, wooden box kite I'd seen in picture books but never actually seen fly and the other was a ripped, transparent polythene kite with a red and black Kung Fu and dragon design on the back, which I could tell Jackie thought was well cool.

'Is it either of these?' the constable said to my father with a smile and, though I couldn't be sure, he winked or blinked one eye in such a way as to say: 'Go on! Go on! Take either of them. Better to see them keeping the kids happy than stuck in a cupboard unclaimed.'

My father was not about to be a party to police corruption, though, however small-scale, and holding himself a little taller, with his shoulders back, he said emphatically: 'No. These don't belong to us. Not ours. Thanks anyway for your time.'

Every year after that, me and Jackie used to go back to the police station on our own to ask if a kite had been handed in, hoping we'd get a selection to choose from, but we never saw our kite or even the Kung Fu kite again.

The little electric cars on the concrete beside the open-air swimming pool were a fascination. They cost 2p a shot round a tiny circuit that was Brands Hatch to me. All the following year at home I saved up two pence pieces in a coffee jar. I must've had about 50. I was going to drive and drive and drive. Then, when we came back to North Berwick in the summer and I ran to the little circuit – pockets full of copper – inflation had beat me to it and the coin slots on the cars had been modified, upgraded, and now only accepted ten pence pieces.

We swam in the allegedly heated outdoor swimming pool. We ate ice creams. We played on the beach. We built elaborate sand-castles with Lion Rampant and Union Jack flags on turrets. We played 'sand-castle wars' to see whose flag would stay up the longest in a battle against the incoming tide, as lapping waves eroded the walls of the houses the foolish men built upon the sand. Science and engineering always won the day, though. My father built concave castles – which didn't look anything like castles, but which reduced the impact of the waves just that little bit longer than our naïve castle-shaped castles. We went fishing off the harbour. Jackie's line got caught on rocks just below the water level and my father shimmied down the vertical wall (like the man in the ad, at the time, who did stupid death-defying stunts all because the lady loves Milk Tray) to dodge the waves, to release the hook, to avoid having to buy new ones. Jackie couldn't watch – he was visualising the funeral and a lifetime of blaming himself. Mission accomplished, my father climbed back up and told us not to worry our mother by mentioning it when we got home. 'Course, Jackie's big, wide 'I've-got-a-secret' eyes gave it away as soon as we walked through the door.

Every year we would moan and whinge our way to the top of the North Berwick Law (the land-locked sister of the Bass Rock) to have our photo taken beside the whale's jawbone – always in the teeth of a gale and, once, even in an unseasonal hailstorm as Tic-tacs rained from the sky.

But everywhere we went, the backdrop to everything we did was the Bass Rock. I felt drawn to it. I felt some kind of strange affinity with it. The Bass Rock was calling. Me – more than anyone else. I never quite thought I had to conquer it 'cause it was there or any of those stiff upper lip, ra-ra British Empire mountaineer clichés, I just felt I had to get up close to satisfy my curiosity and rationalize it. (See on the beach? When there's flotsam and jetsam in the distance which looks like it maybe, could be, something else, something undefined? Same thing with the Rock, I reckon, same curiosity.) I had an unavoidable date with destiny. The day finally arrived in the last summer we ever went to North Berwick. My mother wouldn't leave dry land. James and Jackie weren't there – they'd both left home. It was just me and our father.

On the morning of the boat trip we got up early to prepare for the voyage, taking tuna sandwiches should we get peckish and extra jumpers should it get chilly out there. It felt a little breezy as we walked to the harbour but not so's you'd particularly notice on land (different scales apply on water, we were to discover). The tide was in and the yachts, motor boats and dinghies bobbed gently in the breeze inside the harbour as we joined the queue of daytrippers with cameras and birdwatchers with binoculars swinging round their necks, all waiting to board the boat. Once the 20 or so passengers had paid their money up front to a deckhand, walked the plank and taken their seats, the boat moved off and began to lilt as soon as it was clear of the harbour walls. (How did they build harbours, anyway? How did they stop the incoming tide from washing away the cement?) The wooden boat was slightly shorter than a bus. It looked like the boat on the front of Seaside Mission or Scripture Union song pamphlets. As the vessel struggled to gather speed it slapped into the waves breaking over the bow, sending a delicate spray over us like the squirt from a bottle of perfume. It wasn't exactly unpleasant ... yet. I could taste the salt on my lips. I began to feel the same queasy sensation of leaving my stomach on the ceiling of a fast, downward lift. Only this lift didn't stop. It kept going up and down, with random tilts to outwit my equilibrium. I looked at the other passengers sitting, like me, round the sides of the boat. There was something oddly familiar about these strangers: the young couple dressed identically in chunky fishermen's sweaters and bright yellow cagoules; a golf-widowed and orphaned family of over-nourished North Americans; an elderly English couple with loud but friendly Yorkshire or Lancashire (I can never tell them apart) accents; daytripping families with young children; and a few assorted, earnest-looking twitchers. It was when I noticed the party of three nuns in anoraks and sandals, I realized where I'd seen them all before. They were like a roll-call for a disaster movie.

Only my father and the bearded, weather-beaten captain didn't sit down. The Captain stood at the wheel, eyes focused on the horizon, teeth clenching a pipe, looking every inch a casting agent's stereotype. A couple of paces to one side of the Captain, near the stern, stood my father, holding on to nothing, looking for all the world like it was his boat, hands behind his back, legs slightly apart for balance, jaw set, chest out, in a futile King Canute challenge to the sea: 'Do your worst!' I wanted to take the sea to one side for a word to the wise: 'Look, it's okay, he doesn't mean it, doesn't know what he's saying. I mean, look at him! He's mental!' Unfortunately, the sea was not to be placated. Drinks were being spilled all over the boat. It was taking my father on. The wind blew froth off the tops of waves racing madly in all directions like foaming, wild horses penned in a corral. Then, clear of the shore in deep water, the first few big waves crashed against the bow, sending bucketfuls of freezing water splashing onto the floor inside the boat. People shouted 'Whoa!', shook their wet hair and laughed at the joke shared with strangers. Then as it happened more and more often the laughing stopped and people grimly held on to the side of the boat and each other.

My father, as if he'd sailed the seven seas all his life and seen it all before, remained entirely composed. He was finding it all *so* bracing as he savoured lungfuls of fresh air liberally mixed with sea spray. As the boat smashed head on into the mounting waves, bucking violently, I watched my father's knees bend economically like well-tuned shock absorbers or BMW suspension. His head was like a spirit-level, never out of kilter with the disappearing horizon. I saw a manic look in his eyes. He was enjoying this. He looked like an illustration from a Sunday School book of Jesus during a storm on the Sea of Galilee 'cept, obviously, without the beard, the long hair or robes, or – come to think of it – the ability to walk on water, or change it into wine or, more pertinently, to calm it with outstretched arms and a few salient words. He looked good, though. I have to admit. My dad. I'd have been well proud of him if I wasn't preoccupied with more immediate concerns like keeping my breakfast down and clinging to the railings for dear life.

The Captain gripped the wheel tightly. I looked for signs of concern on the small patch of red face above his bushy beard – I figured if he was relaxed and workaday then I should be too – but he was inscrutable. It was impossible to tell. His expression was impassive, no clues there, but I reckoned he was maybe biting his pipe a little bit tighter than absolutely necessary. Every time we fell to the bottom of a trough between the big waves our view of the Bass Rock ahead of us, and the safety of the coast behind, was completely obscured by six-foot solid walls of water. It didn't help to close my eyes – the waves were even higher in my imagination. Nothing in my survival training had prepared me for this. It would be useful to know how best to stay on a wet wooden seat without slipping off into a growing puddle of sea water splashing from one side of the boat to the other while also maintaining that all-important dignity and decorum – preferably, ideally, a certain air of insouciance – as I frantically scanned the boat for life-jackets.

At last, my father turned round to check I hadn't been lost overboard. He gave me a reassuring smile and wink as if to say 'Aye, this is the life all right!' I smiled weakly back nodding as if I was saying 'Most exhilarating indeed! More wind, more waves, please!' when all I wanted to say was 'Tell Cap'n Birds-Eye there to give us our money back and take us home *now!* I don't want to die!' Children hid whimpering under the wings of their parents' waterproofs as the sea rained in, flooding our floating coffin. People were pale, but seasickness would be a luxury for later: no one dared lean over the side. The elderly husband was popping angina pills supplied by his anxious wife. One of the nuns, eyes tightly shut, clutched what I thought was an unusually big-beaded necklace on her lap and mumbled to herself.

I'd lost all interest in the Bass Rock. All I wanted was the Captain to turn the boat around and head home. I'd have paid him again to abandon the trip. The Bass Rock could wait forever or at least till they built a bridge. I mean, c'mon! There was four inches of timber between me and the sea. Me, my feet, my socks, my trainers, the wood of the hull, the sea, water, water, stinging jellyfish, water, water, killer cod, water, seaweed, crabs, and a million other creatures of the deep which shun the light and are a hundred times bigger than anything that bites in the boating pond.

Finally our captain shouted something in the ear of his deckhand, who shouted to us above the noise of the chugging engine, the wind and the waves: 'The skipper thinks that it might be a little rough today to keep going out to the Bass Rock so he wants to know if you mind if we go round Craigleith instead?' Craigleith rock was much closer to the harbour and everyone agreed that would be for the best though, personally, I thought going straight home would be even better. I said nothing and tried to look miffed we weren't still going to the Bass Rock. Sheltered close to Craigleith the waves were much calmer and, sure enough, there were real seals to see, just like on tv nature programmes, lolling about on rocks fifty feet away from us and even a few birds too to keep the twitchers happy. Then it was back home again with the wind and waves at our back, which seemed to make things more bearable, as did the knowledge it would all soon be over. People cheered up a little, found their voices again. The Captain lit his pipe. Shaky legs disembarked at North Berwick harbour – all survivors, *passengers,* accounted for, all present and correct.

'You disappointed we couldn't go to the rock, son?' asked my father.

'Naw, naw, Craigleith was good.'

'Maybe we could try later in the week if the wind dies down, would you like that, Joe?'

'Well, no, Dad, 'cause remember you promised we'd go swimming in the pool? And then there's the whale's jaw bone to see at the top of the Law, we haven't done that this year yet, and the pictures, we haven't been to the pictures, the putting, and the boating pond, there's really too much we've got to do before we go home. Don't you think? Eh, Dad, eh?'

Out to sea – beyond my wading, swimming or even boating reach – the Bass Rock stood impervious, unchanged, unmoved, unconquered – a great big knot off the coastline to help me remember: keep off the water. Know your place. Know your limitations. Yeah, yeah, *no!* I'm going to go back to that boat one day and circle the Bass Rock like a movie in the tv guide I have to see.

● ● ● ● ● ● ● ● ● ● ● ● ● ● ● ● ● ●

I really tried to follow the book. My father could make sense of it, so why shouldn't I? But it takes more than a leap of faith to understand third-year Physics. Why – apart from the glorious miracle of my electric motor moment – was I so hopeless? Our practical little experiments were supposed to demonstrate to us the unassailable truth of our textbooks but my findings never fitted the neat formulae. My answers defied the laws of physics when all I wanted to do was conform.

We were put into groups of two for our scientific

experiments and I was paired up with Mo, which was great. Mo seemed to know what he was doing and we could set up the experiments pretty well. I quite liked that part of it: messing around with friction-free ramps, little trolleys, ticker-timers and tickertape. But when it came to making sense of our results: measuring the spaces between the dots on the tickertape, the gradient of the ramp, the acceleration of the trolley and making all that match up to the established formulae – work which, unfortunately, we had to do individually – I was lost. Loster than lost, actually.

My father never showed me any favouritism. He was very much Mr Copeland the Science teacher in class and that was that. I tried hard not to let him down or, God forbid, embarrass him, but it was obvious I'd mysteriously missed out on the essential gene for understanding Scottish Certificate of Education 'O' Grade Physics. I'd have looked into it, researched why this should be, but unfortunately I wasn't so hot at biology either. But it was the formulae in Physics I couldn't get my head round. In fact, my head was like a frictionless track through which all Physics theory slipped and slid, in one ear and out the other, without stopping. My mind couldn't get to grips with any of it. Not a Scooby.

'Mo!' I whispered to no visible response. 'Mo!' I hissed, desperately jabbing Moses in the back with a sharpened pencil.

'*Wha-t?*' he hissed back angrily, through clenched teeth, half-turning round to look at me while keeping an eye on my father who was working his way round the front row of the class asking questions in order from the textbook.

'What's the answer to number 12?' I pleaded quietly, like a ventriloquist. I'd worked out that number 12 would be my question because of where I was sitting but there was no hope of me actually working out the answer. Generously, Mo whispered out the side of his mouth: 'Results would depend on the *velocity* of the vehicle as well as the elevation of the ramp.' He turned back round so as not to attract any further attention to himself.

I relaxed. I had the answer. It would soon be bell-time. We'd get a bit of a kickabout at interval. It was Friday. Me, Mo and Finn were planning on going fishing on Saturday after *Swap Shop*. I didn't need to pay attention to the other questions. I was freewheeling into the weekend, repeating the answer to number 12 in my head like a mantra over and over, my lips moving ever so slightly. I didn't hear somebody slip up on number ten so Mo had to answer that instead of 11 as I'd anticipated. I didn't even need to listen to my question, I was so ready with my rehearsed answer.

'Easy one this, Joe. Of the three different types of light listed in your textbook, alongside their normal voltages and currents, which one has the greatest resistance?'

I replied confidently, in a louder than usual, Open University sort of voice: 'Well, *I think*, that *results*, em, would *depend* on the *velocity* of the vehicle as well as the *elevation* of the ramp.' There was a whole moment of puzzled silence, long enough for me to twig all was not right, before the class fell about laughing. Even Mo did. Even my father smiled – through gritted teeth. Russell Bradley was having convulsions. I felt sick.

The glorious miracle of the electric motor moment was a salvation of sorts. Weeks later, when the Number 12 incident had finally been forgotten by everyone else, my father asked the class to follow the instructions on page 196 of our textbook and put together a working electric motor from a heap of components laid out at the top table. To make it more interesting, he told us, once we'd chosen the necessary components, the first person to get their electric motor working would win a Mars Bar. We had to work alone, unfortunately. I knew I didn't have a hope in hell of winning so I was rooting for Moses. When my father gave us the signal to start, I sighed and looked down at the components in front of me: some tangled wire; a wooden spinning reel; some pegs; magnets; a power pack; some more wire; all of which bore little resemblance to the precise illustration on page 196. I began slowly and hopelessly to coil the wire round the spindle. Russell Bradley, a few seats away, was racing ahead of everyone, making a right show of doing everything fast.

'C'mon, Mo, y'gotta beat that swotty bastard!' I whispered under my breath.

I'd wound the coils on but had to start taking them off to start all over because my reel didn't look right, when Russell Bradley shouted 'Finished!'. Everyone turned to watch as he stood back from his motor with a self-satisfied look and theatrically flicked the switch on the power pack. Nothing happened. He switched it on and off a few times in disbelief, like he was about to blame Hydro-Electric but still nothing happened. The apparatus stood motionless. (Ha. Ha.)

We all went back to our work as Russell Bradley dismantled his motor to see where he'd gone wrong. Mo was near completion. 'C'mon Mo, you show 'im!' I told him. But someone else shouted 'Done it!' and we turned to watch as they duly switched on their power pack with great expectancy. But nothing happened to their motor either.

I was beginning to think we all had some vital component missing when Moses reached for the switch on his power pack: 'Here goes!' he said. Again nothing happened. The little motor just sat totally unmoved by all the attention. A couple of others tried too but couldn't make their motor work. So when I finally completed the process – winding the wire onto the reel, making sure it sat freely on the two conductors, checking the magnets, the power pack connections – I reckoned I was on a hiding to nothing. With such low expectations I switched on the power pack and lo, it spun!

Couldn't believe it. It looked so pretty, spinning round in a little blur, making a sweet purring, whirring sound. All my own work. Mo was grinning away, 'Nice one, Joey! Hey, spin on *that*, Bradley! Show us how you did it, Joey, will you?'

Me, the Physics expert. The Mars Bar King.

Explaining it away to Mo and all the rest, as if I had all the answers.

• • • • • • • • • • • • • • • • • • •

Bewildered. We all were. Looking at Georgie, I could tell by her expression she was bewildered too. Her world had just expanded too much, too sudden, she couldn't make sense of it. She looked up to me with those big round eyes. What did she see? How much did she understand? Why should she assume I could explain it away? Did she really imagine I'd have an easy answer? Such misplaced faith in me.

Georgie couldn't escape the news. It was unavoidable.

'A bad man went to that school and killed 16 children and their teacher,' I had to explain, plainly and simply, when she asked. There was no hiding from it.

'Yes, that's right, Daddy,' she said, 'but sure the killed children and the teacher will get better, won't they?'

'No. No I'm afraid they won't, Georgie, they're dead.'

She wore a look of utter incomprehension and denial. We all shared it. I felt compelled to add: 'But they'll be safe now, Georgie ... no one can hurt them in Heaven.'

That night, we tucked Georgie up in bed and were especially attentive to her needs. Every now and again, me and Helen would step quietly into her room and watch her sleep – small, blameless – and we'd start crying again and shake our heads in disbelief. And later still, in the dark, in our bed, we tried to articulate how it felt to see our greatest fears made real. We tried to make sense of it. Tried to rationalize it. Tried to find crumbs of hope from it. But in the end we just held each other close. Didn't row and didn't make love.

• • • • • • • • • • • • • • • • • • •

Audrey Marshall drives me and Chris to the Innovation Convention at the Exhibition Centre. She drives like she lives, putting her foot down hard on the accelerator, hard on the brake. Even on a clear, straight piece of road she pumps the accelerator, making us rock back and forth in our seats. She's a driven woman. A disciple of the 'Blunderbuss' theory of business and economics: if success depends upon who you know, then get to know *everyone*. Everyone in the know. All the movers and the shakers. Make contact and bleed them dry. Audrey fires her business cards off like grapeshot, furiously networking all the time: in her work time, in her spare time, in her dreams, making that chance acquaintance that will be the making of her.

I'm sitting in the backseat in a dwam. Up front, Audrey's rapid-firing questions at Chris about her preparations for today's convention. Chris is struggling – trying to lead Audrey past all the potholes in her work (avoiding altogether the sections which, as ever, lie completely unfinished and hidden behind endless rows of bollards) – so she deploys a remarkably simple but effective tactic which works well on The Chairman, but best on Audrey.

'Since *Friday*?' says Chris, acting astonished, gratefully grasping at some new information, 'I can't believe you've managed to do all that work since *Friday*!' She's pushed the right button all right. Audrey's flattered, doesn't realize she's been given the slip-road.

'That's what weekends are for, isn't it?' Audrey replies zealously, *joyously*, at the recognition of her work above and beyond the call of duty. She describes the work she took home and what it should mean to us, the Institute, and the future of the global economy. I smile to myself at another Chris con trick. Blink and you'd have missed it. The woman's got talent, you've got to admit. It takes a certain resourcefulness for someone to do so little, for so many, for so long, not get caught and still get paid.

'Any thoughts on that, Joseph?' asks Audrey, mascara fluttering in the windscreen mirror.

'I'm sorry, I was miles away, what were you talking about?'

'Position. Display. Any thoughts?'

'Em ...'

'I want you to man the main entrance. Chris and I will take turns on the display.'

'Em, okay.'

Inside the Exhibition Centre we take our places at the Innovation Convention. Me braving the bad Feng Shui by the door, handing out the Institute's glossy information packs. Audrey and Chris smiling like game show hostesses on our dull display stand or working the hall with entrepreneurial spirit. Later in the day I get to wander round the other stalls and stands myself. Turns out ours is one of the best. There's a new kind of petrochemical pipe which does something other petrochemical pipes can't do but – Jesus! – life's too short for me to actually find out what it is. There are innovative new breeze blocks, carpet cleaning equipment, insulation wool, security systems, fertilisers and sunbeds. There's even a ground-breaking new type of pneumatic drill.

It's an inspiration.

And to think I was going to play for Celtic, Mo was going to be lead singer in a band and Finn wanted to be a marine biologist.

. . . .

We were heading for the hills, late Saturday morning, going fishing in the high loch near Ben-y-Vrackie which we knew had been freshly stocked with brown and rainbow trout, when me and Mo first heard Finn's revelation. 'A marine biologist? You're kidding!'

Ben-y-Vrackie – all 2,757 feet of it – looks exactly like a child would paint a mountain. Like the Matterhorn on a packet of Alpen. Well, almost. It's a proper man's mountain, though. Unlike that blousey Ben Nevis – only 4,406 feet – which *claim*s to be the highest in the land but with its rounded summit is not the highest-*looking* which, in my book, is far more important. As far as we were concerned, Ben-y-Vrackie was *numero uno* among all the mountains in all the world and, in our opinion, parties of mountaineers should be booked solid for the next ten years for the opportunity to scale its splendid heights. I mean, Mount Everest – 29,039 feet – was way too high! What was the point of that? You couldn't even see it, lost above the clouds stuck in the middle of nowhere. No, we were happy enough with our own wee mountain, thank you very much. Okay, the mountaineers could leave their ropes and crampons behind – there's just a bit near the top where it gets so steep you find yourself crawling – and there's no glaciers or avalanches or altitude sickness to challenge the thrill-seekers but there's a fine view at the top. Our view. We always felt a dumb pride in being Scottish up there, as if our ancestors had given God a hand during its construction. As if they lugged the rocks there themselves and saw that it was good.

It *was* good. We looked up to Ben-y-Vrackie every day as we walked home from school. It was our weather vane, like the sea is for people on the coast. 'Aye, there's fair snow on the Ben,' people would say and that'd be your first warning winter was on the way. It would turn from dirty grey to green in springtime and dark purple velvet in summer, just like in all those teuchter songs. You could lose yourself for hours up there in the holidays, and we did. Lost, at least, until teatime. We were always gloriously ill-equipped. It was an inverted snobbery of ours to tramp the hills in jeans and Adidas trainers – Mo inevitably in his polyester St Johnstone top – while ramblers and tourists we'd meet on the trail would be dressed from head to serious walking boots in Gore-Tex; Kendal mint cake in their top pockets; compass, map and emergency overnight food in their rucksacks and 'to whom it may concern' messages in their parked cars and guest houses detailing where they intended to walk and what time they expected to return. We mocked the sensible people quietly to ourselves, regarding them as simple amateurs, daytrippers, compared with us, the natives, the sure-footed Sherpas, till the weather changed – as it could be relied upon to do – and we sheltered under dripping evergreens ripping Finn's last stick of Juicy Fruit into three and wishing we'd brought a cagoule or *something*.

Around the 12th of August our wonderland was invaded by rich Belgian and Italian shooters who'd come to live out their perverted Scottish fantasies on moorland kept bare and barren to serve them. We could never understand why landowners didn't plant some proper native trees like birch, aspen, alder, willow or Scots pine. The regimented, fast-growing pine plantations, with imported trees of uniform height fenced in like massed POWs, seemed to us to scar the landscape even more than the cat's cradle of power cables between pylons which at least made no pretence to be green. We liked heather. Heather's fine. But nothing *but* heather was an unnatural desert and we reckoned the likes of Moira Anderson should take a long, hard look at themselves for singing about it like it's all so great. We'd see the shooters in the distance, ludicrous in their tweeds and plus-fours, and blame them for the demise of the Caledonian Forest, squishing them dead between our fingers or shooting the deerstalker hats off their heads with our imaginary long-range semi-automatic rifles as a warning that we – the future – were on to them. We had no idea who owned the land we walked and fished. We sincerely believed it belonged to us. We felt fully justified to go and fish anywhere we damn well pleased.

'This is our home. This is where we live. This is like our garden,' said Finn. But just to make doubly sure, we usually made a courtesy call to the gamekeeper's cottage on the way up, knocked and asked politely if it was okay if we fished for trout in the mountain loch. He'd always take one look at the standard of our fishing rods, smile and say: 'Aye, 'course you can, lads. Long as you're no' using dynamite or cyanide, go ahead!' Truth is, if he'd said no, we'd have walked down the path till we were out of sight then doubled back a different way, keeping an eye out for the gamie's lone-wolf alsatian who might betray us.

We liked to kid ourselves we were masters of the great outdoors and all its birds and animals but really we were like strangers in a strange land. It could be a minefield out there. No matter how carefully I watched my step, grouse would rocket out of nowhere in a panic-stricken flap when I least expected it. It was arguable, in those circumstances, who got the bigger fright – me or the bird. The woods, the moorland and the hills belonged more to the wildlife than it did to us or the people who owned the estates. It was their wild domain. They were the ones in charge. They had superior sense in sight and smell and, I'm sure, would be gone half a mile in the opposite direction without us ever being aware they had been close. We'd only see them long after they'd been monitoring us. But we told such lies to each other. We all claimed we could guddle fish easy, any day, from under stones in the stream but none of us felt the need to actually prove it. We'd all had our individual close encounters with adders, Mo claimed he'd been bitten twice, but the only common factor in our reptile sightings was a lack of witnesses for verification.

Once, inspired by my survival training, I made a 'bolas' – like cowboys from the Argentine use – by fastening three rocks to three separate strings joined in the middle. The idea was to swing it round your head a few times then throw it at an escaping animal to entangle it just long enough to run in for the kill. I swung it once and nearly killed Mo and Finn as the rocks flew off in different directions. I'd forgotten to wrap each stone in cloth *then* tie the end to the string. Gave up on it. Took improvised snares, made from James' snapped electric guitar strings, to the hills instead.

We planned to position them along a trail where rabbits had worn a tiny path. We knew not to walk on the path and leave a scent. We knew vaguely, too, that it was probably illegal, what we were doing, but convinced ourselves of our noble intentions. We were not, in fact, doing this for gratuitous, sadistic pleasure but for essential food to supplement the diet of sandwiches we'd brought with us. Might even have a bash at making a natty rabbit-skin waistcoat to help see us through the winter. We wouldn't waste it. It was justified murder for our own survival. Apparently, eating rabbits – I mean, nothing but rabbits over a period of time – would eventually kill you. Lacking certain vitamins and fats, rabbit meat depletes your own vital minerals and vitamins in the process of digesting it. Sounds like the ultimate posthumous revenge. I was walking away after setting our very first trap when a startled rabbit darted passed me, white tail bobbing like a target. I cursed it for giving me a fright. Next moment, I heard an awful tortured squeal and saw it swinging horribly – plucked from live music to murder by James' guitar string. Its hind legs kept running forward again and again pathetically trying to free itself while only pulling the noose tighter round its neck. I was appalled and exhilarated by the sight of it. Appalled to feel so exhilarated. Me the great hunter. I all but beat my chest. But it squealed with such anguish I rushed over to try and free it. The little bastard bit me. I jumped back, rubbing my hand and cursing again. Couldn't it see I was only trying to help?

'Maybe we should kill it – put it out its misery,' said Mo picking up a rock the size of a grapefruit. I was going to agree in my best 'Yep, it's the right thing to do. It's the way of the country' sort of voice (as if I hadn't been responsible for its agony in the first place) when Mo handed the rock to me and I wasn't so sure. Fortunately, Finn took the initiative, throwing his jacket over the animal, wrapping it up. It struggled but he took a firm hold, loosened the snare round its neck and looped it over its silky ears. He stood up, lifting his jacket like a magician producing a rabbit from under a cloak. I half expected to see a fluffy white rabbit but instead a little wild brown one was revealed with blood at the side of one eye. It stood completely still for a few moments, paralysed with shock. Then it hopped off along the path, slowly and tentatively at first, before making a bolt for it with enough dash to suggest it would survive its ordeal without long-term ill-effects. The same couldn't be said for me. I sheepishly dismantled the snare, explaining to Finn and Mo that now I'd seen how well it worked I didn't need to see it again.

When we fished the high mountain loch – which from the summit is revealed to be shaped, bizarrely, like Charlie Brown's dog, Snoopy – we'd cast from our favourite spots out of sight of each other. I felt as if I was completely alone in the wilderness. There was no sign of other human beings or cars or houses in any direction for miles and miles and miles. And I liked that. I could get my head together. Forgot I was fishing and just laid back on a bed of springy heather and stared at the big blue sky. I breathed in the air so fresh and free from toxins it was intoxicating, till some stupid trout interrupted my reverie. I shouted on Mo and Finn to come and watch me reel it in. It was a thrill to see the fish break through the glass ceiling of divided realms. Utter silence to frantic splashing. Secret silver exposed to an audit by sunlight.

'Two pounds, no more, no less,' said Finn, giving an immediate and irritatingly accurate weight estimation from that first glimpse. I reeled it in, took it off the hook, and stared in wonder as it blew bubbles and gulped in the air.

'Like a fish out of water, isn't it?' I said, not thinking. Mo and Finn laughed, and I pretended I was being clever-funny.

The fish we caught were all so small we couldn't keep them but that didn't matter. The skill was in knowing where best to catch them, and how to reel them in without losing any on the reeds or rocks. We were never bothered with landing nets, or scales, or posing for photos with two slippery fingers up a dead fish's gills. The competition for us was only a matter of numbers.

After a couple of hours me and Mo got bored and edged round the loch till we were close enough to shout mindless insults at each other. By that time we'd given up Finn's angling advice and were singing noisily and casting our shadows over the water but the fish didn't seem to mind. We still seemed to catch them even though we broke the rules. Mo reckoned the fish would be wondering what all the noise was about, they'd come out of the reeds and shady overhangs to investigate, spot a wriggly worm and take the bait.

It was hot that day. So hot that a pocket of snow we noticed high above us near the mountain top inspired a spontaneous expedition. Without further thought, me and Mo left our fishing rods beside Finn and climbed up to reach it because the idea of a snowball fight on that hot August day appealed to our sense of the ridiculous. It was a deceptively long way away but we kept going, stopping only to get our breath back and shout and wave at Finn far below us. We reached the patch of melting snow, trapped and sheltered in a hollow. Sweating from the climb and the heat of the afternoon, we leapt into the middle to cool down and sank waist-deep in cold, wet snow. We laughed with the cold shock of diving into a little pool of shrinking winter. We threw snowballs at each other for a few mad minutes, just for the hell of it, then we ran all the way back down again, feeling like gods 'cause we were young, we could climb fast, we could even subvert the seasons.

Me, Mo and Finn were happy on our mountain. It was all talking, laughing and telling dirty jokes. Fishing was the least of it. It was just a laugh. Something to do while we waited to grow up. You couldn't hope to make a living from it.

'A marine biologist?'

Me and Mo looked at Finn differently from then on. I mean, we all knew, on our fishing expeditions, that Finn was the only one who actually knew anything about fish. Me and Mo didn't hold it against him. The fish took his bait no more than ours. And we'd heard him – one balmy evening at the Mill Pond on West Moulin Road when the trout weren't biting but the midges were – entertain us by catching tens of stickleback in an ice cream tub and pretending they were salmon on a tv documentary. We lay on the grass and, losing all sense of perspective, stared at the tiny fish swimming round and round the tub, as Finn put on a cod French accent like Jacques Cousteau and told us fascinating facts from the life cycle of the salmon: 'When ze bebé feesh are first 'atched from zer strange orange-collured bebé feesh eggs zay are known as *alevins*. Zer coat becomes silvery when zay are two years old and zen zay are no longer *alevins* zey are now called *smolts*. Attention! You stupeed boys! Don't you know zees? Zay spend four years at sea maturing into adult feesh before returning to zee place zay call 'ome. Ze veré reevers and streams from where zay were first spawned. Ow do zay know where to go? Raymarkable, *n'est pas?*'

Well, yes, he'd convinced us that salmon – with the ability to survive in both seawater and freshwater and find their way back to their spawning grounds up some river in the Highlands were, indeed, remarkable. But not as remarkable, surely, as, say, the number of girls who used to scream for those toothy, moon-faced Osmonds? Or the adulation of scoring the winning goal – bending the ball from a free kick into the top corner – in a Scottish Cup final? Or even, say, the *European* Cup final. Was he mad? It seemed ludicrous to me and Mo that Finn should dream of being a marine biologist of all things. We weren't quite sure what to make of it, weren't quite sure what it was, to tell you the truth, but it sounded a bit nerdy.

'Don't you ever want to play at Muirton?' asked Mo.

'No way!' laughed Finn, who was a Rangers man anyway.

'Not even Ibrox?' I asked.

'Nope,' said Finn, shaking his head with conviction, like he'd really thought it all out. We tried to convince him that, though it was something he maybe didn't want to hear right now, he'd understand when he was older. You don't always get what you want in life and maybe Finn should have a more realistic ambition, perhaps something more along the lines of ours. We sympathized, nevertheless, and told him that marine biology – whatever it meant – was something he'd probably grow out of.

'Course now, now I'm giving out brochures at the Innovation Convention, Mo's in between jobs, and Finn's a *bona fide* marine biologist! Works for Fruits of the Ocean, forever in a wet suit, jets round the world on fish business. He's trying to develop a strain of salmon so fresh for the consumer it not only swims upriver to its spawning ground but slaps up the main street to the supermarket as well, slipping neatly onto the ice behind the fish counter all by itself, wearing an 'eat me' grin. Remarkable, *n'est pas?*

• • • • • • • • • • • • • • • • •

Fishing was fun, but football? That was *living*. I couldn't fathom Finn. Ever since I could remember, I'd been hooked on football. My father took me to Hampden for the first time when I was 11 but I'd been there lots of times before. I'd visualised every kick of every big game on the radio. I'd avidly read the match reports. It really felt as if I'd been there – played there, even, a couple of times.

That night, before the Scotland-England game, I searched the linen cupboard for a box which hadn't seen the light of day for years. Inside it, wrapped in tissue, was a child-size kilt James had worn when he was a kid. Clan MacDonald, I think, predominantly dark greens, a tasteful tartan if you were kindly disposed to subdued tweeds, dull if you were not. Jackie had worn it too, a couple of times, and I'd worn it once to a fancy dress birthday party when I was seven (completing the outfit with a white vest and carrying a home-made fabric draught excluder for a caber, I was supposed to be Big Bill Anderson of Highland Games fame). I wasn't keen on kilts, though, or the whole kilt cult. Couldn't be sure of its authenticity. Couldn't be sure we weren't just parodying ourselves to wear it. Couldn't be sure of anything much at all, really, because my grasp of Scottish history was as vague and hazy a mixture of myth and legend as any tourist's. I knew for certain, however, that tartan would be *de rigueur* at the game and in my pre-match preoccupation it didn't occur to me, as I lay the kilt on the bed and carefully cut a length of tartan from it to make a ridiculously short scarf, that kilts – even children's ones – are expensive items and ones wrapped lovingly in tissue and folded neatly in a box hidden in the linen cupboard had added sentimental value. How was I to know you could take your pick of any kind of tartan scarf for a quid from hawkers outside Hampden on the day?

My father didn't take a newspaper on a regular basis. So every Monday (Thursdays, if there'd been a game the night before) I'd go round to Mrs Murray's next door and she'd let me cut out all the Celtic (and any Scotland) match reports from the back page of *The Scotsman*. Floodlit games looked like they'd been played in a permanent fog in the grainy black and white newsprint pictures I stuck on my bedroom wall. But it didn't matter. I could see every game clearly in my head.

My favourite player was Bobby Lennox. He just got on with the job, going for goal, minimum of fuss, totally reliable, always there when you needed him, never let you down, sensible haircut. People took him for granted. He was like somebody's dad. He was my favourite player till Kenny came along. Dalglish was like somebody's big brother. He was like *my* big brother. There he was, my big brother, looking like a shy pop star, scoring goals for Celtic at will.

We motored down to Glasgow in the morning, my

guilt-kilt-scarf hidden in my jacket, excitement mounting with every car or van or coachload of supporters we overtook. It was, I noted, a typical Scottish day: grey, overcast, occasional showers. *Dreich*. I took this to be an omen. We went to meet James for dinner at Dalrymple Hall of Residence in the West End. He was supposed to be studying English Literature but he only went to lectures or tutorials on days it didn't rain. And it rains a lot in Glasgow.

A crowd of long-haired students were watching *Football Focus* in the television room, not listening to the preview at all, just booing and swearing at every Englishman who appeared on screen and cheering every Scotsman. My father talked over my head a bit as we ate in the canteen. He was talking about English Literature, James' future, all sorts of serious stuff and I wasn't really listening, my head was so full of football. Then I heard my father telling James he should be an example to me as it was obvious 'the boy worships you!'. I was embarrassed but let it pass. I'd heard it before.

We got a pudding for second course which even school dinners would have rejected. It was a kind of pink blancmange with hundreds and thousands sprinkled on it, which made it look marginally more appealing but couldn't disguise the taste. James took one spoonful and pushed his plate away in disgust. I ate a spoonful too and reacted the same way.

'See that?' my father, who'd eat sawdust if it was served up to him, said to James: 'He's *so* influenced by you.'

Outside Hampden I was wide-eyed with wonder at the sight of more drunks in one place than I'd ever seen before. Wee fellahs in dirty suits and rosettes, raucous tartan-clad gangs, carry outs clinking, happily sung in discordant harmony: 'Yaba daba doo, we'll support the boys in blue, singing Easy! Easy!' I walked fast through the streets and over wasteground to keep up and keep close to my brother and my father. As we queued at the turnstile, ticketless teenagers in flapping flared jeans took running jumps at the gate to get in. Two or three made it before the police moved the others on. Small boys were lifted over the turnstile for free. The official capacity was limited to 85,000 in the rickety, ageing stadium which held so many attendance records. But if I'd seen an extra five people make it into the ground without paying in only a few minutes at one gate alone then what must the real attendance figures be like? We walked through a prehistoric tunnel with lines of cavemen and caveboys pissing against both walls and a stream of steaming urine flowing out through the gutters. And for the first time, I began to think Hampden might not be what I'd hoped for. This wasn't how I'd imagined it. Then, as the three of us walked out onto the terracing of the North Enclosure, bright sunshine emerged through the rainclouds to greet us.

The covered Rangers end, to our right, was a fluid mass of waving blue and white Saltires, yellow and red Lion Rampants, and garishly coloured scarves from every legitimate clan tartan in the country and several more that looked woven specially for the occasion by blind weavers. My oddly cut, dull-coloured and frayed scarf looked anonymous round my neck (even though it was doubtless the only pleated scarf in the stadium). The grass on the pitch below us was a brilliant, lush green, like the lovingly mowed lawn of an English country garden. The smell of freshly cut grass – with all its subconscious associations with village fêtes and school sports days and summer – mixed incongruously with the smoke from thousands of cigarettes and the smell of strong spirits and men in too close proximity. We found a place to stand on the black ash of the terracing. I was enclosed by four solid walls of sound. I had to shout to speak to my brother or my father. It felt good not to be English.

As the terracing filled up, James, in a long Red Army surplus coat with huge lapels, lifted me onto the barrier and held me up. I was head and shoulders above everyone else. I could see everything. I thought I could see the fear in Kevin Keegan's eyes as the teams ran out of the tunnel into a glue of white noise. The game kicked off. Every time a white shirt touched the ball there was immense, indignant booing (hadn't they read the script?) until a dark blue jersey regained possession, to righteous cheering, and every dark blue pass that stayed under dark blue control was greeted with the same life-affirming enthusiasm as lines of scripture at a revivalist meeting.

The entire match seemed to last no more than ten minutes. Just a blur. A fast-forward. England having the effrontery to score first. And some individual having the effrontery to shout 'Englan'!' during a brief lull in the noise level. The whole of the North Enclosure turned round to see who'd shouted. I never heard him again. Scotland equalized with a penalty. Then sometime in the second half, time switched to slow-mo. The ball found its rightful place at Kenny's feet only ten yards or so from the England goal. Hands were placed on the shoulders of the person in front, necks stretched. The sinews of Kenny's hamstring reacted to a message from his brain, pulling back the trigger to shoot. Index finger pointing at the end of his outstretched arm, the perfect balance of a natural player, the leather of his boot making contact with the leather of the ball. In the urgency of the moment, it wasn't a perfect connection and the ball took off on its decisive journey almost hesitantly, reluctantly. But it travelled not with the power of one man's kick but with the collective power of 85,000, 5,500,000 people, a whole nation, all its ancestors and exiles, willing it forward. It seemed to take the rest of the afternoon but eventually squeezed in, only doing its duty, keeping to the wish-fulfilling screenplay, the reluctant star. The focus of all our rapt attention till then. Who cared where the ball was now? It sat in the back of the England net where it belonged. Its proper home. Its rightful place. Not on the edge of the Scotland penalty area and certainly not flying through the air towards the Scotland 'keeper who might, or might not, reach it in time. Those were the agonies. But who cared where the ball was now? No longer was it a magnet for our eyes, turning our heads this way and that, making us fret, making us hopeful, making us shout a big bruising, ear-bursting 'Yee-s!' in relief and release. As we did then, as Kenny turned with his arms raised, wearing an 85,000-volt smile on his face. The terracing crowds seemed to collapse in on themselves as supporters hugged each other and danced. The noise from the covered Rangers end bounced off the roof and raced up the pitch to join the celebrations at the Celtic end. I thought Kenny had neatly placed the ball between the near post and the goalkeeper to score but that night on Mrs Murray's tv I saw it had gone through the keeper's legs. The noise which accompanied the flap of the netting behind him must still be reverberating round Ray Clemence's head today. He'll carry that to the shops, when he's eating his tea, watching a video, it'll still be there buzzing in his head, keeping him awake at night. Or maybe not. Who knows? Why should I presume what goes on in Ray Clemence's head? How the hell should I know? All I know is: it's still buzzing in *my* head. Still keeps me awake sometimes. The rest of the game was a celebration mixed with anxious whistles for full-time, a long time before full-time, and a scare as Mick Channon rushed in on our goal and Tom Forsyth, of all people, not noted for his finesse in the tackle, judged the timing of his challenge perfectly, stealing the ball like a snatch thief and running up the park with the swagger, for better or worse, that's a part of who we are.

Full-time, we'd won the Home Championship outright and, frankly, Brazil and all her World Cups paled in comparison. We ran through the streets to beat the traffic jams. Said goodbye to my brother at the bus stop, got back in the car and were off up the road home, my kilt-scarf flapping out the window. Kids who'd watched the game on tv stood by the road to wave to the buses. We were subdued driving home. I'd lost my voice. My ears were ringing. All I remember my father saying, summing up a more sober perspective, was 'Aye, well, you'll have increased your vocabulary today, Son'.

.   .   .   .

Georgie was growing fast. Learning fast. She'd just started going to nursery. She was cute. She was clever. We were proud. Judge Helen and I by Georgie. She was our alibi. As long as we had a bright, healthy, happy kid our relationship couldn't be all bad, could it? She never let us down. Never showed signs of anxiety. Never wet the bed. Never cried in the night. She was sociable, outgoing, well-adjusted. But then, she was shielded. Shielded from our dissolution, which we deviously hid and disguised like alcoholics in denial. On the brink of an argument we'd take one look at Georgie and pull back, change the subject, count to ten, but save every petty hurt for later, when the child would be safely asleep. Every trivial, real or imagined, slight was filed, categorized, catalogued, nurtured and cared for, ready to be lovingly recalled in all its potent detail. *Oh, how I have been wronged!* How I have suffered! That delicious, bittersweet, sinking sensation of hurt and despair in the pit of my stomach like freezing cold, ice-cubed water and bubbling, boiling hot water poured simultaneously on the same spot. Again and again.

Alone we would quietly and rationally talk it through like adults. Helen using her sweet, reasonable voice to recall what she'd said earlier then switching to a bitter, unreasonable voice for all my quotes which only made me more bitter and unreasonable. Our quiet, ever-so-rational voices got louder and louder till one of us could take no more and doors were slammed. In the silence which ensued we'd wonder what kept us together at all – as she slept on, oblivious, in her pink room, Spice Girl posters on the wall, clinging to her small, stuffed hippo. Georgie was never affected. We made sure of it. She was always blissfully unaware of the tensions in the house.

My parents came to visit us in our flat. We'd tidied and dusted and hidden the overflowing basket of our dirty washing. Helen and I were going to put on a united front for the sake of the child and the child's grandparents. They arrived. We gave them tea. They fussed over Georgie who played happily with them, singing, drawing pictures. They knelt on the carpet, took an interest in Georgie's dolls and all their accessories. Georgie, delighting in the attention, showed off, supplying the voices as she innocently role-played with her toys.

'Fuck *off!*' said Ken.

'No, *you* fuck off!' said Barbie.

•   •   •   •   •   •   •   •   •   •   •   •   •   •   •   •   •   •   •

Chris' friend Mary has brought her baby into the Institute. I manage to slip past the crowd of cooing women surrounding the child in reception but I can still hear its plaintive crying from our office. I want to go and see what's the matter. What's it trying to tell us? I can't bear the thought of it being misunderstood or ignored. I want to pick it up, take it away from all the peering faces, check if it's too warm or too cold, see if it needs its bottle, see if it needs a change of nappy, make sure it's comfortable, like I used to do with Georgie. Mary carries the baby into our office in its detachable car seat. The short journey from reception has calmed it down and it's gurgling happily, looking this way and that for anything of interest to focus on. Mary puts it on a desk to wait for Chris who she wants to thank for her support through some unspecified 'difficult times'.

And, I know, I know, it would just be *too* rude to ignore it. Can't do it. Prue gets up and stands a little back from the baby with her arms crossed.

'Hel-lo little one! Is it a boy or a girl?'

It's hard to tell at that age. I'm glad she asked. New mums can be touchy. Turns out it's a boy. Mary's beaming. She's all right, used to work in personnel at the Institute in the early days, now she's a proud mum. Thinks compliments for the baby are indirect compliments to her.

'He's beautiful!' says Prue, still maintaining a distance.

'*Thank you!*' says Mary, like she must therefore be beautiful too.

I come over to look at the baby because to stay at my desk would only make me more conspicuous. What can I say? He's a little human being with all that pre-programmed genetic stuff going on and a whole lot of environmental factors starting to kick in and Mary's nurturing about to make him a future Prime Minister or cop killer.

'He's a good looking wee boy, Mary,' I say dutifully.

'*Thank you!*' she says.

I don't really know what to say next and Prue, never usually lost for words, doesn't seem to know either so I'm actually quite relieved when a whole clutch of clucking hens burst into the office in search of Mary's boy child. 'There he is!' they shout, running over to the desk. I look at the baby, half-expecting him to say '*Shit!* They've found me! Y'gotta help me, you're my only hope, man!' but he doesn't seem put out. They crowd the boy and coo some more inanities but there's something genuine going on too. It's not *all* about fulfilling obligations to a mob mentality. He sits there helpless, trying to focus his bright, alert eyes at the big, smiling faces. He stretches his arms a little, waggles his feet like he's trying to shake off his socks. He yawns extravagantly. The women react as if he's just stood up and given a Brahms recital, ooing and ahing their appreciation at the child prodigy.

Audrey arrives – and even though networking leaves her no time for a husband, let alone a baby, she seems to know better than me or Prue the proper etiquette required of the situation, elbowing her way to the front of the congregation.

'It's a boy, isn't it, Mary?' Daring Mary to disagree. 'Oh, he's *gor-geous*! Who's a big boy then?' she asks, poking him in the stomach with a long painted finger nail. She starts her rapid-fire questions: 'Name? Breast-feeding, Mary? Teething yet? D'you have to watch him all the time or is he playing with himself yet?'

There's a change in his demeanour. It may have been coincidence, but his face crumples as if in concentration. New Pampers, please.

• • • • • • • • • • • • • • • • • •

On a hot day, the stench from the dump would waft through the green, leafy glade to the Black Spout. Tourists would sniff the air as they sat on the viewing seat above the waterfall and presume it was some strange, foul-smelling Scottish herb flowering in summer profusion in the forest. Not that many visitors went there – it was well off the usual beaten tourist track. It was pretty much a local secret in Pitlochry, then, for two reasons: the waterfall wasn't actually all that spectacular – it was arguable whether it justified the walk to get there – and the town's land-fill rubbish dump was only a few hundred yards away, masked by birch trees.

No higher than a modest church spire, the Black Spout cascaded with melted snow, rainwater and industrial purpose in winter when no one went to see it. Piqued in summer, it trickled, thin and lazy, at the moist centre of the damp glade like a tap on half twist. Me, Mo and Finn – running wild like savages in the woods on our way to the dump – would always take the necessary detour to look at the waterfall. It was possible – half-closing your eyes and imagining yourself tiny, standing under huge tropical trees of bracken – to make the Black Spout higher than Angel Falls in Venezuela. It was all a matter of hypnotic perspective to stand and stare. To concentrate on one foamy bubble, catch it at the top and follow it down through space, watch it split on jutting rocks into many bubbles and on downwards into the cool pool at the bottom. I'd feel as if I was falling. I'd catch myself in time: 'Fuck this! C'mon, we'll go to the dump!'

It was a favourite haunt of mine, Mo's and Finn's. We all knew – because it *does* happen, albeit *very* occasionally, and *always* to other people – that one day we'd stumble on a bag of swag containing thousands of used tenners thrown out by mistake by a rookie at the Royal Bank of Scotland. Our sharp eyes would spot the bank's logo on a piece of blue cloth in the distance and we'd wade through rotting rubbish to reach it. In our breathless excitement we'd tug and tear at the bag and split it open, scattering hundreds and thousands of ten pound notes to the wind. We'd be furious, there'd be fisticuffs, till we found solace and consolation for our own selfish loss in discovering we'd inadvertently planted Utopia: the trees growing leaves of money in a beautiful, organic redistribution of wealth.

But mostly, to be honest, we went there to throw stones at the car wrecks. Windscreens? Smithereens. Each smithereen a diamond in the mud. It gave us deep, indescribable pleasure to be wantonly destructive, to run like Luddites trashing all the trash. White goods, black with our boot marks. Rocking the heavy washing machines, the fridge freezers and the cookers lined up for scrap metal till they toppled like statues.

Access to this wonderful playground was inexplicably denied to children, even ones like us on the eve of adolescence, on grounds of safety. There were 'Keep Out' signs and fences but the biggest deterrent of all was a giant of a man in a dirty orange boilersuit. All day he bulldozed layers of earth over fresh rubbish, burying the debris of our lives into a compressed methane time capsule. He spooked us. Finn thought he'd seen bolts in his neck. If he ever saw us hanging around, he'd turn the bulldozer violently and head straight for us as we fled into the woods. We reckoned he wouldn't think twice about burying some trespassing kids with the rest of the rubbish.

The orange giant scared us big time. It was an era in our lives when certain adults possessed a strange supernatural mystique, in our own world mythology, and were best avoided. Adults like the wicked witch of the amusement arcade, where we also would gravitate in that awkward, footloose time between childhood and pubhood. We'd eke out any money we had asking for change in two pence pieces and playing the mindlessly stupid 'Pennyfalls' machine. A drawer moved back and forth pushing dropped coins to the brink of a chute where, with luck, they'd fall with a pleasing clatter into a tray where I'd collect my winnings. My big cash jackpot. I'd rejoice, count the coins – all 16p – tell Mo and Finn how many I was up by, then put them all right back into the machine in a process of ever-decreasing totals till I was left with nothing but a gnawing feeling of frustration and injustice. It was only pennies. But that wasn't the point. It only added insult to injury to be able to peer through the glass and see my coins balancing improbably over the lip of the cliff. At that moment – cleaned out, pockets empty – the temptation to give the machine just a little nudge became too much to resist.

And it worked. The pennies dropped. No one noticed. I'd got it sussed. It was natural justice. I was kicking against all the false hope and disappointment of all those flashing fruit machines and one-armed bandits. It was God's work. I put them back in the machine and they stuck on the ledge displacing no others. Emboldened by the success of the earlier nudge, I aimed a swift shoulder charge against the reinforced glass, hoping to hear my favourite percussion, the tambourine rattle of coins in the chute. But instead, the previously passive machine reacted violently, bells and buzzers sounded the alarm and a police light I hadn't noticed started spinning on top of it in red alert. Everyone turned to look in my direction. Mo and Finn took a step back, like they'd never met me before in their entire lives.

'*Don't bang the machines!*' screeched the wicked witch of the change booth, giving me nightmares with her evil eye. She was fearsome. Half human, half Dalek. Her head and torso above the counter moved mechanically and her all-seeing eyes followed me wherever I went in the arcade like a portrait in a haunted house. From then on, I only ever banged the machines when someone else was in the booth. It wasn't until years later I saw her for the first time out of context. She was up the street. She had legs. Human legs. She even had a smile and a kiss for her little granddaughter.

The demonic myth of the amusements would later be as shattered as the glass bottles and light bulbs which made such a satisfying popping noise when they hit the ground at the dump. If the coast was clear, the bulldozer lay dozing, and there was no sign of the giant with the neck bolts and the orange boilersuit, we would wander about and wonder at other people's discarded treasure. It was odd how the stench was almost unbearable at first but soon we hardly noticed it. Like scavengers from the favelas, we searched for objects of any value. Plastic bottles sailed over the man-made mountains of stinking garbage when given an almighty kick. Heaps of magazines disappointed with nothing more stimulating than out of date travel agent brochures. But there was always a chance of finding something valuable the bin men and the orange man had missed.

Then Finn spotted a boat. He really did. A blue, fibreglass dinghy. Perfect condition – or so it looked from the top of the hill. We waded down the soft slope, knee-deep in soggy packaging, newspapers, broken eggs, rotting vegetables, never knowing if the next step would sink into something sharp like dagger glass from a broken mirror, or spokes and spikes off a rusty bike, or just sink into a deep hole of nothing. We thought nothing of the risks as we kept our eyes on the prize. It was obviously some silly mistake someone had made, dumping such a handsome, watertight little boat. Some fool was going to be in big trouble when they realized they'd dumped the wrong boat. We'd better take it quick before the owner came back to claim it.

All the way down the soft slope we discussed how we would use the boat to go fishing in the deepest parts of the loch, which of our friends could use it for free, who we'd charge, and where we would hide it. We couldn't believe our luck. We were so enamoured with the whole idea of it – our own little boat, for God's sake! – that nothing, absolutely nothing, was going to come between us and that cherished fantasy, not least a three-foot tear in a fibreglass hull. The owner had obviously deemed it irreparable.

'We can fix that easy!' said Finn, head full of plans for deep water experiments in the name of marine science, no doubt. We blithely agreed. We all hauled the boat back up the soft, sinking, stinking slope. Every time we pulled it, small pieces of fibreglass would break off and enlarge the hole but we were not to be put off.

It was late and getting dark, so rather than stumble through the fields and over fences and other obstacles, risking further damage, we decided to carry it through the town. It took some brass neck to walk up the main street. The three of us with an upturned dinghy on our heads. No one bothered us. A police patrol drove past, slowing for a few moments – we hid our heads in the hull in embarrassment – before speeding on to more pressing crime-fighting duties in the vast, heaving metropolis. After several rest stops on the journey – it was surprisingly heavy – we reached the bottom of Finn's garden and dropped the boat behind his dad's greenhouse. Finn's mum watched us suspiciously from the back door. We were well pleased with ourselves. It was important work. We'd done well. That night we would sleep dreaming of sailing the little choppy waves of the deepest part of the loch reeling in the big, fat trout for nowt.

In the sober light of the following day our dinghy made a sorry sight. The three-foot gash had grown and a flap of useless fibreglass hung from the hull. We tried to melt various plastics onto the slash to seal it but only succeeded in choking each other with noxious fumes. We thought about taking our boat to the PE teacher at school, who could patch up gashes on canoes, but we knew in our hearts this was no superficial flesh wound – it was terminal. And though we never said, none of us wanted to face the humiliation of carrying the boat through the school playground on our heads with all our school pals watching and laughing at our dumb daydreams. We gave up on the whole idea as easily as we'd first taken it up. The boat stayed where it was behind Finn's dad's greenhouse, neglected and forgotten, as we returned to playing football once more.

Forgotten and neglected it remained till January, when the first heavy snow fell and, with a brainwave, we remembered the boat, pulled it free from the weeds which had entangled it, carried it over a fence, across a road and up a steeply sloping nearby field. Dragging it all the way to the top, pointing it downwards, all piling in, not sure if it was going to work. Sitting there like lemons in a still-life till Mo got out, gave us a wee push and jumped in as it gathered speed. Worked a dream. Like a downhill racer. Like an Olympic bobsleigh. Shooting down the slope at high speed, crashing into the burn at the bottom, pieces of fibreglass breaking off with each go.

That's part of survival training, that is: to make the best and most imaginative use of all available materials to meet the challenges of your environment and circumstances. I *could* claim it but, to be honest, the sledge thing was Mo's idea.

Adapt and survive.

• • • • • • • • • • • • • • • • •

Thursday morning in Aberdeen. I take the car because I'm

running late. I needn't have rushed – Audrey Marshall's at a business conference in Manchester and Chris has the day off – it's just me and Prue in the office.

Prue says 'Morning, Joe!', manically cheery for a change, when I walk in the door, so I say 'Morning, Prue!'

'Nice weekend?'

'Oh, yeah, yeah, it was great,' I say, a little taken aback because Prue usually takes a while to warm up in the morning. 'You?'

'Well, we went to the pictures on Friday. Had my sister and her family round all day Saturday. Did a whole pile of washing and ironing on Sunday afternoon and watched that new mini-series on ITV in the evening. Did you see it?'

'Me? Naw, naw, a couple of pals from school were up. No time for tv, me. Wild weekend.'

'Where did you go?'

'Where did we go? Where did we go? Where *didn't* we go? Oh, it was *wild!*'

'*Must've* been wild if you can't remember a thing about it.'

'Oh yeah! Definitely. Wild, so it was! Hey, you haven't told me what your calendar's saying today. D'you forget to tear a page off? Tut! Tut! Slipping up in your old age.'

It's such a careless, throwaway remark I've forgotten it by the time it's been said.

'I haven't even *read* today's one yet,' Prue says with a catch in her voice like I'm deliberately putting her on the defensive, like her cheeriness is a sham, like she's been found out. 'I didn't know you were so interested in them anyway,' she adds, in a tone that tells me the conversation has been terminated. Strangled at birth.

The office is quiet and self-conscious without Chris' private calls and Audrey marshalling the troops. Without distractions from the boss, Prue and I get through a power of work for an hour then she rolls her chair slightly to one side, reaches into her handbag and takes out a tiny compact. She hides her head behind the computer monitor as she silently pats powder on her nose and cheeks, checks her hair – top, left, right – in the little mirror she closes in her palm. I can see her reflection in the smoked glass partition behind her desk. She doesn't know. She isn't being showy. For a moment, she doesn't look so dangerous. She looks almost like someone I could trust with the truth of me. But no, hold on, she's a killer. A hitman. A character assassinator. Master of the verbal putdown. Risk a retort and she'd win on a KO with a well-timed, killer comeback line.

Prue's got a hospital appointment. She's gone for the rest of the morning and – surprisingly, for someone so conscientious – late into the afternoon. I'm looking for a new roll of Sellotape, A4 envelopes and some Tipp-Ex In the walk-in stationery cupboard when she returns. I can't find the envelopes anywhere. I'm just about to shout through to ask her if she knows where they are when I hear a noise. I hold my breath and listen ... crying. Prue sobbing softly. I don't know what to do. Should I come out and ask her what's the matter? She might be embarrassed. She must've seen the office empty and assumed I was away at a meeting. Should I make a noise in the cupboard, give her time to recover, pretend I heard nothing when I come out? I can't decide what's best. She's still crying. I wait so long I can't come out. She'll wonder what I've been doing in there for a whole ten minutes. I've got visions of being trapped in the cupboard until Prue goes off home. But then she always locks up if she thinks she's last to leave. She'll lock the cupboard. I could be stuck in here all night till the cleaners come in at six. I sigh inwardly, lean back against the wall and knock a roll of bubble wrap onto the floor. It bounces lightly on the carpet but sounds to me like a doll's house-size thunderstorm. I stand like a statue. Monumental stupidity. I can hear Prue getting up out of her chair and walking towards the cupboard. I've been rumbled. I don't breathe. I see her walking straight past the quarter-open cupboard door, wiping her eyes with a handkerchief. I hear the office door closing behind her. I breathe again. She's probably gone to wash her face and tidy herself up. I take my chance, escape solitary confinement, return to my chair ready with a ruse should Prue ask where I was.

Something happened today.

Earlier, when Prue was at the hospital, I'd gone home to my flat for lunch as usual, parked my bashed-up Chevette off George Street, and headed up the permanent night flights of stairs for a quick bite to eat. I'd normally watch the end of the *One O'Clock News* but I was a little later today and watched some old, time-filling Australian soap Sydney saw first in the seventies. It's healthy to get out of the office though. Healthier still, I'm sure, to get out the building altogether. (When she not 'doing' lunch, Audrey patronizes The Tasty Tit-bit sandwich bar in Holburn Street, brings her quarry back to her desk and drops crumbs between the keys of her keyboard. The smell from her choice of filling pervades the office for the rest of the afternoon.) It's a rush hour for all of us wherever we go. Fighting through the traffic lights and queues is as likely to induce indigestion as working on in the office with a sandwich.

On my way back to the Institute, I figured I'd nip to the bank, get some cash out with my Keycard. I swung into the car park, stopped in the first available space, got out, snibbed the door to lock it, and swung it shut in one swift, unthinking, mechanical movement before I realized I'd not only locked the car with the key in the ignition, I'd locked the car with the key in the ignition *and* the engine running.

I lock myself out of my car at a rate of about twice a year, so that wasn't unusual, but locking myself out with the engine still running was a first, even for me. The window on the driver's side was still slightly open, I noticed, by a tantalizing half inch at the top, and I tried to pull it down further with no luck. I walked round the car looking at the options, hoping a door would be unlocked or another window open but it was sealed from all angles. Exhaust fumes began to choke the air. Should I put my foot over the exhaust pipe to cut the engine, I wondered – no, that might do some damage. I could feel a rising panic at the thought of having to ask a couple of laconic coppers for help.

I walked into the bank, trying to walk like a person walking into a bank for a spot of banking. With the open plan in there, everyone hears and takes an unnatural amount of interest when a customer wants to make a temporary withdrawal of a wire coat-hanger. They did have one, fortunately. I explained what it was for and secured a loan. Even walking down the steps of the bank incongruously carrying a coat-hanger was embarrassing. The car was hot now, the fan made a rattly noise and the carbon monoxide fumes were suffocating some shrubs in a border in the car park. I made a hook with the end of the wire and fed it through the window, more in hope than expectation. I became aware I was being watched and looked up. At two first-floor windows, a group of five or six bank staff were leaning out watching. Evidently, I'd made their day. One or two had the decency to look away as I looked up but the rest were brazen enough to keep on staring. I waved, smiled through gritted teeth.

I got back to the work in hand. All distractions put aside – plenty time for humiliation and embarrassment later – I concentrated on the delicate manoeuvring of the wire to try and hook the key in the ignition. It was tricky because when the coat-hanger was stretched out it became very springy. Would my hook bend as I tried to turn the key? Would the key spring out onto the floor when I tried to pull it towards me? I felt as if I was dismantling an unexploded bomb or trying to figure out the combination lock of a safe as the cops were closing in. I surprised myself, but betrayed no hint of it to my audience, as I managed to hook the key, give it a twist and finally silenced the faltering chug of the engine. I had to take the wire out again and make a better, more rounded hook for the final phase of the operation. I actually managed to hook the key again – you'd think it was part of the driving test, I was so good – then I pulled the key ever-so-carefully out of the ignition towards me and – another critical moment – through the half inch of open window.

I'd made it! Reunited with my key, I turned round and jabbed my fist once in the air to spontaneous applause from the bank staff above me. I put on a show of cockiness walking across to the cash machine, taking my money out and returning the misshapen coat-hanger before driving off as if the whole thing had been a routine operation.

It made it a special day. Gave it a reference point. It would stand out from all the other days without contour or contrast. It would forever be 'The-day-I-locked-myself-out-of-my-car-with-the-engine-running'.

Prue returns to the office. She's composed herself only long enough to say 'Hi, Joe' in an absent, preoccupied manner and sit down. But behind the monitor of her computer, she's getting upset all over again. Holding back the tears. Won't tell me what's the matter. She goes home early for the first time in her life. She's not faking it. I'm answering her phone once she's gone and the message on the tear-a-day desk calendar says:

OCTOBER
10
Thursday
A mother alone knows what it is to love and be happy

• • • • • • • • • • • • • • • • • • • •

Big Momma stainless steel safety pins made it into my survival kit despite my prejudices against them. James' survival pamphlet said safety pins were essential items to be included in any self-respecting survival kit. Safety pins were invaluable for securing bandages to broken arms and legs – which, I conceded, was useful – and making improvised fishing hooks – which appealed to me too; but they were also ideal for makeshift repairs to torn clothes – which sounded more Boy's Brigade than Red Brigade. I found a few in a first aid box and placed them reluctantly at the bottom of my tobacco tin along with a tiny sewing kit which was also recommended.

Safety pins seemed a bit nancy boy to me. I mean, weren't they used for holding babies' nappies together? It didn't fit in with my idea of the rugged adventurer who scorned cuts and grazes, laughed in the face of danger but always made sure any wee holes in his jacket were held together with a shiny new safety pin before sewing them up nicely, at the earliest opportunity, with a needle and thread: 'I may be lost in the jungle, miles from civilization, but one must keep up appearances, mustn't one?'

Punk took the safety out of pins for a little while. Made the functional fashionable. Gave them some status, a hint of danger, like pins pulled from grenades. I felt I'd been primed the day punk arrived in Pitlochry in the shape of a peroxide Billy Idol clone called Brendan Doyle from Shettleston (a.k.a. 'Doily' behind his back but *never* to his face) whose father had just become manager of a small, local hotel. He'd seen us kicking a ball and, bold as brass, came up, stood on the sidelines till he knew who was playing which way and joined in without even asking. And we passed to him and tackled him and only asked his name to know what to shout when he got the ball. He had a spiked haircut like we'd only ever seen on tv and wore a fluffy v-neck jumper and black combats with unnecessary zips. He was a good player and a good laugh and he brought us good news from the big city for all the young members of Generation X.

Only from sheer fatigue did the football finally fizzle out and we sat on the gently revolving roundabout – near the swings we'd swung as kids – red-faced, cooling down, chilling out, smoking Brendan's cigarettes, listening to his hypnotic foreign accent tell tall tales of life after school. He was a piss artist – we could tell – but he painted such pleasingly exotic pictures in our heads of parties and girls and speed that it didn't matter. Beyond our sleepy town was a bigger canvas on which to scratch our mark. We'd always known it was there, of course, but now it was here. It was unavoidable. We couldn't hide any more. Brendan had been sent to tell us our time had come, rolling into town on a CityLink bus, ticking over and ready to roll out again.

He asked me who my favourite band was and, thinking fast how to impress him, I told him my brother Jackie's favourite band: 'Led Zepellin,' I said. A blatant lie. Mo and Finn looked surprised but said nothing. Brendan laughed like I'd told him a great joke and sneered his best Billy Idol sneer.

'Aw, they're *shite*, man!' he spat, 'and that's not an opinion that's a fact! Their songs last an hour and a half each, don't they? D'you know why? 'Cause they can't think of anything worth saying so they fill in time with wanky guitar solos. Look at me! I can play guitar! So *fuck!* An' drum solos? That's a fucken joke. That's just a rip off, can't you see? They're making arses of you. All that shitty, self-indulgent crap! You buy their album – all you're doing is buying aviation fuel for their private jet. Don't buy it! It's finished! It's over! Punk's gonna just blow all that away!'

We were ripe for Brendan's cultural revolution. We'd heard sporadic outbursts of punk on the radio and at first we thought, like the newspapers, it was unlistenable but then, like Brendan said, so was Genesis. He told us that all that went before was bad. Only the new wave was good. We had to free the charts of records by anyone over 25 to let the new blood take over. And – 25 being positively geriatric to us – we were all for it. Didn't need much convincing. Made perfect sense to us. We were converts before the end of the conversation. There was consensus on the magic roundabout: 'It's true, right enough. Led Zeppelin really *are* shite.' I didn't mind – I'd never liked them anyway. Brendan said we should denounce all members of the rock music establishment for crimes against the new beat generation: Elton John, Rod Stewart, Pink Floyd, Deep Purple, The Rolling Stones, they were all the same, corporate robots the lot of them! It was easy! I hadn't realized how long I'd been waiting for an excuse to drop them all! Smash the Status Quo!.

Then Brendan goes and oversteps the mark.

'Even The Beatles are shite!'

And, after a moment's shocked hesitation, we denounced them too, even though, in our heart of hearts we knew they – alone – to tell you the truth, actually, in fact, *weren't* shite.

We saw Brendan a lot that summer when he wasn't waiting tables in the hotel. He lent me *The Clash* and *Never Mind the Bollocks* and *In the City.* I listened, then I laughed too at the mere thought of Led Zeppelin. And we laughed at the papers who hadn't got wise to it and still thought punk was a joke. And when we heard it on the radio – all screaming vocals and 100mph train-crash drums – we understood. It was like staring at a Magic Eye painting, just seeing chaos and anarchy till suddenly the hidden picture was revealed in all its precious, secret glory. All the aggression, all the frustration, all the rejection of everything that went before. We loved it. Guitars played like roaring chainsaws cutting through all the deadwood of those flabby, pretentious concept albums my long-haired, hippie brothers had been sold. Me, Mo and Finn were agreed. If it couldn't be done in three minutes with three chords, us three weren't interested. It wasn't a matter of taste but a matter of right and wrong. We'd got it all sussed – and that wasn't an opinion, it was an indisputable, scientific fact.

Growing up in rural Perthshire, obviously, we had to improvise a bit for the necessary punk backdrop of urban decay but we were solid-gold punks at heart. We cultivated an attitude: if those bands who couldn't play or sing played and sang anyway, well, hey, we could do *anything* we wanted too. I could play for Celtic, Mo could top the charts, Finn could even be a marine biologist if he really wanted to be. I never had a spiked haircut or a pierced anything. We didn't have a look, we just looked in the drawer in the morning and wore the first thing we found. In other words, we looked like any of The Undertones except Feargal (who'd want to?). It might sound like I'm polishing my fingernails on my chest to say it but, although we looked anonymous, ours was the purest punk attitude of all because it was just a state of mind and couldn't be copied, exploited, mass-marketed and sold right back to us later in 15-year retro cycles. (Well, maybe it could.) Deliberately cutting up t-shirts and wearing painstakingly styled Mohican haircuts – soon to be so sanitized as to feature on London postcards – wasn't for us.

• • • • • • • • • • • • • • • • • • •

The whole punk uniform of chains and razor blades and safety pins seemed as preeningly self-conscious as anything that went before. We were truly anti-fashion. And what could be more anti-fashion than shopping, as we did, with the lumpen masses at Burton's and Concept Man?

Ideas endure, fashion fades. The punk nadir came a few years later when Brendan – who was championing Crass and The Exploited – grew his hair long specially to fashion it into cone shapes. He used glue to make the cones stick out all over his head and, admittedly, the finished effect was striking. He was a walking work of art. Old women crossed to the other side of the road when they saw him coming. Only thing was, he found it impossible to sleep with his stupid conehead and had to shave them off after a week of insomnia.

Brendan was a restless thrill-seeker who progressed

from glue-sniffing to mushrooms to hard drugs and now he's dead. People'd like that, wouldn't they? Or else he became a lawyer or a doctor. A real old-fashioned, mainstream, establishment success. Oh, the contrast and all. Well, truth is, I don't know. He moved away. Lost touch. Who knows?

Punk's well dead, though. I know that.

• • • • • • • • • • • • • • • • • • •

Georgie's nursery put on a video of *Peter Pan* for all the kids old enough to cope with Captain Hook. It was obvious, when I collected her at hometime, Georgie had not yet returned to Scotland from Never Never Land. She kept running ahead of me, flapping her arms, trying to use the pavement like a runway for take off, believing that, at any moment, her jelly-shoed feet would leave the ground and she'd be airborne. She didn't fly once. Or twice. Or three times. But she didn't give up. She deduced, all by herself, she couldn't fly – not because *she couldn't fly* – but because she must be too heavy. It must be her Sleeping Beauty rucksack – light and empty but for an extra cardie in case she got cold playing outside at nursery – that was weighing her down. She pulled the straps off her shoulders and handed the bag to me to carry. She ran faster, flapping furiously at the air with her featherless wings, oblivious to the bus queue we were passing who watched and smiled. Still she couldn't fly. She handed me her pink anorak. She meant business. She ran. She flapped. She tried to glide. She stood on the spot and tried to jump. I lifted her onto my shoulders. Her head was in the clouds.

'Georgie, d'you not think if people could fly the sky would be as busy as the streets?'

She said nothing 'cause she knew, in her dreams, she flew.

• • • • • • • • • • • • • • • • • • •

Me, Moses and Finn knew every word to every Jam song. Wrote their lyrics on our school jotters and memorised them. Weren't fairweather or fickle fans, we followed them as faithfully as our football teams. Reserved copies of their soon-to-be-released singles before we'd even heard them. Three of us, three of them, we understood each other. We were going through it all together. The Sex Pistols were the trailblazers, we acknowledged, but they were also grotesque caricatures – hard to like or relate to. The Clash were better. We liked them. But we loved The Jam. They were more punk than the punks.

We went to see them at the Edinburgh Playhouse. Outside in the queue someone with an English accent asked me 'Where d'you get your t-shirt, mate?' (It was a tour t-shirt, a cheap replica of official merchandise, I'd just bought from a bootlegger.) I was so immersed in the Mod-Punk persona – which seemed to be wholly focused on London – so wrapped up in it, that I unconsciously replied in pseudo-Cockney: 'Off that geezer up there, mate. See 'im? All right, no problem.' Moses and Finn laughed at me and started taking the piss talking Cockney too: 'Finks 'e's Paul Wella, 'e does!', said Moses.

'S'ere a lot of you Cockney lads from Pitlochry then, Joey?' said Finn.

For a spokesman for a generation Paul Weller didn't actually *say* very much. The songs – as blissfully naïve as they and we were – said it all. His sneery, cigarette voice – like a meadow of nettles, or whistling under the railway bridge, or an Alan Sillitoe novel (as the starstruck fanzines would describe it) – was the soundtrack of our adolescence but he never actually *said* much. During the concert he made a passing reference, between songs, to the Task Force which at that very moment, as we danced, was steaming south to the Falklands in an act of brinkmanship by Margaret Thatcher. But that was all. Didn't introduce the songs, didn't talk to us, didn't patronise us, just careered into each three-chord smash at high speed, like to pause for breath would be selling out.

We were in the balcony seats but we stood for the duration along with everybody else. It wasn't sit-back-and-tap-your-feet music, it was attack, attack, attack! Muscle music driven fast by thumping bass and rattle-gun drumming. A vehicle of overwhelming power. Attack! Attack! Attack! That was what we wanted. That was what me, Mo and Finn demanded of Celtic, St Johnstone and Rangers respectively but not, strangely, of the British Army, Navy and RAF in the South Atlantic. Fuck the Task Force! We responded to the aggression of the delivery. We instinctively understood it, felt it ourselves, felt it was directed at the powers that be who didn't reflect us at all. In front of the stage below us, Mods in their fancy dress uniforms – parkas, drill trousers, Ben Sherman shirts, white socks, Italian slacks, mohair suits, bowling shoes – pogoed violently, throwing broken seats out of their way onto the stage as the very fabric of the building shook and fell apart.

Inspired to revolution but without a map or guidance or any conceivable plan – limited by a leader they'd go over the top with, but who could only sing – the crowd spilled out after the concert, dissipating in all directions into an Edinburgh night, running over parked cars, breaking bottles on the pavement in a directionless release of energy and excitement and pent-up, unfocused anger which punk plugged into like two fingers in a shaving socket. Me, Moses and Finn spilled out too, ears buzzing, dazed by the spectacle and waited on the corner for a light blue Fiesta with my Mum and Dad – who'd been visiting my Aunt Margaret – to pick us up and go for a nice bag of chips each and a bottle of Irn Bru between us. Like the mad, revolutionary punks we were: anti-establishment, anti-fashion and Auntie Margaret.

• • • • • • • • • • • • • • • • • •

Two Thousand 'Ideas in Action' pamphlets finally arrive from the printers late in the afternoon. They're supposed to reach every leading organization or business in and around Aberdeen by tomorrow morning to coincide with an investment announcement from the Scottish Office, so it's all hands on deck to put them into envelopes in time for the last post.

The Chairman hears we're stretched and, showing solidarity in difficult times, pays us a rare royal visit. He finds Chris surrounded by piles of envelopes and pamphlets spreading all over her desk and onto the floor. (Good God, man! The woman evidently works like a coolie for the Institute!) Audrey's pile of envelopes is much smaller, so's mine, and Prue's is smaller still but it's misleading. Prue's so fast and efficient she's already taken three or four piles through to the mail room for franking. I've taken a couple myself. Even Audrey's taken one. Chris hasn't moved from her desk yet but The Chairman's little nod and smile of appreciation towards her shows he's impressed. He even directs a little hurt and disappointed frown towards Prue as if she's been shirking. The Chairman can't be in too much of a hurry as he hangs about talking golf with Chris. At no point during his morale-boosting visit does it occur to him to sit down and give us a hand.

I take another pile of envelopes along the corridor to the mail room. Siobhan, the new mail-room girl, doesn't seem to have grasped the urgency of our mailshot either. She's carefully opening the plastic cover on the bottom of the paper-punch when I go in. She's tapping the tiny, multi-coloured circles of paper onto the worktop, gathering them together with her cupped hands and edging them over the brink into a small cardboard box almost full of hundreds and thousands of pink, white, green, yellow and blue paper dots from the Institute's reports. It's evidently an on-going project for her.

'What you doing, Siobhan?'

She jumps – hadn't realized I was in the room.

'Confetti,' she says, blushing like it's a confession.

'Y'know, I won't need to buy any when my friends get married. Waste not, want not!'

She's young, obviously shy and easily embarrassed, so I don't tease her. Instead I say 'That's a good idea', though I think it's slightly odd, leave the pile of envelopes for her to frank, asking if she can give us a hand with the others when she's finished.

Mindless repetitive work at least frees your mind for higher thoughts. Audrey has to rush off for a 5 o'clock meeting in town. It's one less pair of hands but we'll make it without her. I'm glad to see her go. The pamphlets slide neatly into the A4 envelopes but the flaps aren't self-sealing and the sight of Audrey's big, long, lascivious tongue sliding out from between her lipsticked lips was making me feel quite ill. Then Siobhan arrives to help, decorating the office with her presence. She's pretty in a subtle, understated way. As we chat, as we work, she smiles shyly at me, putting 'Ideas in Action' into envelopes, ideas in my head.

• • • • • • • • • • • • • • • • • • •

The cabbage-stewing kitchen served up a platter of chatter and clatter. I was at the other end of the corridor, alone in the dishwasher room. A large industrial dishwasher made of stainless steel took up most of the space. It was summer time and the grubby panes of magnifying glass in the tall window above the sink overheated the room even before the dishwasher was switched on. I wore a grey, food-stained, waterproof apron, which was functional but no fashion statement. The uniformed waitresses ran past the door carrying the starters and Catriona would smile briefly and say 'Hi, Joe!' as she carefully backed through the opaque plastic curtain strips that separated the guest and staff areas, balancing a tray of prawn cocktails in stemmed glasses.

We'd conduct a staccato conversation as the meals progressed and she brought me trays of dirty dishes and glasses and cutlery from each sitting. There was no time for anything more and more often there was no time for anything. We worked like mute mules. I had to scrape the leftovers into a bin, rinse everything in blistering hot water from the tap in the deep, steel sink, then place the dishes upside down on a crate. When the dishwasher had completed its cycle I'd pull the other crate full of clean dishes out of one end and push the dirty dishes into the other like a non-stop car wash. Everything was hot. The steamy air I breathed was hot. The window misted up with condensation and the rhododendron bushes outside disappeared in the fog. My face glistened with a sheen of sweat. It was hard to keep up: one me, four waitresses, a steady stream of dirty dishes piled high on the worktop – course after course, table after table. As one group of diners reached coffees and mints, another sat down for starters. On and on it went. The noise of the dishwasher. The clinking of the glasses and the chinking of the plates. Tap water running non-stop. The anxious urgency of shouted orders among the kitchen staff. The steam and the heat. *Two hot pots, three steaks, two well done, one rare, more roast potatoes, please!* The tropical humidity. *Bacardi and Coke and a mango juice!*

As well as dishwashing, I had to dry off the hot, clean dishes and glasses with a teatowel and put them away in their exact and proper place in the cupboard or the manager would get mad at me. He'd lose the rag if a particular glass was required in a hurry for a particular drink and he found it wasn't in its particular place. On the other side of the plastic curtain, the manager could be obsequious with the predominantly elderly guests who came to stay. He'd be all smiles and how-are-we-today? But as soon as he stepped through the curtain into the staff area he'd undergo a drastic personality change. *Jekyll and Hyde* meets *Upstairs Downstairs.*

A couple of inches of chilled Coke was left in a bottle he'd used for a mixer. It was like he'd left it on the Formica top to tease me. In the dehydrating heat of the dishwasher room the demure Marilyn Monroe curves of the Coca-Cola bottle were irresistible. I had my head right back gulping it down when he caught me. He grabbed the bottle and threw it in the bin.

'Don't ever let me catch you stealing my property again. If you want a drink, use the cold tap. You're here to work.'

I was so young I accepted it. At least I knew he wasn't picking on me in particular. He was like that with everyone. It was a family-run hotel and his wife, son and daughter all slaved in the kitchen with the rest of us. They'd shout right back at him in the marriage-breaking tension of the backrooms. It was his way of handling the high-pressure times, taking it out on others. Whenever he was around I kept quiet, kept my head down, tried not to provoke him. Whereas now, believe me, I'd tell him where to stick his Coke bottle.

Towards the end of the evening the wine glasses came in, with heavy lipstick stains on the rims which the dishwasher couldn't remove even on the high heat setting. I had to use a cloth on each glass individually before placing them carefully on the dishwasher crate. The cloth would end up blood red. I found those lip stains, with grooves unique as fingerprints, disgusting and obscene. The thought of those bejewelled, elderly women sip, sip, sipping from the glasses with lips too thickly coated with garish grease churned my stomach. I was glad of the thick, grey rubber gloves I wore.

The tiny pots of mustard returned from every table were even worse. The smell of these rinsed clean in steaming hot water always made me want to throw up but at least their arrival signalled the dinner was coming to an end.

I could hear parties of guests walking out of the dining room into the hall in their relaxed holiday moods, talking and laughing after a hearty meal. I'm sure they were all nice people. I'm sure they all led interesting, compassionate lives. I'm sure they wouldn't have turned their noses up at me if they could see through the thick, plastic curtain but all I could make out was the loud, bombastic 'Ra, ra, ra' of the men and the hysterical neighing of the women. They milled around the lobby planning their evening's entertainment, only a couple of steps through the plastic curtain but a world away from the dishwasher room.

Catriona would hang about after she'd finished dressing the tables with fresh white linen and setting them for breakfast. I was self-conscious: red-faced with the work and the heat, dripping sweat and still wearing my ridiculous matching ensemble of grey rubber gloves and mustard-stained apron. She looked clean and starchy in contrast. She'd get a teatowel and dry some of the glasses, cups and saucers and plates and ask 'Where does this go?' and help me put them away even though her shift had started an hour before mine and the other waitresses had all gone home. It was a chance to talk as we worked. She never mentioned the shows or the waltzers or anything from years back, so neither did I. Tried to play it cool as a cucumber but must've looked like red hot chilli.

When I'd finished – put everything back in its proper place, wiped down all the surfaces, cleaned the filter on the dishwasher, refilled the machine with washing powder ready for the morning and dumped the bin bag, brimming full of enough wasted food to feed the five thousand, outside in the industrial bin – we were free to go. We'd say goodnight to the manager – who, sitting drinking coffee in the kitchen with his wife now the pressure was off, had metamorphosed into a perfectly amiable person – and walk out into the evening.

The air tasted as fresh as chilled grapefruit juice in contrast to the unbearable heat and stuffiness of the dishwasher room. I walked my bike as we talked and talked until we had to split at a junction, as her house was a different way from mine. After a couple of weeks our daily conversations seemed too good to curtail and it seemed natural enough to take a detour and walk her all the way to her house. It was a convoluted route to cycle home from there but – after talking to Catriona – it seemed my bike had wings.

In high summer – when the rhododendron bushes in the grounds were at their peak, the hotel full to capacity, the backrooms more pungent than ever with the smell of stewing cabbage, and the flow of dirty dishes, lipstick-stained glasses and smelly mustard pots seemed never ending – Catriona, coolly swishing past in black polyester and flat black shoes, warding off the stale air with Charlie perfume, was my salvation. At the end of a hectic August evening's work, as I finished up, she came into the dishwasher room. She said she was a bit behind tonight and could I help her set the tables for breakfast. Of course I would, I said, I owed her.

First she had to get clean table cloths. She led me through the plastic curtain into the unfamiliar territory of the guests' domain and up the stairs to the second-floor landing where the carpets were thick, light fittings ornamental and, through half-open bedroom doors, I could glimpse velvet seats, tie-back curtains, and huge, inviting double beds. I felt out of place in a grubby Lonsdale t-shirt and jeans but there were few guests to see me – most had gone out for the evening to the theatre or were promenading along the main street or the loch walks down by the dam.

We reached the locked linen cupboard. My stomach felt funny. Catriona dropped the key, picked it up, opened the door. There was a striplight switch on the inside of the door which, I noticed, Catriona didn't touch as we walked in. A warm, natural light emanated from a small skylight window in the high ceiling. The cupboard room smelt of washing powder and fabric conditioner.

'I hide in here sometimes if I need a wee break,' she said, showing me a hidden alcove behind the slatted wood shelves. 'If I'm sent to fetch something, I might stay a few minutes longer, get my head together, it's such a mad rush downstairs, nob'dy misses me.'

We stepped behind the neat piles of starched white linen table cloths and pillow cases and bed sheets and, right enough, I thought, no one would be able to see us here. It was a private, secret place. There was just about enough room for two people to lie down – if they lay close to each other.

Catriona shook open a pressed and laundered sheet, laid it on the floor and sat down, taking my hand and pulling me gently down beside her. We lay down, absolutely still and quiet for ages, listening to our fast, uneven breathing. She was waiting for me to make a move. Christ, *I* was waiting for me to make a move. What move though? I didn't know. I was paralysed.

'It's good here, isn't it?' she whispered, breathing the words on my neck, 'just us.'

She moved her face so close to mine it would have been insulting not to kiss her. She kissed me back.
'Mmmn,' she said, 'salty.'

I was embarrassed. I wasn't at my best after an evening in the sauna of the dishwasher room. I put my hand on her face and placed a strand of dark hair behind her ear, away from her brown eyes. We both laughed for a moment at the strangeness of our closeness then smothered our smiles with kisses. Every kiss and caress was a tactile expedition somewhere we'd never been. It was all new to us. My hands explored a strange uncharted topography, defying the shocked, prudish messages from my brain: 'What *are* you doing? Get your hand off that girl's thigh! Where are you *going*? That's quite high enough! Stop that! You're too young! You're just a boy. Just a boy ...'

Much stronger messages were overriding everything.

'Mmmn,' she murmured in encouragement whenever I unwittingly hit the spot. I pressed my fingers into the wetness of her tights as she clung to me: tightly, tighter, tightest.

Me and Catriona higher than ever before. High

above the hotel and the rhododendrons and the backyard, the industrial bin and my bike. Looking down on Pitlochry and Loch Faskally and the Hydro Electric dam, higher and higher, I could see the A9, the River Tummel joining the Tay, the hills, the mountains, Perth, Dundee, the estuary, the sea. I could recognise the relief of Scotland: 'He's done it! He's actually done it! Way to go, Joey! Knew you could do it, pal. Jo-ey! Jo-ey!' The elation of a nation would cycle home with me that night, sleep in my bed, walk with me to school, stay with me forever.

'*Joey!*' I heard Catriona's smiling voice pulling me gently back down from orbit. 'We better get going.'

We brushed away tell-tale dishevelment, straightened our clothes, our shared secrets staining our underwear. We brought down a pile of pristine, folded table cloths. I threw them over the bare tables in the dining room as she walked round with the cutlery trolley – knives, forks and Catriona still warm from the dishwasher.

• • • • • • • • • • • • • • • • • • •

The Dishwasher, the Shelfpacker and the Shop Assistant – me, Mo and Finn, respectively – would take the train (Finn had free British Rail travel because his dad was a signalman) to Perth on alternate Saturdays. Our little brown wage packets burned holes in our jackets. We'd kick around the clothes and record and music shops in the morning. We went to Wilkie's of Perth and lusted after Gibson and Fender guitars we could neither play nor afford. We were too embarrassed and too shy to try them out because there was always some muso oik showing off his stupid, wanky Eric Clapton fretwork to make us feel inadequate.

And yet, in truth, with our post-punk principles, we felt superior. They'd completely missed the point. And later we'd teach ourselves to play well enough to form a band. We'd have more cool and attitude in a single power chord than all those finger-picking plectrums put together. Me on a *brand new* £60 guitar, Mo defying a bashed-in replica Rickenbacker bass by actually getting a tune out of it, and Finn on a borrowed drum kit he really could play. Me and him had learned drums with the Boy's Brigade band. Finn would practise complicated drum patterns next day on the desks at school with his fingers. He really had it. I didn't. You can't teach rhythm. Marching with the BB's on Remembrance Sunday, Finn and some other lad played for real but they hid me between them and told me to mime.

A plate of chips in the Lite-Bite for dinner then we'd walk the 15 miles, or so it seemed, out to Muirton to watch St Johnstone play East Fife or Meadowbank Thistle. I'd act all blasé – being a veteran of Scotland-England an' all – but it was still a thrill. We'd get there ridiculously early to soak up the atmosphere of the empty, wind-swept terraces, where weeds grew in patches like the beginnings of a rock garden. We'd stand at pitch level opposite the tunnel, lean over the advertising hoardings and watch the players warm up and sign autographs, but the spectacle of the fans arriving was the best pre-match entertainment. They dribbled through the turnstiles at first: alone, fathers and sons, little groups of friends, pausing to buy programmes then huddling together in their favoured vantage points seeking out the comfort of strangers and like-minded souls. Then shortly before kick-off, fans from the nearest pubs would pour through the gates and we'd delight in the arrival of a couple of noisy coachloads of opposition fans who we could shout abuse at through the wire mesh and fence which separated us.

All clean and shiny blue, St Johnstone ran out at five to three and the cheers, though always loud and full-throated, were not deafening. It wasn't like Hampden, where the players were no bigger than they looked on tv. It was more like real life. We could hear the smack of the ball, the crack of gruesome bone-crunching tackles and the players shouting for a pass the same as we did on the Recreation Ground. They could hear us too, though they pretended not to. If John Brogan was about to be tackled from his blind side we'd shout 'Man on!' and he'd dodge the tackle because we'd warned him. We were part of the team. We felt we had an influence on the final score.

Habitually, ritually, we'd pick on some ageing, fat or balding player on the other side and barrack him remorselessly every time he touched the ball. It never once occurred to us that shite though he indisputably was (he'd have no grounds for libel) even he'd achieved dizzy footballing heights we'd never match. Once this guy ran right in front of us to collect the ball for a throw-in and, placing my chewing gum expertly at the back of my top gum for safe-keeping, I shouted 'You're shi-*te*!' as he passed four feet away. It was during one of those unexpected lulls in the noise-level and everyone heard me. He picked up the ball and, instead of turning a deaf ear and taking the shy like a proper professional, had the audacity to make like he was offering the ball to me to have a go. I didn't know where to look. Even the Saints fans laughed. I shut up after that. Only cheered up at half-time when the crowd went loud again as the other scores were displayed and word got round Dundee were 1-0 down.

My mum said I wasn't to go to the football 'cause of the hooligans so I told her we were going to the pictures. I should've been eating popcorn but me, Mo and Finn were pogoing in sympathy with the hardcore, bovver boys in crew cuts and bomber jackets, who adopted and adapted the Sham 69 hit, singing 'Perthshire Boys! Perthshire Boys! Laced up boots and corduroys!'

• • • • • • • • • • • • • • • • • •

Football? Finn? Mo who? Saturdays would never be quite the

same again. Who needs Saints? I'd found me an angel in white linen.

When the heavens opened we found shelter under the grey, box-girder bridge which carried the town's new bypass over Loch Faskally. We'd been walking, self-consciously hand in hand, along the main street, hoping people we knew would see us together. To them, and to everyone else, everything must have seemed typical and ordinary and usual but, to us, Saturday – all its people and cars and shops and trees and children – looked *especially* Saturday. We walked down to the boating station to hire a rowing boat for an hour but it was closed. It didn't matter, we could just walk round the loch instead.

Then it started to rain. I mean, *really* rain, like a power shower, and we ran, laughing for no good reason, scrambling up the banking, off the beaten track to where the gold would sit under a concrete rainbow. We sat, close and cuddling, in our dry urban bubble, surrounded by a wet rural idyll, and tried to articulate our feelings as lorries thundered over our heads. I scraped our initials inside a heart with a stone on a steel girder but kisses succeeded where words failed. I thought I'd died and gone to heaven.

Catriona was a catch. She was pretty in a subtle, understated way. She liked Kate Bush like I liked The Jam – only more so. She had three copies of *The Kick Inside*: one to listen to and enjoy herself; one to lend to friends to get them into Kate Bush; and a third copy to keep safe in cellophane, unscratched and unopened in the wardrobe in case anything should happen to the other two. She crimped her hair like Kate Bush. It seemed very fetching to me at the time. She liked it when people told her she looked like Kate Bush but I never. I had tunnel vision. Catriona was the perfection pop stars, models, all women and all girls could only aspire to. She lent me the lending record, which jumped during *Wuthering Heights* – if I didn't get up and physically move the needle with my finger Kate would sing

'It's me, it's me, it's me … ' over and over again to eternity. Sometimes I liked that and I wouldn't get up and move the needle for ages. I'd wait for that particular moment in the song and she'd never let me down. She sung it differently for me than she did on *Top of the Pops* for the rest of the world. She'd have sung 'It's me, it's me, it's me …' till the stylus broke if I'd let her. It needled my father no end. He'd shout through the door unchivalrously referring to Kate Bush as 'that screeching banshee', and tell me to turn it off.

The rain stopped. We walked round Loch Faskally which looked, in places, like it might date from the Ice Age – but don't be fooled. God created engineers and the North of Scotland Hydro Electric Board formed the loch in 1951. At the dam, each pool in the graded fish ladder swirled with sticks and bark in menacing black water. In the observation chamber we could see the pipes which led from one pool to another to allow the salmon to reach their spawning grounds upstream. A large salmon swam out of the murky shadows obligingly close to the thick glass for us to marvel. I thought of Finn. He'd like this. He'd be at the Lite-Bite in Perth with Mo. Then I looked at Catriona, looking so fine, looking at the fish and forgot Finn.

We walked up the steps and across the top of the dam, peering through high windows into a giant room below us, like the nave of a cathedral, where turbines hummed with mysterious power and glory. Warm air from the room wafted up through half-open slats and smelt familiar and particular. It was the smell of crayons melting behind wrought iron radiators in infant school. We were so pleased to classify it we didn't question why it should occur in the big, deserted room. We thought only of tiny chairs, round tiny tables and a long forgotten memory of tiny hands holding tiny hands as a scraggy crocodile of kids were led round the dam on a school visit.

Outside in the cool, fresh air we stood on the

walkway. On one side, down below us, the River Tummel, dizzy from the turbines, turned its back on the dam, regained its original purpose and composure and headed swiftly towards the sea. On our other side, the high water of Loch Faskally looked tame and domesticated, content in its unnatural containment. There was no visible surface tension but in its hidden depths the wild forces of nature pushed and pulled to break free of man-made constraints. I put my hand on the granite-topped, concrete wall. I could feel the vibrations of the turbines.

'Can you feel it throbbing?' I said in all innocence.

Catriona raised an eyebrow. I started to blush, she just laughed, pulled me closer and kissed me. Catriona's tiny tongue in my head. Catriona, Catriona, Catriona.

Our lips were the conductors for an overwhelming electrical charge which carried in an instant to our toes, through the concrete, through the water, shocking the fish, along the connecting aqueducts and pipes and rivers and burns before, ultimately, leaping – like lightning in reverse – to the very cloud from where the raindrop had first fallen. We caused a soaring, megawatt blip on the power station's ammeters, exploding, in an instant, man-made pretensions of indestructibility. A torrent of water escaped through a gaping hole near the top of the drum gate at the centre of the dam. We watched from our grandstand view on the concrete walkway, as cracks drew in all directions and raging water ripped open the metal barrier below us like turning the key on a sardine tin. The first huge tidal wave crashed down the River Tummel followed by a mighty, unstoppable outpouring. We watched, transfixed, as the servant loch became master. The theatre, the hamlet of Port-na-Craig, the swing bridge, the swings and climbing frame and playing fields of the Recreation Ground were immediately subsumed. Wave after wave escaped down the engorged river, flooding low-lying roads and railway lines and farmland all the way to Ballinluig where it joined the Tay, gathered strength, smashed over Dunkeld Bridge and on and on to Perth Bridge, Queen's Bridge, Moncrieff Island, overturning boats in the harbour, into deeper water, to the estuary at Dundee, washing over the rail bridge, the road bridge, sending shock waves into the North Sea and rocking the rigs. What have we done? What did we do?

Catriona redrew the map of my world. It was spectacular while it lasted. How was I to know how ugly, scarred and desolate the stinking, empty loch would look when the waves died down?

• • • • • • • • • • • • • • • • • • •

Georgie was puzzled and disappointed with the fish ladder at the dam when I took her there in pilgrimage. She'd envisaged something a little more vertical with a little less water. Where were the acrobatic salmon climbing the fish ladder rung by rung with their fins? Didn't look like any ladder she'd ever seen.

The Forth Rail Bridge let her down too. Where were the other three? And why didn't the trains go up and down it like a rollercoaster? Why else would they build it like that? The fundraising May Fayre at her nursery was just a bunch of trestle tables with jumble and bric-à-brac! Where was the helter skelter? Where was the roundabout with the skewered horses? The *Teletubbies* were just people dressed up:

'They are! You can see the join where their heads join their bodies. Look! D'you see it?' There was no sign of the King at His Majesty's for the panto, no snow inside the Winter Gardens in Duthie Park, and no monkeys at the Lewis Grassic Gibbon Centre. So many disappointments, so much disillusionment. People can't fly like Peter Pan. She couldn't fly, no matter how hard she wished. She couldn't even keep her parents together. How could it be? Would she get an answer praying religiously, night after night, to the Holy Trinity of Jesus, Santa and the Tooth Fairy?

• • • • • • • • • • • • • • • • • • •

Georgie's mum and I met at Perth College. She was re-sitting Higher Maths too. Fate and Mrs Humphrey-Jackson sat us together at the back of the class. Mrs Humphrey-Jackson had the quaint notion that a boy-girl, boy-girl seating arrangement would cut down on idle gossip and chit-chat, bless her. (It would be worth a medical research grant to see how this policy affected Perthshire's teenage pregnancy rates.) I was struck by the naffness of Helen's skull-on-a-cross earrings and matching skull rings. (I wasn't to know I'd met her during a short-lived Goth period.) I copied some of her answers for a multiple-choice maths test at the end of the first week and it turned out she was as thick as I was (which I found quite endearing). I started looking forward to maths for the first time in my life. Helen was nothing like Catriona which had – by that time – become an attractive trait.

Mrs Humphrey-Jackson was one of those really nice toffs with an eternally sunny disposition who seem to think the best of everyone and make you feel like you're getting their full attention, you're worth it, you're important and you're special even when you know you're not. I felt loathe to let her down. I tried to listen. I tried hard to understand. I tried hard to follow her sweet, forgiving posh accent as she tried to shine a torch through the dark labyrinth of calculus formulae to show me the way ahead but I knew I had no business there. It was a dead end. The numbers and symbols on the blackboard were as foreign and indecipherable to me as hieroglyphics and it was clear they always would be.

I had better ways to waste my time. I persuaded Helen to skive off some afternoons and she'd reluctantly agree. We felt like Bonnie and Clyde. It was a heady excitement not to return to class from lunch. To bus into town. To walk to the park in the sunshine, feeling like freewheeling fugitives from all and everything that would restrict our freedom. But it was never as good in reality as it had been in anticipation. We'd sit on the grass of the North Inch and chill out, literally, because the sunshine would be weak and intermittent and it almost always felt cold beside the river. Then we'd retreat to a cafe to warm up, nursing hot cappuccinos, making them last as long as possible, pretending to the waitress and even ourselves that there was still some left, when all that remained was cold froth.

• • • • • • • • • • • • • • • • • •

Friday night and The Salmon Bar was leaping. The juke-box was cranked up really loud and every now and then a song worthy of our discerning, post-punk seal of approval would come on and we'd sing the chorus as loud as we'd have sung at a game. There was a sweet smell, a little like burnt fireworks, wafting around and after a couple of pints – even though the fluorescent lights were harsh and unforgiving – I didn't feel so self-conscious about the rash of spots on my forehead. Plan was, we'd all troop out to the only disco in town (two miles *out* of town at a country hotel, to be precise) once we'd all tanked up in The Salmon Bar. We were jumping already, the weekend was here, we were young, school was out and, frankly, there wasn't nothing worth knowing we didn't know. There was me, Mo, Finn, Craig, Alastair, Graeme, Sid the Copper's Kid, Katherine, Mairi, Joyce the Voice, wee Mags but no sign of Catriona.

Every time the main door opened, I'd sneak a wee fly glance, hoping to see her before she saw me so I could adjust my expression from relief to congenial, easy-going, good-time guy. I was gauche, I was green, but I didn't ever want her to see me pine. If it wasn't Catriona it was always a familiar face at the door. I'd know their name or I'd have seen them about.

Occasionally, it's true, English or American tourists would walk confidently through the door and we'd watch their steps slow up and stop before they made it to the bar, as they checked out the clientele, the bare stone floor, the pool-cue pock marks above the pool table, the perforated wall round the dartboard and, most of all, old Hughie Henderson dancing arthritically between the tables. A permanent feature of the place, Hugh was such a familiar sight none of the locals took a blind bit of notice but tourists – seeing him, eyes closed in concentration, moving to some old teuchter tune only he could hear – would do a sudden *volte-face* and leave. I reckon we were secretly proud of that. The Salmon Bar remained our exclusive domain. The United Nations on vacation were welcome everywhere else, we didn't mind sharing, but it was good to have a retreat too. A tourist-free snug.

From my seat I could look out the window and see the Citylink and Stagecoach buses draw up, heading down to Glasgow or up to Inverness. It gave me wanderlust just to see them but also made me jealously possessive of all that was here. Those who didn't alight would never know. It was a small town but it was on the map, not off it. We were pretty much at the heart of it all. Easy to reach, easy to leave. We slagged the place off all the time amongst ourselves but would defend it to the death if an outsider did it down. Mo wanted to stay, get a job, settle down. Me and Finn were getting out, going to college: Finn following his marine biologist dream, me just following, seeing what happened next.

A whole bunch of Liverpool lads came into the bar, about five or six of them. They looked just like us. I mean, they didn't look any more worldly-wise just because they'd come from the city. They weren't put off by the clientele or the décor or Hughie's dancing and, once they'd got their drinks in, sat at a couple of tables adjacent to us. Mo, hearing their accents, got the crack going.

'Look out! Echo and the Bunnymen are in town,' he said loud enough so's they'd hear him.

One of them took him on: 'Yeah, I'm Ian McCulloch, want me autograph?'

We got talking: they were all right. They'd sneaked out from the YMCA on a school trip; they were about the same underage as us; turned out they liked the same bands; sadly, though, they appeared not to appreciate that Glasgow Celtic was way bigger than Everton and they mortally offended Mo having never even heard of Perth Saints. Like I said, they weren't very worldly-wise.

One of them had a lighter the shape of an ocean liner.

'Hey, I like yer lighter, pal.' said Mo crashing a fag.

'Yeah, my sister works on that ship,' the guy explained with pride.

'Small, is she?' said Mo, deadpan. We nearly choked on our lager, laughing so much.

There was still no sign of Catriona by the time the taxis were arriving to take everyone out to the disco at Dunfallandy. Saving a fare, we piled into Graeme's Capri like rag-week students in a telephone box. It was an interminably claustrophobic drive to the disco. But I kept quiet, endured it, focused my thoughts on Catriona. She'll be there. She'll be there.

We arrived. Tumbled, crumpled, out of the car. I hoped my new black combat jacket, cheap from the Army and Navy store, made me look a pleasing blend of street chic and don't-give-a-fuck fashion as I walked, shoulders back, eyes straight ahead, towards the bar in the disco, searching desperately for Catriona with my peripheral vision.

Liverpool accents rang out now and again at the bar like chirpy harmonicas in the middle eight of a pop song. It was dark at the disco. I carried two full pints round the edge of the dancefloor pretending I was taking a short cut to someone while really I was ticking off a roll-call of who was sitting at each table. In the parlance of the Hawaiian-shirted, sunlamp-tanned DJ, who talked like he was from Nashville,

Tennessee, when everyone knew he came from Luncarty: 'What we have here, folks, is a Catriona-no-show situation.' That's how I heard it in my head, as I leant against a pillar, detached from the gang, drinking too fast, brooding, thinking black thoughts. The music was as loud and tasteless as the DJ's clothes. In charge of a sound system without the musical savvy or suss to make the vibes right he was a danger to himself and others. I hated the DJ, for something to hate, and there was a real danger I was going to pour the dregs of my pint over his turntable or over his head. In Pitlochry that night, if you didn't dance to the Bee Gees, Elton John or Queen you didn't dance at all. I didn't dance at all.

Finn handed me a fresh, dripping pint.

'S'up?' he shouted in my ear, above the noise.

'Nothing,' I shook my head, smiled wanly.

'Great music though, eh?' he winked, going back to the table where he had something going on with wee Mags.

One drink blended into another in a cocktail of misery till I was rudely awoken from my elbow space in the shadows when the lights switched on, the music switched off and the slow-dance couples were caught in mid-smooch. People blinked their eyes in the glare, grabbed their coats and scuttled into the night.

I was consumed by a black mood. I waited at the bottom of the steps outside for Finn or Mo or someone I knew, anyone who wasn't wrapped up in the arms of a secret lover, to walk the long walk home when, with only a shout for warning, a big rammy broke out. Fists were flying, legs kicking, there were shouts and high-pitched girly screams. I took one step back, trying to figure out who was fighting who – whose side was I on? Finn was in the thick of it and Mo got in a couple of telling punches. One of the Liverpool lads lay on the ground, his mouth bleeding. The others were almost in a circle round him, fighting back the restless natives. Bouncers and bar staff leapt down the steps and pushed back the rival gangs. The fight was over, almost as soon as it had begun. The lad on the ground got up, unsteady on his feet, picked up his glasses, checked the lenses, adjusted the stem and tried to walk back to his pals with dignity but a limp surprised him. He looked shook up.

The Liverpool lads were ushered back into the disco. The doors were locked on us. Finn had already disappeared into the night with wee Mags. Me and Mo zig-zagged home in the pitch dark of the country lane with no streetlights.

'Why didn't you tell me?'

'I knew you were too busy looking out for Catriona.'

'But I wanted a fight. I *really, really* wanted to fight tonight. Why didn't you tell me?'

'Christ, man, did you have your eyes closed? It'd been brewing all night. Did you not see Ian McCulloch ask wee Mags to dance? Finn was away for a piss.'

'No. Is that what started it?'

'Ach, naw, not really, it was just the excuse. The final straw. They were up for it as much as we were. He was just chancing it, seeing how far he could push us.'

'Aw, Mo, why didn't you tell me? I'd have *loved* to fight tonight.'

'We managed fine without you, didn't we? Did you see me get the big guy? Not bad, eh?'

I could just make out Mo's arm swishing the air with a right jab.

'What d'you mean, "you managed fine without me"? What *exactly* d'you mean?'

'Just the numbers were pretty even so we didn't need you.'

'Didn't need me? What? You didn't think I'd be much use. Is that what you're saying, is it?'

I gave Mo a heavy push in the chest and he almost fell over in the dark. He jumped up and pushed me right back. I nearly fell over too. We kept on walking. Saying nothing, breathing harder. I felt sober. Felt adrenaline rushing in my veins.

'You're lucky they didn't have blades. Scouse kids an' all. They could've had blades.'

That's what I said, 'blades', like I was a finger-clicking extra in *West Side Story*.

'Wouldn't have bothered me,' said Mo the Macho, 'what you do is whip off yer jacket, right? Wrap it round your left hand like this' – he actually did a demonstration – 'and use it as a shield while you knock him down with your right. Or, you do this' – he swung his jacket in the air – 'and wrap yer jacket round the hand that's got the knife.'

'Oh, *fuck off*, Mo! You're not Bruce Lee. You'd have run a fucken mile if they'd had knives.'

'Oh yeah, y'think?' He was well irked. 'Least I took 'em on, didn't stand around like a lemon.'

I don't know who was first but next thing I knew there was a flurry of fists, two of them mine, flailing wildly. We crashed off the road into a boggy ditch. We stood up again, shoving, pushing, trying to get an arm free for a punch. I whacked him just above his right eye. It made a sickening crack. We both fell back, momentarily stunned. We'd been mock fighting since we were kids but always with claws retracted. No harm done. I was scared I'd hurt him. I didn't even think to follow up. I just wanted to say 'Right, Mo, let's stop it there', but I knew he owed me one. He pushed me off the road. I slipped into the ditch again. He put his two hands round my neck, squeezing hard. There was a pause for a few seconds. I didn't try to fight my way out. I just waited. His grip, which was tight but not as tight as he was capable of, gradually loosened. The anger subsided. He let go, stood up, brushed the dirt from his hands and walked off ahead. I didn't try to catch him up. Didn't move. The last stragglers passed by, mumbling incoherently to themselves in the dark. I lay quiet. No one bothered me. No one knew I was there. The last tyres zipped past on the tarmac but the headlights couldn't dip into the dark ditch. I knew I really should be getting going but I was getting to like it there. I could smell the grass and bracken and nettles and the mulch of leaves and mud. Water trickled close to my ear. Something scratched and scraped in the undergrowth. Cows on the other side of the hedge and the fence and broken dry-stane dyke ripped the grass from the field, chewing and breathing loudly. It was quite nice in the ditch. Maybe I shouldn't get cremated. Maybe I should just stay here, slowly decompose to a wet mulch, regenerate the plants, feed the animals. The clouds stood fixed and still as the earth raced past.

As the drink wore off, the cold wrapped around me like a shroud. After I don't know how long, I got up, stone cold sober, and walked fast into town, collar up on my muddy jacket, hands deep in my pockets. No more warming up for the next life. The Salmon Bar was closed now and deserted. There was no traffic, no lights on in the flats above the shops. It looked as if I had the whole town to myself but as I turned up West Moulin Road I caught sight of a couple necking in the brightly lit doorway of John Menzies. Eating each other's faces, so they were. I deliberately looked away to give them the privacy I'd want but something made me look back: it was Catriona with Russell Bradley.

• • • • • • • • • • • • • • • • • • • •

Audrey Marshall has a breakfast meeting with The Chairman. Prue knows from the grapevine – well, The Chairman's personal assistant who's a personal friend – what it's all about. There are to be compulsory redundancies at the Institute of Business and Entrepreneurship. Prue's seen it all before. A £235,000 study on work practices at the Institute by a team of outside consultants (two little gel-haired boys just out of accounting college) has concluded that five jobs are surplus to optimum operative requirements. We reckon – judging by the way Audrey kept anxiously rubbing her neck the day before – that she knows she's for the chop. But as she returns from the meeting her concealer can barely hide her relief.

Audrey calls me and Prue into her office. Her face mask is moulded in a fixed expression of deep, deep concern, compassion even, but there's a tell-tale manic look in her eyes which could almost be mistaken for a suppressed giggle.

We sit down. Audrey walks over to the window with her back to us and looks meaningfully out for a few moments, no doubt drawing inspiration from the awesome vista of the Institute's car park. Prue and I exchange quizzical looks. Audrey starts pacing the room with her hands behind her back (she must imagine it looks very senior management) saying: 'The Institute's got to run a tight ship. We're here to encourage business and industry to locate in our area, advise and support them when they do. Crucially, we have to ensure the competitiveness of our skills base in the Institute itself as well as the region as a whole. We simply can't afford to make a loss – it would be very bad PR. We'd risk losing the very credibility that an organization such as ours depends on. We have to lead by example and not be afraid to make the tough decisions when they come along. Our department doesn't generate money in the same way as, say, Enterprise Consultancy does, and we have to ask ourselves where savings and economies can best be made. As you probably know, The Chairman's commissioned a whole team of financial consultants to look at the way we run things here and – though I know, and I accept, they haven't actually visited our office here or met us in person – they've come up with some useful recommendations.'

She sits down in her little office swivel chair just like ours (she aspires to a high-backed leather one, one day, one day). She faces us. She's blunt.

'There's no easy way to tell you this ... '

She gathers herself heroically.

'The Chairman has informed me that we will not

be able to offer either of you extended contracts when they come up for renewal in January.'

Prue hasn't grasped the full implications or is in some kind of denial.

'You mean,' she hesitates, 'you mean, we're getting our permanent staff positions?'

'No, er, no, that's not what I mean,' says Audrey, struggling a bit, to her credit, seeing Prue's earnest expression. 'We must remember ...' Audrey looks sincere (and I doubt her sincerity no more than her hair colour). 'It's nothing personal. It's business.'

'You mean ... we're being sacked?' says Prue, her voice hardening with realization.

'No, er, no.' Audrey's voice is hardening too (she's tried so hard to be nice). 'I've made it quite clear, as I understand it, you're not being sacked, no one is saying you're being sacked, no one is being sacked, what I am saying is: the Institute is not, unfortunately, in a position to be able to renew your contracts in the New Year.'

Ah, the nuances of business and entrepreneurship. Free enterprise works!

Prue looks crushed. Of course, she'd heard rumours about a possible shake-up of personnel, that was nothing new, but she'd never imagined for a moment she'd be one of those shook up. I feel really sorry for her, she's filling up, she's taking it bad, but at the same time I feel a strange, guilty elation for myself, like my release date's been put forward for good behaviour. What have I got to lose? Nothing worth more than I've lost already. Will I miss that stupid tree outside the window? Will I miss my many, dear golfing friends at the card-swiping, rat-racing, go-getting, mirrored magnificence of the Institute of Business and Entrepreneurship?

The possibilities are endless. I can do anything, anytime, any day (and now I'll have to). It's a rush, isn't it? Will I miss the money? I've saved up, what, nearly £2,000 maybe, since

I've worked here. Sell my car for a few hundred and I could buy a one-way ticket somewhere far off. Wing it from there. Swim with dolphins, dance in the Mardi Gras, run for my life in Pamplona, that sort of bullshit. Live it up till the money runs out. Then get a job washing dishes in a downtown hotel. And if things get so low, so bad, I can prise open my tobacco tin, take out the razor blade that's in there, take the last option, quietly ebb away in opium-den Chinatown or mud-hut Mozambique or Ice Station Zebra. That'd be defeat, though. That'd be missing the whole point. That'd be an insult to the boy who packed the tin in the first place. I couldn't live with that.

How am I going to live? (Reality's sinking in.) Where'm I going to get another job by Christmas? Haven't I got enough to deal with? I can't give Helen the satisfaction of seeing me fall behind with Georgie's maintenance payments. But then, why be surprised? Why should the Institute for Business and Entrepreneurship be any different from the inevitable, intrinsic, limping boom and bust of the market economy? Seeing Prue's hard work and loyalty rewarded like this, I feel I ought to say something, make a stand. Ought to climb onto Audrey's desk, shout and swear and throw her papers into the air, watch them flutter and fall, out of order around her head. Ought to wrench her computer from its sockets and throw it out the window for the smash of the glass, the dull thud as it hits the ground outside. Quite the anarchist, me. Audrey's hard disk leaching memory irreparably onto the tarmac. All that hard work and dedication. All that empire building. All that faith and worship in flawless systems.

I *could* do all that – 'cept I don't.

I'm a paragon of self-control, me, but I'm seething inside. Prue's too choked up to speak. Audrey addresses me.

'Do you have anything you want to say?'

'Would anything I have to say make any difference?'

'Em, no, the decision has already been made.'

'Then I've nothing to say.'

'I'm sorry about this, Joseph, I really am, dreadful business, very hard for me too, you know.'

There's a real danger I could self-destruct at any moment with the sheer effort of keeping my counsel. Implode, with a loud bang and a puff of smoke, leaving only the buckle from my belt, the metal eyelets from my shoes and the faint smell of Lynx deodorant.

Chris, bless her, is in her element when she hears the news. She insists the three of us go for a drink after work. It's the first time we've ever been out together. They're like different people away from the pressures of the Institute. A couple of gin and tonics later, Prue's cheered up no end. We're having a laugh at Audrey's expense.

'She's never really grown out of that powder pink, eighties power-dressing thing, has she?'

'I know! She could take somebody's eye out with those shoulder pads!'

'That gunk she puts on her face! Other day she missed a bit. I saw what was underneath – *stainless steel!* No kidding, she's a robot!'

'Got to admire her though. Never stops, does she?'

'First into work, last away. Work, work, busy, busy!'

'Never missed a day's work through illness in her life, she's always telling us.'

'Not that she doesn't get ill.'

'Those six-week colds she can never shake off?'

'I quite like it when she loses her voice.'

'Not so good when she's up close whispering in your ear, sharing out her germs!'

'Got energy to spare, though, hasn't she?'

'Yeah, stick a plug up her arse and she'd power a small town!'

We try to keep it light but as the drink takes effect the conversation keeps lurching back to the serious.

'This couldn't have happened at a worse time for me,' says Prue. 'Alan and I have been trying to start a family. Well, we've been trying since we got married.' She laughs nervously, looking up for reassurance. 'We've had to have a few tests done to see what the problem is, Alan's been checked out and he's okay, but me? You don't want to know the gory details.' (She's right). 'Last month I had a laparoscopy.'

'A what?' asks Chris, only encouraging her.

'A laparoscopy. It's when they put this long needle in your tummy under local anaesthetic, right? Inside the needle's a titchy, tiny telescope and a fibre optic light so they can poke around looking for signs of infection. Turns out I haven't got any. No congenital abnormalities. I've got a satisfactorily pear-shaped uterus, apparently. My ovaries are in fine fettle and my fallopian tubes aren't blocked. No fibroids. No salpingitus. I know all the words now. I've studied it. They even took a wee sample of the lining of my uterus with a titchy, tiny spoon that's inside the needle too. Amazing, eh? What they can do. Whole thing only took half an hour but they kept me under observation for a couple hours after. Told me to go home but I went back to work. I felt okay, except my shoulder hurt a bit afterwards but that's a normal reaction for some reason, I'm told.'

Prue holds up her hand to indicate parenthesis, takes a quick gulp of her drink, then continues.

'So they did some analysis on my sample and d'you know what they've come up with? D'you know what their diagnosis is from all that magical, medical science? Apparently – it's official – I have "Unexplained Infertility". Wow! Thanks for your help, boys! I can explain it, all right. Why I can't seem to get pregnant. All this endless talk about it, all this poking around, Alan's mum desperate for grandkids ... well, you know, it doesn't half put you off actually *doing* it.'

Chris and me aren't sure whether to laugh at this so we just smile and nod our heads ambiguously.

'Alan wants us to get on the waiting list for IVF treatment ASAP but the doctor's been explaining the process to me and, I'm telling you, it's no easy option. Anyway, you only get one treatment on the NHS and if that doesn't work out you have to go private. I don't see how we'll be able to afford it if I'm not working.'

Chris is shaking her head, tutting gently, saying: 'Aw, Prue.'

I'm trying to think of the right thing to say in the circumstances.

'Does it really mean that much to you to start a family?'

Prue snaps back: 'Well, you're all right aren't you? You've got a child. Does it mean that much to you?'

'You know about Georgie?'

I'm not angry, just surprised. I thought I'd kept it so quiet. Prue sees she's hit a raw nerve, pats my hand a couple of times across the table.

'We knew from your CV, silly. Married with one child. I filed it myself. Plus Caroline from reception saw you at the art gallery with the wee lass in tow, Georgia, isn't it?'

'Yeah, *Georgie*,' something weird's happening, 'she's five,' washing over me like a tidal wave, 'she's great,' a couple of rogue tears breach the barriers. I'm embarrassed at my deception. My situation. Ashamed.

'It must be hard for you,' says Chris, putting her arm round my shoulders and giving me a squeeze. Prue's offering me a clean paper handkerchief from her handbag. I wipe my eyes. Take a deep breath, gather it all back in again. Wipe my nose quickly once, like I've just had a mild and sudden attack of hayfever. Chris and Prue are looking at me as if for the first time and I'm looking at them like they've changed.

'What is this? *Ricki Lake* or something?'

We laugh. Break the tension.

'I hardly see her. You know me and Helen split up. That's why I came to Aberdeen. Fresh start. But I never wanted, never thought I'd *lose* Georgie. But there's such bad feeling between me and her mum. Every time I see her, she makes it difficult. Says they can't put their lives on hold for me. Georgie's growing up fast, I can't keep up, I still talk to her like she's four but she's moved on, learning new stuff. She gets annoyed when I underestimate her. But what can I do? We don't have that day-to-day contact. I don't know what she's into now, what toys she likes, what songs she's singing, who her new pals are at school. Then if we do spend enough time together to get over that awkward stage and we're just about getting some kind of rapport going again, it's time for her to go back home to Mum. It's getting to the stage I think maybe ... maybe it might be better for all of us if I broke off all contact altogether. Less disruptive for her, less painful for me.'

It's an unwanted thought that's been gestating in my mind. I can't believe I'm telling this to Chris and Prue who, a couple of drinks ago, were as good as complete strangers to me.

'How come you never let on you knew about Georgie?'

'Well, you never mentioned her. It was none of our business. We reckoned it was best to keep quiet about it.'

There's a long lull in the conversation. Then me and Prue, like she's reading my mind, both look at Chris as if to say 'So, that was us, it's your turn now'. She gets the message and laughs: '*Oh* no!' she says, 'I've got nothing for *Ricki Lake* at the moment!' And we have a few more drinks. Laugh it all off like it doesn't really matter.

•   •   •   •   •   •   •   •   •   •   •   •   •   •   •   •   •

I'm a fallen man ...

No one could've been more surprised than I was to observe with curious detachment my hand reaching into my inside jacket pocket and pulling out a little black velvet box. I reached over the table – careful not to knock over the wine glasses or put my cuffs in the leftover pasta sauce congealing on our empty plates – held Helen's hand with one hand and placed the box in her open palm with the other. It was how she'd wanted it.

Her friends from school and college were marrying like it was going out of fashion. She'd sigh, receiving another wedding invitation, and say what a nice couple they made, they were a bit younger than us, hadn't been going out as long as we had. We made a nice couple, too, didn't we?

One evening, as the credits rolled on *EastEnders*, I looked at her at the other end of the second-hand sofa. There she was. She was pretty, said she loved me, we made a nice couple, what more did I need?

'How would you like to be *Mrs* Helen *Copeland*?' I said.

Now in retrospect, I can see it was ill advised on several counts – the wording wasn't very PC (all that surname stuff is really besides the point, isn't it?); the timing, squeezed between *EastEnders* and *Brookside*, was bad; and the setting was unimaginative – but, hey, start as you mean to go on, I say. Our marriage was all those things too. At least it was spontaneous.

Helen stared straight ahead towards the tv as if she hadn't heard me but I could sense great crunching machinations going on in her head as I waited for a response, feeling more sheepish by the second, bracing myself for an outright refusal. Instead she stared dreamily into the middle distance and spoke as if she was talking to herself: 'Y'know, I've always dreamt of Mr Right going down on one knee in a high-class restaurant, popping the question with a diamond cluster ring. Ah, maybe one day ... '

Falling in love with Helen was as easy as falling off

a log – assuming you hit the log with your head on the way down and spent the next five years heavily concussed and not thinking straight. Falling is a talent of mine. Falling into primary, secondary, college, university, more by accident than design, passing like a shadow under the cloisters. Studiously unremarkable. Falling into work, out of work, into work. Falling like Alice in Wonderland. Swept along with convention. Never swimming against the tide. Never trying to swim. Never even trying. My ambitions were always fuzzy, unmapped, unclear, iffy and haphazard. I fell into things. The only thing I ever really wanted to do, was blindly ambitious for (wildly unfashionable though it is to admit), was to fall in love.

Helen's mouth opened in direct proportion to the lid of the black velvet box, stopping fixedly on its hinges. There was a ring inside, obviously. My God! An engagement ring. I stared at it too in utter disbelief. I mean, I know I went to the jewellers, I chose it, I agreed terms to pay for it monthly for the next year and a half but I couldn't believe how far I'd allowed the whole charade to go. We were just trying it all on for size, weren't we? I had a get-out clause, a cooling off period, didn't I? This was getting out of hand.

'Oh, Joe! That's so sweet,' she said in mock surprise, taking out the ring with a swift pincer movement, slipping it on her wedding finger. It was a perfect fit (I'd taken one of her other rings to the jewellers to make sure I got the right size). It was the most expensive object I'd ever bought. The clustered diamonds sparkled so brightly they seemed to throw dots of light indiscriminately round the restaurant's ceiling and walls like a glitter ball (and at that price, so they should). The whole thing seemed so dazzling I thought the other diners would complain but no one else appeared to notice.

She snapped the velvet box shut. It wasn't a reassuring click like a safety belt, more like the harness of a rollercoaster locking into position at the very moment you've changed your mind.

'So. When's the wedding? Let's do it soon, eh? No sense in hanging about?' she said contentedly, her eyes burning with new purpose, mental lists forming in her head.

'Well, I was thinking, maybe, if we skip a holiday this year and save up instead, we should be all right for next summer? As long as we keep things modest.'

'Modest?' She said the word with contempt. 'I don't want a modest wedding! C'mon, Joey, wise up! This is something you only do once, right? It's time to push the boat out. You can see that, can't you? I'll see if my dad wants to contribute to the eternal happiness of his only daughter.'

'Naw, Helen, let's pay for it ourselves, c'mon, show we're independent.'

'No way! Are you mad? D'you know how much weddings cost these days? You can't afford it. Dad would love to pay for it anyway. You know what he's like. He'll be delighted.'

She looked at me. Her eyes were shining. She was happy. She'd made a few plans in advance, already, it seemed.

'I've seen a dress I like. It's a small fortune but it's worth it. You'll need to hire a kilt.'

'I don't want to wear a kilt.'

She wasn't listening.

'Copeland doesn't really have a proper tartan, does it? I've checked it out. Would be nice if you matched what Dad'll wear – our clan, our tartan – wouldn't it? We need to put an announcement in the paper. It has to be in St John's Kirk, doesn't it? Where we going on our honeymoon? Money should be no object, mind. Barbados, Borneo, Bali?'

'Ballymoney, more like,' I whispered under my breath. She didn't hear.

I sat there with my arms crossed, listening to

happy Helen describe the mother of all weddings, as the cuffs on my jacket lengthened over my hands and slowly wrapped around my back where they tightened up, tied and fastened securely.

　　… call a somnambulance.

　·　·　·　·　·　·　·　·　·　·　·　·　·　·　·　·　·　·

Twice a day, Siobhan, the new mail-room girl, comes into our office to collect the outgoing mail from a wire basket on top of the filing cabinet. She smiles shyly at me and I smile back. She smiles at everyone, I know, and I smile back at anyone who smiles at me. I do. It's only polite. I'm not claiming there's some kind of *frisson* between us or anything like that. I mean, all right, okay, she does remind me a lot of how Catriona looked then, but that was then. Siobhan's way too young for me now, though I always forget I'm older. I'm certainly not entertaining any thoughts of a relationship with her or anything like that. Get real! That would be ridiculous. The girl looks like she's never had a boyfriend in her life. I've got history, me. I'm a married man with a child. I have a life. It's just that my life no longer lives with me.

　　　Sixth sense or something tells me I'll see Siobhan Saturday, even though I've never seen her up the street before. Third shop I go into, there she is. Like she's waiting for me. She sees me, I'm pretty sure, though she doesn't let on, just keeps looking at the racks of CDs. My mouth goes dry. It's essential to affect nonchalance in these circumstances – I know that much – but I can't trust myself to speak without my voice betraying me. I can't think what I'd say. I'd surely say the wrong thing. No, she hasn't seen me, I'm pretty sure, she's moved round to another rack. Got her back to me, now. I'll make my escape. I turn around, step outside, walk into the bookshop next door. I'm looking at a book but I'm also keeping an eye on the door to see if she'll walk past. She walks in. She's following me! Or maybe it's coincidence. Not much of a coincidence, though, is it? I mean, she's shopping, I'm shopping, sort of. It's not exactly unheard of to peruse the books after the records when the shops are next door to each other, is it? She's seen me. She's coming over. What'll I say? Just be totally natural. Pretend this book jacket is fascinating. Is it an appropriate book to be interested in? *Ajax, Barcelona and Cruyff.* No, she'll think I'm an oik, an anorak. I should have the complete poems of Byron or something. I've got heart palpitations like a love-sick teenager: H.O.L.L.A.N.D. (Hope Our Love Lasts And Never Dies). I could collapse on the floor at any moment. My eyes are clouding over. I feel dizzy. I could swoon (were that not such a girly, Victorian sort of thing to do). She walks past, two feet away from me. I can see her sensible shoes above the book I'm looking down at. My neck hurts, locked in this position, but I have to keep pretending to read or else it'll be obvious to her I'm just pretending if I look up now and she sees me looking. I put the book back after a couple of minutes. Look up, ever-so-casual-like, frantic for her. She's gone.

Wait now, wait now, Joey, calm down. You've been too long without the close company of a woman. Be rational. I see her in HMV. She sees me, right? I leave. Go into Ottakars, she follows me! Then she walks right past me, real close, deliberately, I could smell her perfume. But, get this, she *doesn't* stop to say 'hello' like you would do normally if you saw someone from work. That can only mean me and her have got something going but she's too shy to initiate anything, right? She must want me to make the first move. I have to find her. Find out.

Siobhan's nowhere to be seen. And there's no chance I'll find her either: Union Street's awash with Saturday shoppers walking the dirty, bubble-gummed pavements. Several shop windows have Christmas displays already. It's depressing. They could at least wait till after Halloween, couldn't they? I make a mental note to boycott, wherever possible, the shops that look a little too keen, too eager, too early to exploit the annual retail bonanza. (As if my bristling indignance'll make a blind bit of difference.) I can feel my pulse rate returning to normal as I resume my usual weekend routine. I'll get a paper, head home for the football results, watch wall-to-wall tv. It's high time I got myself a video recorder. Get a video out. It's a wonderful life.

Then I catch a glimpse of Siobhan crossing the road towards me. I keep walking in the direction I was going. She must be right behind me. If there's something in this she'll catch up and we'll get talking. I'm walking over Union Bridge. I'm slowing down, can't look back, reach the traffic lights. It's a legitimate place for me to stop, wait for the green man. I look around. She's there! A couple of shoppers away from me. She doesn't stop though. She's jay-walking over the road, skipping between the cars swinging a white Warehouse poly bag. She's ahead of me now. It's up to me then, is it? The green man guides me over with the crowd. We're dancing, aren't we? She's only a few steps ahead. I could jog up to her. We're passing the Music Hall – I could talk music, I could say 'want to see a gig with me?' She's walking really fast. She's got somewhere to go. I'm having doubts. If she's aware of me, if we've got something going, if we're dancing, what's the hurry? This is all in my head, this. This is a figment of my imagination. I'm making a fool of myself here. I slow up, watch her disappear into the distance, hoping she'll turn round to check if I'm there. But I've lost her in the crowd before she ever does, if she does.

I feel empty. I should've said something instead of this stupid dancing. It's the not knowing that's the worst. Maybe she's mad at me for following her. That's not good, is it? Maybe she's mad at me for not catching up with her. That's not good either. What am I doing? Compelled to pursue her like this. Not thinking straight. Really losing it. Not shopping at all. Completely consumed by my search for her. Is it really only in my head? Is it just me? Is this a phantom affair? Siobhan, how was it for you?

• • • • • • • • • • • • • • • • • •

Georgie's impatience, a forward-planning meeting at the Dundee Chamber of Commerce and roadworks at Kinfauns conspired to make me miss the big event. By the time I got to Perth Royal Infirmary – responding to the pager message that Georgie was destined to arrive prematurely – everything had been cleaned up and sanitized nicely. All cut and dried. Childbirth's heaven and hell and all things in between, I'd always imagined. Always said I wanted to be there, to be a part of it, albeit a bit-part. That was the plan anyway. But I was secretly – guiltily – relieved to be too late.

When I arrived, Helen was sitting up, back in the same tidy hospital bed where I'd last seen her in an earlier false alarm, looking much the same as before, maybe a little washed out, wearing the new cotton nightie she'd bought specially for the hospital and a what-time-d'you-call-this? expression on her face. A crumple-faced bundle of Georgie lay in her arms, wearing a blue plastic identity bracelet like a price tag. It was hard to imagine she could be a product of Helen's own blood, sweat and tears. One minute, or so it seemed, there was no Georgie; the next there she was, fully formed and breathing. More credible surely, easier for me, to imagine she must be shop-bought – which, knowing Helen, was almost conceivable. She was how much? Six pounds two ounces.

• • • • • • • • • • • • • • • • • •

I'm telling myself I'm only going out to buy a newspaper, maybe buy a new book or a CD. That must be why I'm picking out my best clothes – I always wear my best clothes to buy a newspaper.

I take the lead role in a faithful and detailed reconstruction of last Saturday's events. Retracing my steps with forensic precision, I go to all the same places at all the same times as previous sightings, hoping Siobhan's a creature of habit too. But there's no sign of her anywhere. I feel I ought to be handing out leaflets to passers-by, saying 'HAVE YOU SEEN THIS GIRL? If so ring this number – we're waiting for your call'. It starts to rain hard and the sky's dark and brooding. I've walked through the Bon Accord Centre, the St Nicholas Centre, up Union Street, through the Trinity Centre, up Union Street a little further and all the way back again. I've hung around the appropriate shops and attracted only the suspicions of security men who see me all watchful but with obviously no intent to buy.

I give up. The girl has disappeared. I head home, the pavements and the streets are awash with artificial light dripping and distorted in the puddles. I'm cold and dispirited and walking fast when I almost bump right into Siobhan walking round a corner. She squints at me from under the hood of her jacket, there's a pause – she must be wrestling with the same inner turmoil and confusion of the heart as I am.

'Joe! Hi Joe! Wasn't sure for a second there – can't see a thing without my glasses.'

'Didn't know you wore glasses.'

'Well, I wear contacts at work but don't bother with them at weekends, usually just wear my glasses. People think I'm being a snob when I walk right past them but I never recognize anyone unless they come up close to me. You just doing a bit of shopping, are you?'

'Yeah, yeah ... '

'Fancy a coffee or something?' she says.

I instinctively look at my watch as if I've got plans. It must look like she's twisting my arm.

We go to a cheap Italian restaurant nearby and I'm gone. She's Maria, I'm Luigi, this is Napoli. We're in the window seats looking out at the road. It's well and truly Aberdeen out there, with the granite buildings a duller shade of grey with the rain robbing the street of colour. But time and place is a state of mind. She's chit-chattering away, I'm half-listening. We're only talking English because it's been dubbed over our fluent Italian. There's a billboard poster opposite us advertising a car and I pretend it's a Fiat. All the cars going past the window are Fiats, in fact. All the motorbikes are Vespas. And all the people passing are native Italians. This really works. They start to look Italian. All those Aberdonians under umbrellas, hurrying home with their shopping bags, with their collars up, with their eyes screwed up against the lashing rain, see the way they look? See the way they hold themselves? The curve of their noses? That's typical of the Campania region, that is. I've tried this before. It's great. Look out your window, pretend you're in Italy, or France if you prefer, whatever, and pretend all those people in the street are French, let's say. Then, I swear this happens, they all start taking on typically French characteristics, Gallic shrugs and all, and you can imagine if you could only eavesdrop on their conversations you'd hear these Torry quines gabbing on in the nasal tones of perfect Parisian patois.

Our steaming cappuccinos are served in very un-Italian mugs like people have at home. I get a Dennis the Menace mug and Siobhan gets a Mars Bars mug like the ones you get free with Easter Eggs (actually, not 'like', it obviously 'was'). It isn't classy but it has a certain homely charm and at least with a big mug it lasts longer. Finally, we finish our coffees. Up close she's no Catriona but it's been nice. Me and Maria. Maybe we can do this again sometime, I'm not going to rush her.

'D'you live near here?' asks Siobhan.

'Yeah, just up George Street a bit.'

'C'mon, I'll make your tea,' she says, waving her Tesco bag for an alibi.

The outside door closes heavily and we're left in total darkness to climb the stairs. She reaches for my hand and I guide her up the wooden staircase. I worry how presentable my flat is. I'm getting nervous. I feel my way under the door knob, fingering for the keyhole, unlock the door. I show her round.

'That's the kitchen, that's the bathroom, this is the living room, want another coffee?'

She puts down the Tesco bag, takes my hand and pulls me into the room I've made conspicuous by omission. She pulls me onto the bed, kissing and fumbling, like perfect strangers. She lies down with her hands above her head: 'Tie me up,' she whispers dramatically.

I try not to show surprise. Try not to appear an amateur at this sort of thing. Try to look as if I have a large selection of handcuffs and chains and ropes for this very purpose that perhaps Madam would like to choose her preference from. Try to make out this sort of thing happens to me most Saturday afternoons. But, *go, Joe, go!*, if I don't hurry she'll change her mind.

I grab a couple of old office ties from the wardrobe, ham-fistedly tie her wrists to the headboard. It's fiddly work – I mean, it really ought to be done in advance, 'Here's a natty reef knot I prepared earlier!'—because it's difficult to judge, in the urgency of the moment, whether the bind is tight enough to give her the thrill she seeks while not so tight it actually hurts or chafes (even if that might be what she's after).

'You're not used to this sort of thing, are you?' she says, patiently, holding her arms in place as if I was measuring her for a spot of dressmaking.

'Er, no, not really,' I admit.

She closes her eyes, doesn't inspect my finished work, which is just as well because my old Paisley patterned tie with its indelible soup stain and a bobbled, polyester Marks and Spencer number on her wrists look more tragic-comic than erotic. I'm sure she's aware – disappointed, even – that the binds are so loose she could release them at any moment. But so's not to waste any further time, she's thoughtfully gripping the ties herself so they don't fall off.

We go through the motions. It's all so painfully self-conscious. Feels like we're actually wearing our emotional baggage in huge rucksacks on our backs and are only pretending to enjoy the occasion out of politeness to a stranger. It's the worst possible moment for me to realize my desire for Siobhan peaked last week when I saw her disappear into the distance and imagined her forever out of my reach. The proceedings continue, eyes tight closed in awkward embarrassment. She whispers in my ear again: 'Talk dirty! Tell me how you'd like to rape me.'

I can feel myself shrinking.

'But I don't want to rape you.'

'I know, I know, just pretend, that's all. Tell me a story, I like it.'

I'm thinking fast.

'You're walking through a meadow full of alpine flowers wearing a beautiful white dress' – I'm actually using a fabric conditioner advert as my inspiration – 'and who should come a-walking by, but a handsome young farmhand in a brilliant white collarless shirt, leather waistcoat and brown corduroys' – I always imagine it's the important little details women like to know – 'overcome with a hot passion he ignores your protestations, gently lowers you to the ground and ... '

'No, no, no, *no!*' she hisses, 'I want a dark alley and a gang of skinheads!'

• • • • • • • • • • • • • • • • • • •

When I first met Helen – sitting beside her in Mrs Humphrey-Jackson's class re-sitting our Maths Highers – she had afternoon Secretarial Studies classes which she didn't like to miss. On days when I did manage to persuade her to skip class and we'd skive off to the park I used to think it must be our truancy that made her nervous because I noticed – you couldn't help but notice – she could hardly keep still for a moment and was always fidgeting. She used to shoogle her legs nearly non-stop and her feet seemed to be permanently on tip-toe. I figured – like the bighead I am – maybe she was nervous and shy to be in the company of a real live boy-man and all, but I had to admit that didn't square with the confident, self-assured way she spoke to me. It was a noticeable shake, though. Looked like the onset of Parkinson's disease. Jig, jig, jigging legs. Was she aware she was doing it? Was it ballet-in-her-head she was doing, pointing those toes? It became too much to ignore.

Helen was only too pleased to put me out my misery: 'Oh, you've noticed that? Oops! I thought I was being discreet. Well, I'll tell you if you don't think it's *too* kooky.'

She waited for me to respond but, to be honest, I hadn't given the boundaries of kookiness much thought and even if I knew for certain where cute kookiness ended and vulgar madness began I could hardly make a judgement before I even knew what the hell she was talking about. She could sense I was perplexed and gave in.

'Okay, okay, okay, I'll tell you anyway. It's speed-typing. I'm speed-typing. Practising for my Secreterial Studies exam. Typing out my thoughts as I think them. Like my toes are my fingers and there's an imaginary QWERTY keyboard on the ground. Typing out my thoughts wherever I am, in the classroom, on the bus, in my sleep, whenever you're talking, actually, as a matter of fact! The only time I don't do it is when I'm speaking or not thinking at all.'

I should, perhaps, have found this revelation deeply disconcerting but, of course, I chose to find it charmingly kooky. And at first, you can imagine, it seemed harmless enough. I liked to watch her knees shoogling up and down. To see her feet making minuscule movements hither and thither. To be in on her secret. It was humbling, really. This shared intimacy. Her toes crunching and stretching like a Jane Fonda workout to reach each letter, articulating her every thought and whim to no one in particular. No one at all actually. Her thoughts disappeared without trace where she'd typed them. Invisible graffiti on pavements, floors and stairs, stone, wood, concrete, grass and carpet. Big toe on her left foot tapping often near the heel of her right foot as she hit the imaginary space bar. Backspacing to correct mistakes if she hit a wrong key or hadn't put on the shift for capitals. Because, of course, it had to be just right. Wouldn't do to type out shabby work on imaginary paper on an imaginary keyboard that no one would ever see to correct. Had to be perfect.

If I'd been really clever, I'd have taught myself to read those shoogles like deaf people read lips. That would've saved time, wouldn't it? That would've cut to the quick. Cut the crap. To be able to read her thoughts like a newspaper for the day. Or more like an encyclopaedia of trivia for the day. The girl packed a lot of thoughts into her waking hours. Not to mention her toes twitching in her sleep as she typed out her dreams – I didn't know that then. Would have been good, though, to be able to read her restless legs tip-tapping away. No more misunderstandings. I'd always have known exactly what she was thinking.

'What d'you reckon, Helen? Do you fancy chips and a burger or would you prefer to eat in a fancy restaurant?'

'Oh, I don't mind, Joe. You decide,' she'd *say*, feigning easy going when really she was thinking: J-e-s-u-s J-o-e! I d-o-n-'t w-a-n-t t-o e-a-t i-n s-o-m-e c-h-e-a-p b-u-r-g-e-r j-o-i-n-t!

After she passed her speed-typing exam – in the conventional way – Helen's legs gradually grew still. I thought she'd conquered the compulsion till she confided that she'd actually become so adept at it she could type out her thoughts on a tiny, imaginary keyboard no bigger than a stamp with only microscopic movements of her big toe.

Helen's idiosyncrasies seemed less charmingly kooky to be married to. It was a useful tip of hers, when boiling water for coffee or tea, to let the cold water tap run for a minute before filling the kettle because then the water would be more oxygenated than the stagnant stuff in the house pipes. If the tea tasted better it was a difference too fine for my palate to detect. But sometimes I'd forget and she'd always be able to tell. She'd pour the cup out and make it *properly* herself. And I'd get that sinking feeling again. Like a jug of freezing ice-cubed water and a steaming hot kettle just boiled pouring onto the same spot in the pit of my stomach at the same time. Used to get that a lot with Helen. She came home once from work in a distressed state – I thought she'd been mugged. Turns out she'd got chewing gum stuck to one of her shoes and spent the entire day disabled by the horrible stickiness on her foot. She felt violated. I scraped the gum off while she was cleansing herself in the bath but she insisted on throwing the shoes out. It disgusted her to walk the city streets awash with dog excrement, phlegm and gob, chewing gum and cigarette ends. Worst of all, with the chewing gum on her shoes, she'd typed her thoughts out all day with a lisp.

She loved to arrange and re-arrange things. Not flowers, which would be nice, but food tins in the cupboard, making sure our Heinz and Baxters and Tesco labels were facing out the way, ready for inspection. She'd dust the ornaments daily and position and re-position them till they were just right, in a laborious comfort ritual. Clothes should be hung on the clothes horse in such a way as to allow the maximum air flow around them and so they'd dry with minimum creases for easy ironing. She arranged and decorated the flat tastefully enough with all the latest, choicest, most expensive wallpaper, carpets and fittings (Helen harboured ambitions to be an interior designer, I think) but it was a kind of sterile perfection she craved and achieved. Always looked like a showhouse, like we were expecting visitors. She couldn't pass a fabric shop without wanting to go in and look at the cushion covers, duvet covers, sheets, curtains. She always wanted to buy something even though I'd err on the side of caution and say we couldn't afford it. This only made her all the more determined to buy it. She was a material girl living in a material world.

I must've made the place look untidy. When I was unemployed for a while, before the job at the Perth Institute for Business and Enterprise, she'd bustle off to work at the retail park in a blue suit with her name badge on the lapel leaving me watching breakfast tv with a bowl of Weetabix in my hand. She'd come home after a hectic day, a rushed lunch, a ladder in her tights, to find me watching *Home and Away* on the same sofa and sometimes, shame on me, still in my boxers.

At least, I suppose you could say, with our spotless little flat and the gap between us in bed, baby Georgia was born into a sterile environment. Georgie had colic and cried non-stop for three months, announcing her arrival to the world and to all our neighbours.

Sometimes, in the middle of the night, in desperation, I would take screaming Georgie a run in the car with the radio switched on to low-volume white noise between the stations, which seemed to help soothe her to sleep. Late one night, when Helen was at a work's night out and Georgie was insufferable with her screaming I took her out in the car and drove aimlessly round and round the town. In the warm car she quietened down and fell asleep hypnotised by the rhythms of the engine and the radio. When we got back, Helen was naked on the bed in a deep sleep. Her balled tights and rumpled clothes in a warm heap. She lay awkwardly on her side, duvet draped loosely low around her waist, one arm hidden under the pillow, a shadow across the childhood inoculations on her other arm. Hellenistic. The Venus de Milo. Marble made woman. So very beautiful. So smoothly curved. And so very drunk.

•   •   •   •   •   •   •   •   •   •   •   •   •   •   •   •   •   •   •

Disingenuous, I am. A liar, more like. Drunk on bitter. Picking and choosing the worst of Helen, the best of me. What's my angle? That Georgie would be better off with me? It's not the whole truth. Before Helen and I lived together, before we got engaged, before she got pregnant, before I ruined the wedding, before Georgie was born (in that holy order) and before we saw only the worst in each other – before all that, I saw Helen for what she really was. What she really is. The way God made her. A glimpse of her shining, true self. Because, fact is, all the poets and all the pop singers who witter on about being *blinded* by love are wrong. It's the other way round, of course. Normally we're blind. Partially sighted. Usually see the everyday world through cynical, jaundice-tinted spectacles. But when you're in love, *true* love – not the imaginary pink, fluffy, sentimental, fictional candy floss peddled by the likes of Barbara Cartland but real-life, down-our-street, can't-live-without-it *true* love (a survival priority up there with water, food and shelter in my book)—you get a glimpse of how someone must look to God. You see into the shining soul of someone.

That's why when you lose that, it's easier to lie, be selective with your memories. Block out the trusted intimacies once shared. The reasons I fell in the first place. Pretend I never did see her for what she really is. And if I ever did, it was only because I was blinded by love. Like I was blind drunk at the time. Don't remember a thing. Otherwise how could I ever move on?

Helen (me too, if the truth be told) once saved and hoarded every possible souvenir of romance like people save newspaper front pages on days of particularly earth-shattering news. TITANIC SINKS. KENNEDY IS DEAD. MAN WALKS ON THE MOON. JOE LOVES HELEN. Our lives will never be the same. Collecting, treasuring souvenirs, as if future generations would bid for them at Sotheby's or Christie's like Beatles memorabilia. Of course, we know they were of sentimental value only, and only to us, ever. Oddities too eclectic and obscure for others to understand, like half a stick and wrapper of Wrigleys spearmint gum ripped down the middle 'cause we'd imitated a stupid advert, just fooling around, and she got the other half. Romantic, eh? (You had to be there.) Pressed flowers. Twigs. Shells. Leaves. Clover. Almost anything could qualify as long as it triggered a memory and had raw sentiment attached. Lots of ticket stubs: bands long out of fashion; movies long since gone to video; bus journeys to Crieff and Aberfeldy that were workaday for the drivers and the other passengers but were something else to us. And a whole heap of love letters and love cards and love notes and love tokens in the large, frayed manilla envelope bursting with mawkish sentiment which didn't seem mawkish then. 'Cause frankly, it wasn't. Even if it was expressed clumsily in red felt-tip love hearts on Valentine's Day it doesn't mean we were making it up, acting, or pretending. It was sincere – once – then. But d'you know what? All that stuff. All those souvenirs. They just look like rubbish now. Just look like Aberdeen did on bin days, before the wheelie bins arrived, when the seagulls would rip open the bags and scatter a week's worth of living history all over the pavements.

But I can't sweep away the past. In its time, it was sincere. Heartfelt. Wasn't forced like scentless factory-farmed carnations or corporate and sold to us like Coca-Cola. It was free. It was the real thing. And that's what we'll tell Georgie. Because it's the truth. She was born of love. Not some clumsy, loveless fumble in the dark. But in the darkened room of our flat, lit a glowing orange from the street lights, a train rumbling past in the distance. Helen wet from the shower, hair in a towel turban, humming a tune to herself, self-contained, content. Drying herself ritualistically, the air humid and heavy with anticipation. Her short, satin nightie, coolly fresh from the drawer, slipping over her shoulders and dropping to the tops of her thighs, the material sparking blue and crackling with static. The air charged with electricity.

•   •   •   •   •   •   •   •   •   •   •   •   •   •   •   •   •   •   •

Jackie, who wants to be known as Jack now he's all grown up and an insurance salesman in Chislehurst no less (living not far from my older brother James in Sevenoaks who's a radical, revolutionary Bolshevik Finance Manager), bounded into Helen's and my room, flung open the curtains, and shook my big toe through the duvet. I know this happened, exactly as I've just described, because I didn't just live it – I've seen the movie.

It was Jackie's latest fad. He'd just bought a brand new camcorder and offered to film the wedding free of charge. Helen wasn't at all keen but, after the silly money her dad had already spent on a long list of the best of everything, including hiring the most expensive wedding photographer in Perth, she was under pressure to concede *some* economies. And, anyway, as Jackie pointed out, he was family after all and everyone would be more relaxed with him around. He'd be able to capture informal, behind-the-scenes footage to contrast with the official photographer's portfolio. And d'you know, *sometimes,* he said, it's actually the spontaneous candid shots of a formal event that people treasure the most. Few people can resist Jackie's eager-to-please expression, Helen finally relented and it was agreed he would film the wedding. What his sales pitch neglected to mention, however, was that he'd never quite finished reading the camcorder instruction book. Practising with the camcorder, Jackie admitted to me that one or two of the functions were still a mystery to him. I should have read the warnings but I was persuaded against my better judgement by Jackie's infectious enthusiasm.

'No worries,' he said, 'by the time the wedding comes round I'll have it taped.'

Only other thing was, he confessed later, he'd yet to master the art of editing. Everything he filmed would end up in the final version of the uncut, uncensored, all-singing, all-dancing, feature-length epic: *Joe and Helen get Hitched.*

I've watched our wedding video once and once only. The big mistake was to watch it for the very first time in the plush comfort of Helen's parents' house with Helen's parents and her extended family of aunties, uncles and cousins – all in town for the wedding – in a dubious spirit of post-match analysis. I don't know what we were expecting – what does anyone expect of their wedding video? I suppose I'd been hoping for a good Hollywood romance – lovely leading lady, handsome leading man, that sort of thing – *Love Story* without one of the partners dying before the end. But somehow Jackie – who was there for the British première and totally unrepentant – had unwittingly made a gritty, fly-on-wall docu-drama. A *World in Action* exposé filmed by Martin Scorsese. Mostly it was unwatchable – laughable, really – with all the jerky camera movements and Jackie's odd sense of what made an interesting shot. His taste for avant-garde shots of the cake from odd angles and, bizarrely, a cat on a wheely bin at the back of the hotel.

'Aw, fair dos, Joey, black cat, good luck, wedding, makes sense. Elements of Hitchcock there, I thought.'

But there was one scene which was the show-stopper and augured very badly for our marriage. In fairness, Jackie couldn't have avoided it during filming. Mind you, if he'd only worked out how to edit in time, he could have cut it before we all sat and watched in horror while Helen's mischief-making cousins shouted for replays and slow-mo and 'There! Freeze frame, there!'

The scene so upset Helen that she banned the video from our house and we never spoke of it, never mind watched it, ever again. I kept the master copy – the only copy – in my manilla envelope, took it with me when I left. It wouldn't be missed. I'd watch it now, here in Aberdeen, here in this scummy flat but I don't have a VCR. The one I bought is at Helen's and I don't begrudge her it. Georgie likes to watch the Disney cartoons. Anyway, I don't need to see it again. Once seen, never forgotten. It's funny, but it's become the definitive version of the wedding in my head. It was the objective perspective. It was odd to see myself like an actor in a movie. To see myself as others must see me. No film star, no distinguishing features, undistinguished: Mr Average. The camera doesn't love me. I had no on-screen wedding presence. I looked so ordinary, so unremarkable, I could hardly believe it was me. Is that all that people see when they see me? Is that all there is to me? It's actually more bearable to pretend I was acting. Yes, look! Look at me master this part. I play the husband-to-be. Marvel at my method acting. See how I've suppressed my own dazzling personality and made myself look like any old Joe.

Organizing the Mother of All Weddings was a complicated business and I recognized early on there could be no place for sentiment or airy fairy democratic consultations. Someone had to seize control. Make things work. Make things run to schedule. Helen, naturally, assumed the mantle. And I gratefully let her: 'It's your baby, Baby.' Frankly, I defy most men to even feign an interest in the colour and contents of the little sewn bags of potpourri given out as favours to the female wedding guests. Helen planned every minute detail with military precision. She was very thorough. She even phoned Tayside Police and Perth and Kinross District Council to make sure there would be no roadworks en route to the church which might delay her stately progress in the white-ribboned classic car. And when they told her there *would* be roadworks on Tay Street, she asked them in all seriousness if they wouldn't mind delaying work till after 3pm on Saturday 5 July. They politely declined – explaining that there were, in fact, weddings almost every week and they could hardly stop work for all of them – before helpfully suggesting an alternative route. Taking responsibility. Taking charge. Helen was in her element. She was the Cecil B. DeMille of the whole production. It was going to be *The Greatest Show on Earth.*

The video started well enough with a slow pan of the mantlepiece at our flat, with all our wedding cards from family and friends, then it stopped in the middle to zoom in on a piece of white cardboard propped up against the clock with Jackie's handwritten, black felt-tip, opening title: *Joe and Helen get Hitched.*

Cut to black, as the camera's automatic lighting adjusted to the dark of Helen's and my bedroom. We could just make out Jackie's arm flinging open the curtains before everything turned a dazzling white with psychedelic Paisley patterns in red as the camera struggled to cope with the sudden change of light. Then there was me. Or at least the top of my head, with straw hair sticking out of an untidy wrap of duvet. On any other day, Helen would have been sleeping beside me but as it was our wedding day and she wanted to do everything by the book – the traditional way – she'd decided to stay at her mother's. She wouldn't see me till the church. Gave it all a cloak of respectability, she reckoned. Naked hypocrisy, others might've called it.

Jackie nipped my big toe in a big brotherly sort of way. And I grumbled and groaned into the pillow. We heard Jackie's voice booming like Charlton Heston in *The Ten Commandments* because he was so close to the microphone: 'C'mon, Joey, the big day has arrived! Mustn't be late. Last chance for any second thoughts ...'

I'm not at my peak in the morning at the best of times and Jackie was really getting my goat, kneeling on the bed for a close up of my potato face, podgy with sleep. I was getting really mad at him. All I wanted was another half hour. I hate bells and buzzers and must-be-at-a-meeting Monday mornings. We weren't designed to wake up to stress like that. I think it's really dangerous. We're supposed to be woken in gradual stages by the gentle rays of the sun. That's why cavemen could run after antelope: they'd had such a good night's sleep.

'Go away, Jackie. Give us five minutes, will you?' I

pleaded. I was on my best behaviour already, minding my language 'cause I knew the candid camera was on.

'No way, Joe, it's my solemn duty as your big brother and official wedding cameraman to make sure you're up and ready for action. I promised Helen.' He started shouting instructions and suggestions for a video diary: 'Sit up. Scratch your head and yawn. Go on! What are your first thoughts on this day of days? Say something profound, go on!'

He moved closer because the microphone wasn't catching my mumbles under the duvet.

'Please Jackie, please, just ... I just need a few minutes, take the camera away. All right?'

I was pretty angry by then. Me, still in a half-sleep. Jackie hyper. He seemed more excited than I was. He was really nipping my head. He nosed the camera into my face.

'Hey, Mr Groom, man, anything to say to your future wife on camera?'

'Look, just piss off, will you? I mean it!'

Jackie was unperturbed. He just laughed but at least he finally got the message. Switched off the camera for a moment. There was so much else to worry about we both forgot what had been captured and preserved on tape. It was a busy house that day. Jackie, Mo and Finn were all staying. Next scene on tape: the breakfast table in the kitchen. Me and Finn bleary-eyed munching Shreddies, Mo putting bread in the toaster. No one talked except Jackie who'd had his customary shot of extra strong coffee and was buzzing on a caffeine high. (We only had instant in the flat but he takes it with a good three or four heaped spoonfuls. Keeps him going, he says. Keeps him hyper, more like.) Jackie's pinky finger at the top right-hand side of the tv screen looked enormous. It kept appearing and disappearing like a cheap special effect in a sci-fi 'B' movie. Me, Mo and Finn sounded really muted. Like we were talking in whispers while Jackie's voice close to the mike bellowed all over the place.

'Moses, you do your best man speech, right?' he

shouted at the top of his voice or so it seemed, 'then you introduce him here – little bruvver, the Bold Boy, the Groom, the new Mr ... shit! What's Helen's second name again?'

I was almost inaudible in comparison, saying, 'Campbell. You know that.'

'Yeah. Yeah. You should say that, Moses. My brother's so cool, so modern, he takes the bride's surname. They'd laugh. So Joe, you'll stand up, right after the introduction and Moses sits down, okay?'

'Yeah, obviously.'

'Moses, you've got the ring, haven't you? *Have you* got the ring? Where's the ring? Where is the ring?'

'I've got the ring, Jackie, 'member we agreed. I keep it till we get to the church then I give it to Mo and he gives it back to me inside when Helen arrives, right? So Helen sees we're doing it right – keeping it traditional.'

Mo and Finn seemed numbed by the whole occasion. Finn was tanned, tired and jet-lagged, having flown in long-haul only a couple of days before from a study of fish-farming he was carrying out for Fruits of the Ocean in Tasmania. Mo was morose, having recently split up with his girlfriend and wasn't his usual self. I hadn't seen either of them for five, maybe six, years. They hadn't changed. Not really. We could still talk in the same old easy banter like we'd last met Tuesday week. But seeing them there, in that unreal situation, made me realize what was actually happening. I was getting *married*, for God's sake. We were doing all those things grown-ups do. I owned a car: albeit, a stunning, third-hand, boxy Chevette, but I owned it. I had all the documents to prove it. I paid insurance and everything. It was so weird. I'd always imagined we'd stay 15. Forever on the threshold of things. Always exhibiting potential and promise. But never actually having to fulfil it. Never actually having to prove ourselves. Never failing. Never disappointing. Forever the best buddy. The baby brother. Easy things. Not, not-so-easy things like being a good husband or a good father. Owning a flat, I thought, would be beyond belief. But then, I didn't own it. Helen and her father, a successful antiques dealer and all round good bloke, owned it. I tried my best to do it up but when my wallpaper was squint, had bubbles and peeled at the edges, they sorted it out themselves. Leaky tap? Dad'd fix that. Washing machine broken? Dad knew a good plumber. Telly on the blink? Dad'd get us a good deal on a new one. I did wonder sometimes why Helen couldn't just marry her dad.

We'd all trooped down to Moss Bros for a dress rehearsal the day before. Helen had given them a list of our vital statistics a few weeks in advance and, in theory, all we had to do was go for a final fitting and take the gear home. Me, Mo, Finn and Jackie stood there in full tartan regalia feeling as awkward and self-conscious as we would to wear a pirate's outfit or a gorilla suit for a fancy dress party. I looked splendid, of course, Helen had seen to that. She'd been to the shop earlier to ensure the groom's outfit was just right. I should have felt poised and ready to enter the wedding fray but it all felt about as real as *Brigadoon*. Like I'd only have to pick at a random loose thread for the whole sham to unravel.

Our family doesn't appear to have a clan associated with it. The people who make these things up seemed to have inexplicably overlooked the Copelands. My brother James told me once it was because the Copelands had been conscientious objectors in the '45 and wouldn't fight for either the Lowlanders *or* any stupid clan chieftain o' the pudding race. (I actually believed that for several years. I *told* people. They'll remember. Wee Joe Blethers. Thanks for nothing, James.) Helen helpfully, quite forcefully actually, suggested we should all wear Campbell of Breadalbane tartan. Not only was this her maiden name's official tartan, it would also, more importantly, colour-coordinate nicely with the green satin sashes of the bridesmaids.

Jackie couldn't resist the temptation to fool around in his Highlander's outfit. He started jigging his leg and toe-tapping his big brogues, singing 'A Scottish Soldier' out of the side of his mouth like Andy Stewart. *Songs of Scotland* and all those old programmes with Moira Anderson, Peter Morrison and Alistair (The Wee Kirkcudbright Centipede) McDonald came flooding back. Our mum took strange comfort from these programmes while we'd all groan to see them miming old standards with some spectacular mountain backdrop behind them. Moira would be in a knitted sweater or sometimes, incongruously, wearing an evening dress way up there in the middle of nowhere like she'd just been teleported to a mountain top by Scottie off *Star Trek*.

Mo really fancied himself in his kilt. He stood in front of the full-length mirror admiring his new look for far too long. He'd put on the beef since I last saw him. And what with the big silver buckle on his belt stuck out over his sporran and the tight-fitting jacket and black bow-tie he looked for all the world like a strutting, hooded gull. His kilt was a fraction too short, edging above the knee, and he tied the laces of his brogues too high up the calf so that he unwittingly achieved a unique Fran-and-Anna-*cum*-ballerina look. Adjusting his three-buttoned cuffs and slipping a plastic skean-dhu down his sock for the final touches, he harboured hopes of favourable seating arrangements at the reception for him to exploit his lady-killer looks. He thought he looked the business. The bee's knees. Finn's kilt, in contrast, erred towards the other extreme, almost nudging the top of his coarse woollen socks for the National Trust lady tour-guide look. Maybe they'd got their kilts mixed up. My brother and my best friends looked a motley crew of fancy dressers. And though Sir Walter Scott would doubtless approve, we looked a right bunch of Charlies.

Next shot on the video was of the outside of St John's Kirk as one or two guests arrived early for the service. Cut to interior, shots of the minister, the organist, Helen's side of the expectant congregation, my side – my mother, my father, my brother James, his wife and kids, a few other friends – people in hats and starchy collars self-consciously ignoring the camera trained on them, then a shot of the vestibule, with the ushers waiting for expectant Helen, and a shaky, hand-held walk outside again.

The classic car drew up, an old green Bentley, and a piper at the door breathed and squeezed some life into the pipes to announce the bride's safe arrival: localized flooding due to a burst water main and Tay Street roadworks notwithstanding. Everything was going swimmingly. Helen's dad leapt out the car and round to the door to open it for her. He opened and shut the door two or three times for the benefit of the official photographer, who wanted the right shot of Helen as she regally disembarked. The resulting wedding album looked perfect but Jackie's video didn't lie and it all looked a bit stagey and silly as the photographer twice asked Helen to get back in the car so he could get a few more shots of her coming out. Even so, she looked radiant. Isn't that what they always say? Quite stunning, actually, in a white off-the-shoulder bodice dress, which was a pretty racy choice for an apparent virgin but, hey, it's traditional. The rain came on a little but you'd never know from the photos or even the video, Helen looked so poised and assured. She posed on her own, beside the car, outside the church, with the chauffeur, the piper, her father, the three little bridesmaids from Bridesmaids-R-Us (Helen resorted to second cousins, I think, to recruit the child stars she required). She waved to the shoppers and passers-by who'd stopped to gawp. She was every inch the leading lady. A film star. Cut.

Jackie raced inside ahead of Helen to get the next shot of her walking into the church. She smiled at everyone on both sides as she walked down the aisle on her father's arm. She'd never looked more beautiful. Never looked so happy.

It makes me feel physically sick to recall what happened next.

Jackie zoomed in for an arty close up of Helen's face as she was scanning the top of the aisle, searching for me. The camera is ruthless and unforgiving. I could see my whole marriage collapse in her eyes before it had even begun. She saw my best man Mo at the front of the church in his kilt and there was a flicker of incomprehension as she recognized me beside him wearing a dark, understated, rather-tasteful-I-thought suit, smiling nervously at her. Disbelief blinked into a moment of seething rage before her expression fixed into a grim, steely smile – she was a trooper, a pro – but her eyes were killer cold. *The Bride of Frankenstein.* I expected her, at any moment, to shout 'Cut' and storm off to her trailer till the director placated her with the promise of star billing and a new leading man for the inevitable sequel. But instead, she stoically smiled on through, as if it all were still perfect and dreamlike and just how she'd always imagined it would be. I feel terrible pangs of guilt and remorse and shame to recall it. Terrible pangs of guilt and remorse as Helen's cousins froze the frame on the VCR with her gritted teeth fixed in a forced smile but her eyes betraying murderous intent.

As we stood together to exchange vows, the minister kept whispering little reassurances because he sensed things were getting overwrought and tense. We sung hymn 600 in the Church Hymnary Third Edition then it was down to business. When the minister turned to the congregation and asked 'Does anyone know of any lawful impediment why this man and this woman should not be joined in holy matrimony?' there was utter silence in the church except for a rogue cough and a shuffling of feet – a pregnant silence from Helen – but it was screamingly noisy in my head: 'Yeah, man! I do! Stop this charade! This woman is not Catriona. Nothing like Catriona. I don't know why Catriona's married to someone else. I don't know why she's got a kid. I don't know why I'm getting married at all. Stop this at once! Arrest me! I'm a charlatan. I'm a deserter from the Foreign Legion. I'm too young, I'm just a boy. This isn't legal. It's bigamy. I'm married to Catriona. We exchanged vows in the linen cupboard with the floor polisher as our witness ...'

Mo had told me who was doing what in Pitlochry, who was going out with whom, who was getting married, who was dead. But neither Mo nor Finn mentioned Catriona till I asked. Russell Bradley was long gone, last heard of working for a construction company in Wolverhampton. Catriona was married to someone else. Someone Mo didn't know. Someone from out of town. A son, already. Very happy, by all accounts.

I wanna be happy too. We all deserve to be happy, don't we?

'And do you, Joseph Andrew Copeland, take this woman, Helen Cecilia Campbell, to be your lawful wedded wife?'

'I do.'

• • • • • • • • • • • • • • • • • •

I would say it is a scientific fact you never meet, by chance, people from your past who you've long lost touch with who you'd really *love* to see again. The girl on the CityLink bus to London who rested her head on your shoulder all the way from Preston to Birmingham. The guy at university, as lost as you among the cloisters on Freshers' Week, who became a stalwart friend for three whole years before inexplicably disappearing, presumably on a manned space probe to Mars, and never seen again. The guy you worked with at your first job whose mocking impressions of the boss made the unpaid overtime almost bearable. Oh sure, you're *always* bumping into that kid from primary school who used to shout 'Hey, listen to this everybody, listen!' before raising a bum cheek and farting. You often see him in the street and give him a little nod of acknowledgement – yes, uh-huh, you sat across from me in Primary Four, yes, uh-huh we're hicks from the sticks in the big city, aren't we just – without actually breaking stride as you walk past him for fear he'll run to catch you up in his

Gucci loafers and say 'Hey, Jo-ey! Listen to this ...'

But you never meet, by chance, the people you'd really love to meet again. Like maybe even your best friends, say, who hadn't been in touch for years before dutifully attending your wedding then immediately losing touch again in the years since. Oh sure, I get Christmas cards from Mo and Finn. I'm on their lists. Finn's wife writes his: he's married too now. Mo even follows St Johnstone to Pittodrie sometimes and doesn't bother to get in touch. He knows I'm here. Bastard! You'd think the past was meaningless. But anyway, it's a proven, indisputable scientific fact: you never meet by chance the people you really would love to meet again.

So when I clearly heard Catriona's unmistakable voice shouting 'Joe! Jo-ey!' in Union Street I did the only sensible thing and completely ignored it, absolutely certain as I was that it was some other Joe and some other Catriona. 'Cept the shout got louder and closer until I turned round subtly, I hope, like I was looking back at something in a shop window which had caught my eye.

It really *was* Catriona. All smiles. She was carrying a couple of shopping bags and a huge bulky bag of Pampers balanced precariously under the buggie she was wheeling with a kid of about two asleep in it. Ten years or more didn't seem to have changed Catriona very much.

'Jo-ey! Jo-ey Copeland! It *is* you. Long time no see.'

'Catriona? It was you shouting on me, was it? Sorry, I was day-dreaming.'

'Haven't changed then!'

'You neither. You look great! Can't believe it!' (Oops, badly phrased, that.) 'Who's this then?'

'This is Annie, my second. Apple of her daddy's eye, she is! Her big brother's seven and a half now. Staying at his granny's. We're on a daytrip here, y'know, just for the day.'

'Wow, she's cute, isn't she? Sleeping without a care in the world. How do they do that with all the noise and traffic around them?'

'Picture of innocence, isn't it? Doesn't know the conventions. Sleeps whenever she feels the urge. Plus the fact she's had a hard day's shopping with Mum.'

'You married, are you?' I know she is.

'Yeah, to Peter. We're rushing to meet him, actually. He's got a meeting at Shell. Picking us up after.'

There's an awkward silence but it needn't be. I don't feel awkward. She's looks a million dollars. Nah, a million pounds. A million whatever is the top currency of the moment. She's happy. I'm happy for her. To see her now is to know her place in my scheme. A permanent fixture from the best of my past. Nothing more, nothing else, no part of my future. We're both just staring down at the sleeping kid, not quite knowing what to say. The buses, the cars, the people and time rushes by, the blood rushes through our arteries into our hearts and out again.

'He's a lot like you, Joe, Peter is,' she says. 'Had to be.'

We look each other straight in the eye, transmitting, receiving and disseminating more information in a split second than could be written in a long, loving scented letter.

'Anyway. Gotta rush, nice to see you, Joe, I was hoping we might bump into you. Heard you were in Aberdeen now. All the best, take care!'

And she's off down the street into the crowd of strangers. And I reckon maybe, maybe it's just as well you never meet again, by chance, the people you'd really love to meet.

• • • • • • • • • • • • • • • •

Me and Prue put up the same old scabby, shabby Christmas decorations around the office as last year. She'd put them up the year before that, and the year before that: threadbare lengths of tinsel in silver, red and blue; a MERRY CHRISTMAS banner with gold tassels; a bashed and bruised plastic Santa ornament with sleigh and reindeer; spray-on snow for the windows; lots and lots of broken and repeatedly repaired paper chains; and a wreath of evergreens.

It's funny – plastic, paper and pathetic they may be, but they still have the power to transform the office and, at the very least, no one can be in any doubt what time of year it is. The weather's no Christmas card, mind you. It's wet, cold and windy. No hint of snow yet. The lights on Union Street have been ceremoniously switched on by the tv soap stars wintering in *Robinson Crusoe* at His Majesty's, twinkling intermittently, illustrating *The Twelve Days of Christmas*, as they swing in the furious, biting wind that whips up and down the granite gorge. From the ephemeral earthly riches of the Bank of Scotland at one end, to the everlasting riches promised by the Salvation Army Citadel at the other, the pavements heave with over-indulgence in the annual shopping glut. From the highest lords-a-leaping to the lowliest maids-a-milking, everyone wants to buy a piece of Christmas to call their own.

A few days before the Christmas break, Audrey marches me, Chris, and Prue upstairs to the canteen for the Institute's Christmas lunch. She's been unbearable since she heard I've got an offer of a job at the City Council starting in the New Year. Keeps saying what a blessing in disguise it must have been for me that my contract here wasn't going to be renewed. She's convinced herself she's done me a favour. It's a peculiar self-deluding logic of the kind that sustains the Institute of Business and Entrepreneurship. Audrey's never thought to question her faith. The guy who interviewed me at the Council's met her. He's got three business cards she's forced upon him on different occasions. He joked that anyone who'd survived Audrey Marshall for a couple of years had shown loyalty above and beyond the call of duty and I ought to put it in my CV like a medal or a certificate.

The canteen's decked out with Christmas decorations

too. There's holly and ivy centrepieces on each table and red paper tablecloths with matching napkins. Most of the Institute's personnel are there already, or arriving behind us, as we mill around looking for appropriate company to sit beside. Audrey's found herself a seat to the right of The Chairman, who's an unusual sight himself in the canteen and is busy over-compensating, wearing the paper crown from a cracker and desperately small-talking with an embarrassed waitress. I'm very, very keen to avoid sitting anywhere near Siobhan, the mail-room girl, but I needn't have worried since she's already set her sights on someone else on the male rounds.

I find myself the ham in a Chris and Prue sandwich. It's okay sitting between them – we've all been getting on a lot better since we found out our time together is drawing to a close. We pull our crackers. Tell each other the crappy jokes. Someone starts singing a carol and, though it seems corny, we all join in. The canteen manageress dims the lights a little and what with the weather so dull and overcast outside it starts to look really quite cosy in the canteen. I'm prone to sentimentality at these moments but why fight it?

As the first course is served, everyone starts to relax and chat away quite the thing. I offer to pour Prue some white wine but she puts a hand over the empty glass.

'Aw, go on, Prue, it's Christmas! It's not often the Institute buys us a drink.'

She smiles a strange broad grin which doesn't fit what I've just said at all. She leans towards me, I tilt my head, she cups her hand around my ear and whispers confidentially:

'I'm pregnant!' She leans back, looks at my face to gauge my reaction, her eyes shining.

'That's fantastic news, Prue, really great.'

'It's a secret, mind. Don't tell anyone,' she says, pouring herself some sparkling water, 'might not be straightforward, things can go wrong. I'd rather no one knew.'

'Aw, but that's great news though, eh? Best of luck, Prue.' I raise my glass, she raises hers too.

• • • • • • • • • • • • • • • • •

Mo and Finn should be along in a minute. We're meeting here: Moulin Square, 8.30am. I'll sit under this tree. Copper beech it is, I think. Something like that anyway. There's a wooden seat round it on the village green. Tourists love it. Always stop to take a picture here. What with Moulin Kirk over there and the black and whitewashed Moulin Hotel over there and the wee rows of cottages on the other two sides. Looks like a film set. But you'd see it on film and think they'd overdone it. Made it too nicey nicey. You would! But here it is, for real. Makes me want to take a picture. I haven't brought a camera. Got everything else I need though. Got my pack lunch: bottle of American Cream Soda, can of Coke, some Marmite sarnies, an apple, a packet of Golden Wonder Salt and Vinegar Crisps, a Fry's Chocolate Cream and an I've-got-five-pence-what-can-I-get-for-five-pence? Caramac Bar. My fishing rod. My survival kit. Everything I need. Ready for anything, I am. Mo and Finn shouldn't be too long. Must be getting on for half past eight now. Sharp morning, this is. Bit of a bite to it. Start of autumn. Kinda cloudy and sunny. Could go either way. Bit misty too but that'll clear later, I reckon. Yep, that's what I say – me being a world authority on it and all – Copeland the famous Meateororogist, Meteoroligist, bit of a tongue twister that one, weatherman, that's me. What's keeping the lads? Maybe they haven't made it past the dreaded Hanging Tree. Round the back of the church there – can't see it from here – the old ash tree that people say people were hung from in olden days. Criminals. Murderers. Long time ago. Lynched. But actually, most probably, they weren't. I don't think so, anyway. We did a project in school – 'Our Town' – turns out there used to be a Baron's Court right enough but guilty people would only be tied to the tree like being locked in the stakes (I dunno if people actually threw rotten tomatoes and cabbages at them – I'd quite like to do that, throw things at criminals and get away with it, eggs would be brilliant, splat!)

– it was actually called the Judging Tree then. I don't think they ever hanged anyone from it, don't think they were allowed, but you know how people from wee towns think it's only polite to make a story more dramatic in the telling. That's how ordinary things become the stuff of legend – people just trying to tell you what they know you want to hear. Anyway, somewhere along the line the Judging Tree became known as the Hanging Tree 'cause people wanted it that way. It's a hideous sight now. Old and broken down and stumpy, smothered in climbing ivy, only a few branches of new growth to let you know it's still alive but, I tell you, walking home from BBs on dark nights you don't take chances, do you? I always walk real fast past the Hanging Tree, old and broken down though it is, keep my fists clenched, ready for trouble. Sometimes I think I see it move like there's someone inside. How freaky is that? Way I see it, whichever way you look at it though, it's a spooky thing, that tree, so old, there in the graveyard which, we know, for sure, no doubts, no debate, is definitely full of dead bodies. Ghosts? They don't bother me. I could take a ghost, me, no problem. Don't know how you'd fight one, mind you, if you swung your fist it would just go right through them like thin air, wouldn't it? On the other hand, how could they hurt you when they're about as tough as a puff of smoke? Don't scare me. Wouldn't want to inhale one, though. Why would a ghost want to kill me anyway? What did I do? Even so, on dark nights, I reckon it's best to run past the tree. No place to hang around. (Gotta tell Mo and Finn that one!) Where are they? I'm fed up waiting. Must be well after half past eight now. Should've brought my watch. Ach, they can just catch me up. I know the way. I'll just keep walking, slow-steady, no hurry, and any minute I'll hear a shout behind me and they'll be racing up the high drive to catch up. It really is misty, the higher you get up the road. The grass and weeds on the verge of the road are heavy, dripping with dew. Everywhere's a deathly hush. This must be what it's like in China right now. 'Cause Chairman

Mao died on Thursday. John Craven's Newsround *said so. He was 82. (Mao that is, not John.) See if I die at 82, I've got what?, 71 years left. Poor old Mao. Didn't make me cry, though. The news. It's not like I knew him or anything. But there's 800 million people, right now, in China, pretty cut up about it. Well, some of them are. That must be a helluva lot of mourning going on. They do say that by the year 2000 – that's what? 24 years time – there'll be more Chinese than anyone. We'll be overrun by the Yellow Peril. But I reckon by that time there'll be hundreds of millions of Scottish people 'cause we'll have multiplied too, am I right? The so-called experts sometimes overlook the most blatantly obvious things, don't they? Tell you what I think – you gotta think for yourself. That's how to get by. That's how to survive. We won't be overrun by anything 'cause you could drown the entire population of the world ten times over in Loch Ness. It's true! No messing! We got that in Geography. Mrs MacCarthy didn't say 'drown', exactly, she said 'immerse' but, y'know, it stands to reason a lot of the ones lower down would probably drown, eh? If you ever tried it. The ones in wheelchairs, for example, and maybe really heavy people, and people who can't swim. Like me. See on Fridays? When we go swimming at Perth Baths? I'm really going to practise hard till I can swim a whole length without grabbing the side of the pool halfway, as I still have to do, for a breather. Puts it all into perspective though, doesn't it? To think, I used to worry a lot there'd be no place to put everyone 'cause of the world population boom. But there you go, in actual fact, turns out there's plenty room for everyone and if it ever gets too crowded we could always drown a few. John Craven says that before Mao got ill he told everyone to be cool when he dies and carry on as normal. That's what he instructed them to do. Keep on living like I told you to in my Wee Red Book: Never kick, or trip, or strike, or spit at, or obstruct an opponent. Never pull the shirt of an opponent. Never feign injury. Never re-enter the field of play without the referee's permission. Never handle the ball unless you are a goalkeeper within the penalty area. Least that's what it says in the* Evening Times' Wee Red Book! *(I gotta tell Mo and Finn this!) 'Cept, thing is, the crowds won't have it, they won't do as they've been told, they've been weeping and wailing ever since they heard the news. They reckon there'll be hundreds of thousands – millions maybe – wanting to file past his body when it lies in state. He'll be in a state all right, he's dead! Shouldn't mock the dead, though, should you? Mao's one of the main men, I think. James – my brother – he used to have an English translation of Mao's* Little Red Book. *I doubt if he ever read it, though. Wasn't really a fan. He never had a poster of Mao up on the wall beside Che and Lennon. Mao's way too ugly to be a pop hero. Miaow! I was frozen stiff before, but I'm warming up a bit now with all the walking. I'm onto the trail now, through the woods. I'm going to leave a message for Mo and Finn so they know I'm up ahead. Scrape my initials on the dirt here, 'JC' with a big arrow pointing up the path. See my survival manual? It tells you how to get the message across. Sending signals. Mostly for help, right enough, which is not relevant here. But there's others too, I'll just tie this clump of grass in an ever-so-simple granny knot with the top pointing up the path. The boys'll get the idea. Also, if I just place a small stone on top of this big stone with another wee stone ahead of the other two, that tells people which direction I'm headed. There you are! See that? They cannae miss it. That's like phoning, writing a letter and sending a telegram to us Jungle Jims. The fog's lifting a bit, I think. Yeah, it's definitely lifting. Once I get to higher ground I'll be able to see over it. This is what you expect in autumn, isn't it? I love the autumn. I like wearing a jacket. A little bit of body armour. It's my favourite season by far. Can't stand the prickly heat of summer. This summer's been unreal. The hottest this century, they say. People will remember the 'Heatwave of 76', they say. Grass on the playing fields got burnt and went brown. It was like playing on ash. 'Cept you didn't feel like playing, it was so hot you just wanted to sit in the shade. It's funny, but I remember a few years back, after a couple of really cold winters, all the talk was about a new Ice Age. They had scientific proof an' all. It was on the BBC so you had to take it for fact. I had it in my head there'd be woolly mammoths roaming the Highlands and we'd all be living in igloos. But it's all gone a bit quiet on the Ice Age theory now. That's all forgotten. I must have missed the news which had all the Ice Age scientists lined up to apologize for their mistake. See on the weather report, when they say it's the hottest or the wettest or the snowiest summer in living memory? I'm not impressed really. That's only 80-odd years, isn't it? So what? Big deal. There's been weather for since time began. You might watch 80 seconds of a game and declare Stenhousemuir are the greatest football team that ever played in all the games in all the leagues in all the world 'cause they just so happened to be attacking during the time you were paying attention. But you'd fair make a fool of yourself, wouldn't you? Who's Celtic playing today? Dundee United away, I think. It'll be weird to see Pat Stanton playing for us. You hear his name and think Hibs, don't you? He's been their captain forever. Jock Stein swapped Jackie McNamara for him last week like we'd swap bubble gum cards at school. Which is funny 'cause I've got a Pat Stanton bubble gum card and d'you know what – everyone laughed – I got Tipp-Ex and painted white hoops round his Hibs top! Here's the stile. Takes you over the high fence to keep the deer out of the wood. The trees stop sudden and it's nothing but heather moorland all the way to the top of the mountain. Can't actually see Ben-y-Vrackie right now. I can follow the path up the moor only so far then it's lost in the mist but down here it's clearing away. I'll wait here for Mo and Finn. Sit on the grass by the burn. Have a sandwich. It's a bit eerie 'cause the fog makes everything so still and quiet. I can hear the rustle of my anorak when I move my arms and the fast running water in the burn. The babbling brook, if you're a poet. Little creek, if you're a cowboy. Stream of consciousness, if you're Mrs*

MacCarthy. Write what you think, she says. That's what stream of consciousness is, she says. Okay, okay, I thought, I can do that. Why are you making us do this? Why can't we do stuff like Mr Keith's next door? His class is always laughing and enjoying themselves. They get to do outdoor stuff. They get to write about stuff they see outside in the sunshine not stuck in here in a boiling hot classroom on a hot day. So why, eh? Why? And how come you're so biased to the girls anyway, Mrs MacCarthy? How come they always get out first at interval and dinner time and home time? How come you always pick a girl's painting to put up on the wall or a girl's poem to read out as good work? How come you're always getting at the boys every chance you get? Doing us down? How come you're always going on about women's rights like it's our fault? What did we do? We're 11 years old! I swear, it never even crossed my mind that boys were better than girls till you put the thought in my head and made us stand up and have a big classroom debate about it. Used to all get along fine with the girls. Now everything's an issue. That's why we – all the boys, that is – started chanting 'biased, biased, biased' under our breath when you let the girls out first again, as usual, the other day. It's just not fair. We think you've got a real chip on your shoulder about something but, you know, we never put it there. Why should we suffer for it? At least, that's what I would've written if I'd done stream of consciousness for real like Mrs MacCarthy told us to. But I'm no fool. She was only gathering intelligence on us. Seeing who was against her. It was a trick. I just made up a whole lot of drivel like I'd been helluva inspired by the word 'stream' in stream of consciousness. That's where I got the idea of babbling brooks and poets and little creeks and cowboys, that sort of thing. She liked what I'd written a lot. Told me so. She'd probably have read it out to the class as an example of good work 'cept, of course, I'm handicapped: I'm a boy. So she read out Mairi MacLeod's one instead, all about Mairi's poncey pony called Prince, and how Mairi wishes he had wings like Pegasus, the *amazing flying horse of Greek legend, and how she'd like to go flying around on his back, and all the exciting places she'd like to go to visit like Arabia and the pyramids in Egypt and that. It was really quite good, actually. We were rapt. Mairi's pretty good at that sort of stuff. I don't know where she gets it. I'd never even heard of Pegasus. That's maybe not such a good example of Mrs MacCarthy's bias, is it? Mo and Finn could tell you better ones. Where are they? You don't think I've got our plans mixed up? Where else could they be on a Saturday? Aw, shit! I know: Muirton Park. I remember now. Saints-Raith Rovers. That's where they've gone. We had arranged to go fishing. That was the plan. Then there were the gales a couple of days ago and we weren't so keen, said we'd see how the weather looked on Saturday. Then Mo says his dad had offered to drive us to the football and his dad had even okayed it with my mum over the phone, said he'd look after us, keep us out of trouble, take us to the stand. It was all set. So they're not going to catch up with me after all. Aw, man, I really wanted to see the game. They've gone without me. I'm stuck up this stupid mountain. I don't want to go fishing. I just wanna go home. Ach, but then, I've come this far. I may as well go all the way. That sex education we got last week was a joke, man. The girls went to one end of the classroom to talk to Mrs MacCarthy and we went to the other end to talk to Mr Keith. I kept taking peeks behind my back at Mrs McCarthy's group, trying to lipread. I wanted to know what Mrs MacCarthy was saying to them. I was worried. She was probably telling them how shitty all boys are, always. That'd be Mrs MacCarthy. She's got a bee in her bonnet about something. All Mr Keith talked to us about was 'cleanliness'. How it's next to 'Godliness'. How we should keep our private parts very clean. But not rub ourselves too long with a towel to get dry 'cause that might lead to unclean thoughts. He must've talked for about an hour and I was really paying attention but I didn't get it. It was like he was speaking in crossword clues. I didn't like to ask any questions in case I was the only one who didn't understand what he was saying. Nobody asked any questions. So Mr Keith (Mr Keech, older boys call him, for some reason) said: 'Well, that's it. Thanks for listening, boys. Glad I don't have to do this for another year.' I was more confused than ever. I mean, I know what goes where – I am 11, y'know. It's just there are a few wee mysteries to me, I was hoping for a few wee reassurances about this and that, nothing serious like, just wanted to know a bit more, but I sure wasn't going to ask any stupid questions in front of everyone else. Later, I asked Karen Lynch what the girls had been talking about and she said: 'Sanitary towels and stuff.' And I nodded like I knew all about them but, fact is, I don't. Are they like bath towels? Thing is, towels came up in our talk too. I never realized how important towels are in all this. I never knew they were so significant. Nobody tells you. Next time James or Jackie's home I'm gonna get all the gen on towels. I can see the way ahead now. What the hell! I'll keep on going. I don't need my pals. This'll be my epic, solo, one-man adventure. The mist's lifted enough for me to see high up the Ben, not to the very top, that's still in the clouds, but most of the way up. I'll have a wee drink from the babbling brook before I leave base camp for good. It may be some time before I reach water again. I mean, fair do's, I've still got half a bottle of Cream Soda and a can of Coke in my haversack, but there's nothing quite like the taste of a mountain burn, is there? It's easy for me to put my hands down like I'm praying to Mecca and stoop till my lips are kissing the water and I can sook some up. I can hear a sheep baaing. They piss in this water, y'know. I dunno, how fresh is water that's filtered by heather and nothing else? How come the banks of the stream look so brown, like rusting iron? That's rusting iron ore probably. Rusting iron and sheep's piss, that's what I'm drinking. Mmn! Still, doesn't rot yer teeth like cola does. I'm off up the hill. A solo expedition now. Only one man brave enough to attempt it. Air Commodore Brigadier Admiral Sir Joseph Copeland the third, Esquire of the Marine Commando Corps of the SAS. Me. James wouldn't approve of that. His own brother in the army. James used to come out in a rash at the mere sight of a uniform. He'd never wear one and actually mean it. I mean, he's got a Red Army surplus coat for the winter, like. Yeah, but say I'm a double agent, right? I've infiltrated the military at every possible level. I've won all kinds of medals of distinction. But really all the time I'm working for the Communists. Not the Soviets. They're really not doing it right. Nah, the proper, brand new, practise-what-they-preach freedom-fighters. That's who I'm really working for. That's who I'm undertaking this dangerous solo expedition for. Them and Great Britain. Well, Scotland first and foremost. Me, I'm f-u-c-k-e-n fearless! My only weak spot. My only Achilles heel. Is Catriona. 'Specially now. After The Shows last Friday. After The Waltzers. Just me and her. If the enemy were to capture Catriona and threaten to kill her unless I gave up my mission I'd have to put my ideals on hold. She's more important than any principles. Your principles are worth nothing if you put them before love. Mind you, what I'd do, right, is find out where they were holding her captive; slip a gas mask through the bars of her window; slide a smoke grenade under the front door and take all the guards out; run through the smoke – so fast I wouldn't need a mask – fix dynamite to the lock on Catriona's cell, tell her to lie down behind a mattress or something and blow the door open. Ka-boom! We'd run out of there, me and Catriona, hand in hand. I'd probably have injured my chest a bit and she'd have to wrap bandages round my torso and I'd wince a little but try not to show how much it hurt. I'd obviously be taller than I am, without such a moon face and such a stupid haircut 'cause my barber just never listens. A bit older-looking than I am now and she'd actually have a bit of a chest herself – I mean she wears a bra now but she doesn't really need to – and we'd kiss and cuddle and, you know what, prob'ly get some towels involved somewhere, my injury permitting. There's a second stile up here where the path divides. I have a choice. I could follow the well-worn path which I know eventually leads to the high loch at the bottom of the mountain or the two or three other paths here which have been worn by the sheep and could lead to the lower loch or way into the wild purple nowhere. Moorland oblivion. Ach, live a little. I'll go off the usual track. Try to reach the other loch. The lower loch of fabled legend to the East. I've been once before, with the school, though we didn't go this way. Visibility is about half a mile I'd say but it's hard to judge when the landscape's so samey. All undulating heather. Sounds a bit rude that, doesn't it? (Mo and Finn'd laugh.) Big Heather always picks me, for some unknown reason, when it's the girls' choice at Scottish Country Dancing in the gym the month before the Christmas party. It's embarrassing. I get a right beamer. Catriona's too cool to run. Which is all good and well. But sometimes I just wish she'd sprint for me. I always end up getting flung around by Big Heather who, although she's an awful nice person and I do quite like her, is a very dominant dancer – very much in charge, very much the lead. I think Catriona will have to think about running this year otherwise she'll end up with the dregs, y'know, after a catch like me's been caught. She's had to dance a couple of times with Paul and he's a stranger to soap. Me and Catriona – it's a bit special now, after The Waltzers last Friday. We never get to waltz in the gym. Just as well, all that twirling might make Catriona puke again. The dancing's all right. Can be quite a laugh, actually. I wouldn't probably tell anyone that, though. Don't get me wrong, I'd rather play football, I honestly would, but it's nice sometimes, holding a girl's hand and trying to be nice to them and show them we're maybe not the enemy Mrs McCarthy would have us after all. Sooner play football, though. Best games I ever play are at interval or dinner times which it's just a couple of coats for goals. Not a full-sized pitch, Boy's Brigade game where, by the time you've ran the length of the pitch, you're too out of puff to do anything. Just a wee pitch, the same size for us proportionally as a big pitch is for professionals. Although the likes of wee Jimmy Johnstone, he could play on our pitch.*

It'd be proportional for him. It's a blast. A rush. Getting the ball, bit of Jinky dribbling, past one, past two, and then an inch-perfect cross to whoever's waiting in the middle. Sometimes just hitting it high across, not so much to aim for someone's head as to feel the whack of the ball on my foot and just watch it arc so sweetly into space. And if it falls in a good position just out from the goal I can always bawl at my team-mates and ask where were you? Like they should've read what I was trying to do. Passing's my thing. I'm not bragging, I'm just telling it like it is. But I can pass a ball exactly where I want to nine times out of ten. It's a pretty good ratio. I can place it just ahead of someone to run onto so they don't break their stride. I do it so sweet. Feels so good. But, put me in front of open goal. A clear-cut chance to score, just the keeper to beat, all I need to do is keep my shot on target and we've won the game, next goal's the winner, Scotland-wins-the-World Cup sort of scenario? That's when I bottle it. Balloon it. Sky it, high over the bar. Or wide past the post. Or, worst of all, slice it so it spins behind me like a clowning trick shot. Or even worse than worst of all, I take a big hefty swipe at the ball, miss it completely and fall on my arse. Scoring's not my strong point. The blood rushes to my head. It's too much. I know the answer to my problem is that I should be passing the ball into the net. Then I'd place it just right. But I can't delude myself into treating a scoring opportunity like a simple pass. It's the glory of scoring, I'm anticipating too early, which puts me off. I'm hearing the crowd cheering and celebrating before I even shoot. Hear the whistling? It's the wild wind you get on the mountain. It's almost like an animal in the distance crying out in pain or like a wolf howling. It is just the wind I think. I'm not scared. Even on my own. There used to be wolves up here. Packs of Highland wolves. Finn says they had to bury dead people deep in the 15th century 'cause wolves would dig up their bones to eat. Imagine that! There were wild boar then as well. Bears too. Scottish bears used to fight in the colosseum in Rome. Finn said! Finn's a great one for finding things that sound like they're as made up as the bullshit the rest of us say to impress each other but actually turn out to be true. All manner of things used to live in Scotland once. But they've all died out. Extinct. Dead as a dodo. But what if, say, a small pack of wolves manage to survive unbeknown to everyone through the centuries in an isolated little cave up in the mountains? It's possible, isn't it? I think so. More possible than a prehistoric monster surviving through the centuries in Loch Ness, waiting for the entire population of the world to be dropped in for it to feed on. I feel a little uneasy. Wolves and bears and monsters. It's okay to talk about stuff like that when there's a whole bunch of you and you can have a laugh but it's not so good when you're on your own. I feel like I'm being watched or something. Or something is watching me. I turn my shoulder real quick to try and catch whatever it is unawares but I don't see anything. And now that I've done that it knows I know it's there. Which can't be good. I'm not scared, though. Not me. I'm just going to keep on going where I'm going. The lower loch. This way. Walking a bit faster to get there. Can't give up or show any fear 'cause the thing is I'm actually being filmed for a survival documentary. 'You join me as I undertake to make the perilous descent through dense vegetation into an uncharted area of the Amazon basin never before walked by a white man. A place infamous among the local tribespeople for the dangers of such dangerous creatures as the anaconda. The anaconda snake has been known to grow to the size of 17 double decker buses and to crush cars into metal boxes like car crushing machines. Imagine, if you will, what such a creature such as this could do to a person. It would be a fate worse, much worse even, than Big Heather stepping on your toes in the military two step.' Heather has a natural bounciness. A springiness. The old highlanders used to use it to stuff their mattresses. Probably. 'Will y'go lassie, go? And we'll all go together to pluck wild mountain thyme all around the blooming heather, will y'go lassie go?' I can sing that at the top of my voice here, just for the hell of it, and no one's going to hear me or wonder why I'm singing that song. Makes me forget I'm on my own if I belt it out. But it's awful, extra quiet when I stop. Don't think I'll sing again. Too much of a contrast to stop and just hear the wind whistling and a few sheep baaing. More of a meh, anyway. I can survive out here no bother. My survival book tells me how to use all the plants of the forest and the jungle for food and medicines and dyes and clothes and teas and food and all sorts really. Heather moorland like this is to me what William Low's supermarket is to you. If only I had The Knowledge. We've lost The Knowledge of how to use the everyday stuff that grows for free. Y'know how you pick dock leaves when you get stung by nettles? Well, with The Knowledge you'd know all the right things to pick to cure everything from cancer to the common cold. Thyme – that might be all it takes. I mean, when was the last time scientists checked out the properties of thyme? Maybe it's evolved into something else. Maybe now they've got new stuff they can add to thyme that'll make it a cure-all. Who knows? I'm not a scientist, I only know the song: 'Will y'go lassie, go?' I love Catriona. I wish she was here. Just me and her. Can you imagine? That'd be so cool. Me and Catriona alone. We could kiss! See if we like it. I'm hungry. I wonder what time it is now? Should've brought my watch. I reckon it must be about lunchtime. The mist's cleared away enough for me to see the top of Ben-y-Vrackie. I can see a couple of walkers in the far distance on the usual path. They haven't seen me, no way. You'd have to know where to look. I see them 'cause I know where the path is and 'cause they're wearing bright yellow and red cagoules. Can't miss them. They don't know there's a trail down here to where I am overlooking the lower loch now. I've got a dark anorak on. Camouflage. There's no way they'd see me. They're just keeping on walking. They might be a search party. A hit squad. Despatched with a mission to assassinate me before I can complete my solo expedition to reach the lower loch where the special documents on the atomic bomb ingredients are stored. I must reach them first and deactivate them before they fall into enemy hands. Save the world before teatime, man, that's my mission. First, I'll sit in this wee hollow – it's dead comfortable and it's a nice view above the loch – and open up my sandwiches bag again, have my last Marmite sandwich. Crack open a lukewarm can of Coke. Most of it fizzes over my hand, sticky and brown onto the heather. I've been here before on a school trip. Here, at the lower loch. Earlier in the summer, in fact. During the heatwave. Mr Keith took us. Just the boys. Mrs MacCarthy took the girls to a matinée at the theatre. It was a really hot day and Mr Keith suggested we go skinny-dipping in the loch. 'Course we couldn't believe it. Thought it was a great idea. Like we were American or Australian kids or something. Mr Keith swore us to secrecy afterwards. Because obviously, as he said, he wouldn't ever be able to take us to the loch again if the teaching authorities heard about it. There were safety rules to adhere to and he'd only let us swim 'cause he knew we were very responsible. Mind you, I don't know why we couldn't have just kept our underpants on. It was so hot they'd have soon dried out but Mr Keith insisted we took them off. He didn't go in. He just sat on a rock and watched us all intently in case any of us got into difficulties. It seemed like a great idea, in theory, and we didn't need much persuading: it was a blistering hot day, we were hot from walking, we needed to cool off. Only problem was it was a mountain loch, for God's sake, it was absolutely freezing and your feet sunk to over your ankles in the brown squelchy mud at the bottom. We all pretended we went skinny-dipping every day of the week and weren't embarrassed at all. As we concentrated on looking at each other only above shoulder height and tried to stay in water above our waists. What with all of us splashing about, having a laugh, the pure, clear water turned shit brown. I went home covered in a thin layer of silt. Had to have a bath soon as I got in. So much for Mr Keith's ideas of cleanliness. Still, nobody grassed him. I wouldn't have gone in if it had been the Amazon River, mind you. I read in my survival book about this tiny catfish they've got there. Well, it's not pleasant but, fact is, say you're pissing into the Amazon? Well, this catfish, apparently, can swim right up your thing, actually inside it! Imagine that! Then it gets stuck by its fins. I'm not messing. I'm not making it up. That's what my survival manual says. That's only Brazil, of course, but, to tell you the truth I'm not at all keen on wading into the water with nothing on, not here, not there, not anywhere. All I need's my worms and I'll have a few casts into the loch from here. See how I get on. Where are my worms? Aw, man, don't believe it! No Mo, no Finn, and now I've forgotten to bring the jar of worms. Must've left it by the back door. I'll have to find some up here. Under that stone, for instance. No, nothing there. It's actually very dry. The roots of the heather look a bit like worms, maybe I could put a heather root on the end of my hook. Would that fool the trout, d'you think? Doubt it. Okay, okay, what would Joe Copeland SAS man do in these testing circumstances? He'd make do, wouldn't he? Improvise and survive. I can make a delicious fly to catch a trout. Use a little bit of stick, like this one off the ground, no bigger than half a match. That's the fly's body. Now I need a feather. That'd be the thing to make it look like a fly. No feathers around that I can see. C'mon, Joey, improvise to survive. Okay, maybe if I use a little bit of sheep's wool left on the trail somewhere. Ach, you can never find things when you need them, can you? What'll I do? Maybe if I take a little of the lining out of the hole in the sleeve of my anorak I can use that. Tie it round the little stick. You only need a tiny bit of fluff. It's a fiddly operation. Loop the fishing line round here and tie it – oops! – dropped it. Shit, it's blown away. Okay, here we go again, get another piece of fluff from the lining, loop it round and around again, tie it in an ever-so-sophisticated double granny knot. And there it is! A monster mutant fluff fly. But will the trout know the difference? 'Course they won't. They're thick, they are. Couple of tiny lead weights on the line and I'm ready to cast. Here goes. Swish! Whoa! The wind's actually blown the line behind me about six feet into the heather. Wind it back in again. Hey, I like that! My monster mutant fluff fly's got a bit of colour now with a pink, purply flower off the heather stuck on the hook. Might just do the trick if I could only get it in the water. I'll walk round a bit and get my back to the prevailing wind. Cast wind-assisted. Swish! That's better. A good 12 feet into the water. Good, all things considered. Those fly-fishing guys. What do they know? With their fancy flies in their hats and their fishing permits and their wee hip flasks and all. Not like me here, battling with the elements, improvising, making do. Me against the world. See if I do catch a fish, right now? That'll mean not only am I going to play for Celtic but I'm also going to marry Catriona and we'll have three kids, one boy, one girl and one other of either. I'll leave the last one up to God. Ach, I know they're all up to God. See up here? Where the air is fresh and it's so quiet? It's a lot easier to imagine God, isn't it? Feel like you could speak to him. Have a heart to heart. 'Hey, Big G! How y'doing? It's me, Joe Copeland, but then you know that, don't you? I know you know that 'cause you know everything I'm thinking. Everything I've ever thought so I'd probably be boring you to say anything out loud, wouldn't I?' See me? Out here in the middle of nowhere on my own like this? It's like Jesus in the wilderness. My mum says everyone has to serve their time in the wilderness to understand and appreciate everything when they get back. See if I catch a fish now? Ach, it'd just be nice to catch a fish. See there! See the splash? That's a monster-sized trout after my mutant monster fluff fly, that is. I'll cast again. Get it out as far as I can beyond the reeds. Get it near to where that trout jumped. Doesn't half look stupid that fly. The heather's fallen off. Doesn't look like any fly I've ever seen. Maybe some undiscovered fly in Madagascar. I'll wind it in. If only I could tie some yellow and orange thread on it, y'know, brighten it up. Might look more appetizing. Everything I'm wearing is blue or black. Blue jeans. Blue jumper, black t-shirt, blue anorak. Pants are ... red! If I just take a wee piece of thread off the hip side of my pants where the stitching joins up, that'll maybe do the trick. Right, here we go ... six centimetres of red thread ... wrap it round the fly and tie it in a knot. Okay, I admit, it's not a pretty fly, but it looks fat and some hungry trout with poor eyesight might think it's a treat. Here goes. I'll cast it far into the very deepest part of the loch. Swish! Or even just a few feet out. That'll have to do. Maybe, if I leave it there. I suppose you're meant to keep whipping it out of the water and back again to look like a fly landing in the water for a moment before flying off. That's supposed to make the trout jump and get it straight away. Maybe I'll develop a new kind of fishing. Mutant Monster Fluff Fishing. Aw, fuck this! I've had enough. I'm catching nothing today. Wind in the line, hook the hook onto the fishing rod. Time to go a wee dander, see where it takes me. Off the beaten track along another of these wee sheep tracks for a while. On patrol. Hold my fishing rod pointing down to the ground like a rifle. Eyes watchful for snipers and vipers. I've never been along this way before. If I just go over the brow of that hill there. See what I see. The heather's bouncy. I'm springing along like a kangaroo. If my friends could see me now. I wish Mo and Finn were here. Hey, look how far I am from the loch already! Don't seem any nearer the top of the hill, though. Keep right on to the end of the road! Keep right on to the ... Jee-sus! Those grouse freak me out when they jump out of the heather in a right flap. Oh, yeah, now I find some feathers, when it's too late. There's one there, I'll take it just in case I want to make a super mutant feather fly. I'm warming up again with the walking. The sun's come out for the first time but it isn't warm enough to just stand about. It's been pretty overcast. The weather becomes pretty important out here. Most of the time it doesn't matter a jot. My father watches the weather every night on tv avidly, like it's vital he should know, as if it's going to affect the way he drives the car to the school and stands in the classroom teaching Physics. It matters out here, though. At the mercy of the elements. The mist's all but gone now. I quite like being all alone out here on my own. I don't mind. James and Jackie, they always were around for each other, fighting all the time, and now they've left home it's just me, but I don't mind. It's hard work walking over the heather when there is no path. Funny stuff. They burn it, you know. To encourage fresh green shoots to grow 'cause the grouse like it better that way and it means there'll be more grouse for shooters to shoot. Sometimes, when they're burning it, Ben-y-Vrackie looks like an erupting volcano. From West Moulin Road, it looks like the whole mountain's on fire. And it's easy to imagine it spewing out molten rocks and lava. Real easy. Krakatoa. East of Java. Here I am at the brow of the hill and what is there to see? Another wee brow of another wee heather hill. More undulating heather. A great big bouncy desert. 'Cept what's that? It's looks from here like a wee wooden door in the middle of nowhere. I'll go take a closer look, see what it really is. It is a wee wooden door. I've stumbled upon the gateway to another dimension. Or maybe it's just a hide for the shooters. Built into the ground. I'll open it, go inside. Feels warm to be out the wind. There's a wooden bench to kneel on and a slit opening at eye level to place the barrel of your gun and watch for prey. The ground is littered with empty Eley shotgun cartridges. What would they shoot, though? I've seen nothing ... Shhh-it! There's a deer. Aw, man, it's beautiful. A wee lost Bambi. Where's ma gun? Naw, it's really pretty. I'll just crouch down here and watch a while, see what it does. D'you know who it looks like? Nadia Comaneci. She's only three years older than me. Winning gold medals in Montreal. Getting perfect ten-out-of-tens. She's coming up real close to the bunker. Not often you get this close to a deer. Aw man, does that dumb doe not see me? It's only 20 feet away. The wind's towards my face, it's making my eyes water. It can't pick up my scent. If I was a shooter I could just pop it right now. Couldn't miss. Venison, anyone? Never tasted it. I could open the door and jump up now and scream and give it a fright like grouse do to me. Like a jack-in-the-box. That'd be a laugh, to see it's face. Might die of fright, though. Do does die of fright? Oh, it's off. Off at some pace too. Something's spooked it. Me, probably. Must've heard me thinking. But would it notice me in here? Maybe it was something else. Something big that might know I'm trapped in this cubby-hole. Wild wolves. Bears. I'll just stay here till I'm sure the coast is clear. Have a bite to eat. Must be about teatime, d'you think? Gotta keep my strength up if I'm to fight off some wild animal attack. I should maybe think of getting back. What have I got left to eat? An apple, a packet of crisps, my Fry's Chocolate Cream and the I've-got-five-pence-what-can-I-get-for-five-pence? Caramac Bar. Well, I'm not going to starve, am I? 'Course, I wouldn't starve anyway 'cause I can live off the land. I can survive just eating stuff that grows naturally. James winked for some reason when he told me the wild mushroom illustrations were the most useful things in the book but I don't get it. There's plenty other useful stuff, I think. I never did get it when grown-ups winked at me when I was a little kid. Me, on the bus, in the park, sitting in the supermarket trolley, some old guy winking and pulling faces behind my mother's back like we shared some kind of secret. It was a mystery to me. 'Do I know you?' I wanted to say. It was innocent enough, though, I'm not talking about the ones who mean any harm. These old guys were just winking as if to say, 'Hey, kid! I was a kid once too y'know and I know what it's like. You don't want to be trailing round the soup and sauces aisle with your mum, do you? Naw! You'd rather be looking at the toys in Woolies or at home blowing watery paint with a straw.' Little kids don't get it though. They just get all shy and embarrassed and perplexed and cling to their mums. It's all right in here. A safe place. Safe from the elements. I may as well stay here a while till the rain goes off. It's a good place to have a wee nap after my tea then I'll get on down the hill before it starts getting dark. Check around for any adders. That's the one thing up here that spooks me. Though I've never seen one. I'm pretty tired now with all that fresh air. Use my haversack for a pillow. Have a wee rest then get going.

Special Agent Copeland, that's me. Daredevil Joe. Going home. Mission accomplished. Whatever it was. Just have a wee rest. The wind's getting up again. Whistling and howling like a pack of wolves. There are wolves up here, y'know, Finn says so. So it must be so, Joe. A whole pack of wolves that's survived the Ice Age and the Industrial Revolution and the French Revolution and the Second World War and Vietnam. That's what scared off Nadia. There's one! I can see a wolf! Really, I can. That'll be the leader of the pack. Look at him sniffing the air. He's picked up my scent. I'm a goner. It's real close to the opening of the hide. I'll have to try and scare him off. 'Gawngetouttavit!' He's startled. He's scarpered. Barking. Baying. Stops running abruptly when he senses he's out of range of any danger. He's reassessing things from a safe distance. It's only me, after all. He's not very scared. He's moving back, edging closer to me. What I need here, apart from a gun obviously, is fire. I'll start a fire. I've got some matches somewhere. There's some in my tobacco tin, peel off the seal, here they are. 'Gawngetouttahereyafleabittinold-muttya!' He's moved off again but not as far as last time. He's moving in. I grab a few dry sticks and dead bits of heather. C'mon, c'mon, burn, baby, burn. These matches are rubbish! That's two I've wasted. They can't be damp, it must be there's too much of a draft blowing in under the door. Ah, there it goes! We have light. We have fire. Light this smoking torch of dry tinder. 'Cept the smoke is choking me. Making me cough. Shit! The draft under the door's blown it out again anyway. Start again. The wolf is baying for my blood. Scratching at the door. I'll have to fight him with my bare hands. Kick him with the Hong Kong Phooey chop! C'mon! Come ahead, Mr Wolf. He's snarling real bad. I'm kicking at the door to scare him off. Psyching myself up for the scrap when I finally fling open the door. But wait. I've got something in my eyes. Smoke. A piece of ash. I rub my eye with my hands. I'm okay. It's all gone quiet. He must've given up and gone. I check through the gun-hole of the hide. I can't believe it, it's dark outside. Everything's unfamiliar and altered and sinister without daylight. I have to get back home in a hurry. The mist is forming again. It feels really cold outside the bunker. Which way now? I feel disorientated. Up to the brow of this hill, I think. I don't recognise anything. Everything looks completely different on the way back. I have to keep looking behind me to see if I remember anything from walking in the opposite direction. It's hard to tell. I run fast, stumbling and tumbling through the heather, panic rising. What if my mum calls the cops? My father will have kittens. The embarrassment of it. He'll kill me if I make it home alive. Just over the brow of this wee hill here is the loch, I'm sure, and I know where I am from there. Downhill all the way, shouldn't take me too long. 'Cept the loch's not there! Not where I left it anyway. No sign at all. This is not good. It's a deep corrie. Which way out? The mist is creeping down from higher ground like a fire blanket to snuff me out. The mountain rescue people and the police will be getting their gear together. RAF Search and Rescue will be sending out the yellow chopper from Leuchars. A Nimrod too, I daresay. A whole squadron of crack paratroopers. Who might shoot me by mistake. Calm down, Joe. What would the survival book say? I could navigate using the stars! Yeah, the stars. But I can only see one through the mist and the low clouds. Can you navigate with a single star? Nope. Plain truth is, I couldn't navigate from the constellations even if I could see the entire galaxy. I need to find a path or a trail heading down. Power lines. A road. So first I have to go uphill to get out of this corrie. The body of Joseph A. Copeland from Pitlochry was found in a remote corrie near Ben-y-Vrackie. No suspicious circumstances. Just a suspicion of stupidity. That's what they'd say. Wonder what kind of turn out there'd be for my funeral? Mum, Dad, Gran, James, Jackie, Mo, Finn, Catriona. Would the press turn up? Would they leave my bedroom as a shrine? Or would they turn it upside down and give everything to charity? Shit! The things I stole off Jackie I don't want them to find. I have to get back alive. I can't die now – the shame of it. I'm lost. I'm really lost. I don't know where I am. It's so cold. I can't find the main path. Just these thin, wandering, aimless sheep trails. It looks so deeply, densely dark. It must be getting on for three or four o'clock in the morning by now. On and on, along animal trails, through featureless moorland. I'm exhausted. I must rest. But if I lie down in the heather I might never get up again. I'll be eaten alive by adders and wolves and Great Caledonian Bears. What's that ahead? It's a house! I'm saved! I'll just ask to borrow their phone for a minute. 'Cept there's no lights on. No smoke from the chimney. No one lives here. No one's lived here for a very long time judging by the tree which is growing about 60 feet tall in the middle of the living room. It's all tumbled down. It's just a ruin. I ought to make a den here. A bivouac. It'd make sense. Use the ruined walls as two thirds of a shelter. Cover the rest with branches of the beech tree that's growing beside the fireplace. Make a move at first light. That'd be the sensible thing to do. That'd be what the survival book would advise. That's what Captain Lieutenant Joe 'Fearless' Copeland of the Green Berets would do in the circumstances. He'd make a den where the hearth used to be in the tumbled down cottage. But y'know, a lot more people lived up in these kinds of places once before the clearances. Before being turfed out for sheep. I don't know if there was violence involved here or what. I don't know if maybe some old witch lived here. Or if there was the Black Death or something here and they burned the place to the ground with everyone barricaded in. I don't want to hang about here. Might be disrespectful to stay uninvited. Can't just wander into someone's house and set up camp, can you? I'll collect a couple of broken branches which might come in useful for building a shelter far away from the haunted house. They make such a fearful noise as I drag them along, though. Drop them, leave them behind. I need to be able to listen for any dangers in the dark. I'm searching for a path. You'd think there might be one near an old house. I'm tripping over roots as I walk aimlessly away from the ruin.

Shh! I can hear a burn. That's a good sign. Head towards the sound of the water, find the burn, no bother. It's so flat where I am in the night that I have to crouch down to see which way the water's flowing to know for sure which way is downhill from this spot. Follow the burn downwards. Walk first on one bank and then, when rocks and heather and sloping banks get in the way, jump over to the other side. Easy peasy. Just follow the water down. Joe Copeland saves the day. The Epic Adventures of Joe Copeland. I'll reach civilization this way, or at least the coast. I keep walking. Stumbling. The dark gets even darker as I'm walking into these woods and there's trees overhead. And power lines. Pylons humming with electricity. Telephone wires on telegraph poles, nearby. Now we're talking! Now we're cooking with gas! Now I'm getting somewhere. If I can just grab the grass and the baby trees and pull myself up the banking I might get a better idea where I am now. I'm in a wood. But which wood, where? I've no idea. The birds have eaten the crumbs I left as a trail to find my way home. There's the lights of a house, though! The moving lights of a house? Headlights! A road. Maybe they're part of the search party who've been looking for me all night. Must be nearly dawn now. I'm not going to give myself up yet. Crouch down till this car has passed. Land Rover. The gamie's Land Rover with his big bad Alsatian dog in the back, barking like mad. All I have to do is follow the road and I'll get somewhere or other. Keep on going. My poor parents must be beside themselves with worry. They've probably had all the press round. Asking awkward questions. Has your son Joseph ever been convicted of a felony? Well, no, it was never proved. Okay, they were a type of apple they don't sell in the supermarket. But what does that prove? Apples. Lots of them. Stuffed down my football socks under my jeans till I walked like a zombie. But even so, your honour, your high holiness Mr Sheriff man, they tasted really sour anyway. They weren't even ready. They weren't even worth the worry of getting caught. There's the lights of Pitlochry now! I know where I am. Not far to walk. The raid was brilliantly planned and executed. Mrs Miller's garden. Me, Mo, Finn and Douglas Strachan wriggling along on our bellies, trying to avoid detection by the light sensor above the kitchen window. Through to the back garden where the five trees were. Dougie balancing on Mo's shoulders, Me on Finn trying to reach the apples without falling over and without laughing too much. The press would know all about it. They know everything bad about everyone. They have pictures in a drawer and they keep them till the time's right to print them. Dougie wouldn't have sold his story, would he? Hey, a signpost! Welcome to Pitlochry and 'A Hundred Thousand Welcomes' in Gaelic, which I can never pronounce or spell. There's a telephone box. I ought to call in. Tell everyone I'm okay, they can send the Nimrod home. How could you doubt I'd survive? I had my tin with me. I'm none the worse for a whole long night in the wilderness. But ach, that'd only hold me up, let's just keep on going till I get there. It's easy, downhill all the way. There's a car. Will I wave? They'll probably stop. There's the wee lost boy off the news. They're going to stop, are they? Do you realize the fuss you've caused young man? Your mother's been worried sick. Yeah, aye, I know, I know, I'm sorry, I'm sorry. No, they're not stopping. They don't maybe realize who I am. Maybe they haven't listened to the news. I'll take a short cut over these fields. I know the way. It's actually not far at all now. I'm tired. I don't know if I can face the press conference they're bound to want. Here we are. Home at last. Over this fence. Through the gap in the hedge. Cross the road. Slip in the back door and try to avoid all the police and press out front. It's pretty quiet. Everyone must be at police station headquarters co-ordinating the search. Feel for the key under the doormat. Open the door. The kitchen's warm. What time is it now on the cooker clock? Quarter to ten? Quarter to ten in the evening? No way! That can't be right. The fridge is humming to itself like nothing's changed. All's well. There's a message pinned under a magnet on the door: 'Watching The Duchess of Duke

Street *at Mrs Murray's. Dinner in fridge. Preheat oven to 220ºC. Cook for 25mins. Back about 10pm. Hope you enjoyed the match. Love M&D. XXX'*

• • • • • • • • • • • • • • • • •

Some kinds of aches and pains and misery are so self-conscious you've got time to choose a suitable location and even an accompanying soundtrack. *Georgy Girl* won't make the final playlist. Doesn't fit. Too bright, too breezy, too damn cheesy. Ray Charles' *Georgia on my Mind,* however, is a plaintive cert. So's *Rainy Night in Georgia* (the contrast of the lyrics and Randy Crawford's million-dollar smile only adding to the poignancy) and, hey, how apt, because it's raining tonight, here, in Aberdeen. Finally, *Midnight Train to Georgia* makes the list because, railway timetables permitting, it's actually an option. I could do that. Stand dripping on Helen's doorstep at an ungodly hour. Make a big statement. Some histrionics. Thing is, the thing I've been wondering lately is, if it's all so knowing and self-conscious does that mean it's insincere? What's best for Georgie? To try to hold on or to let her go?

Georgie used to cry in the night. Not often, but sometimes, like anyone does, well, any kid anyway. I'd go through to her room. She'd have had a bad dream. I'd give her a cuddle, whisper in reassuring tones about stuff to look forward to tomorrow at nursery, at school, make her forget her dream, take her to the toilet, tuck her in again, make sure she's warm, not too warm. And she'd fall asleep before I'd left the room. The only times she'd be hard to placate would be when she caught sight of herself in the dressing table mirror. Then she'd experiment with all the faces of misery she could pull, revelling in her tears, as if she was the only person who's ever cried. And then I'd get annoyed. Wouldn't be so patient. Not such a perfect father. It smacked of self-indulgence.

It's one of those nights. I watch trash tv till late,

hoping to fall asleep on the sofa but can't. I go to bed, try to sleep, but can't. Try to read, can't concentrate, try to sleep again, but can't. My chosen tracks go spinning round and round and round my head on a continuous dizzy playloop. Every time I look at the alarm clock it seems to say the same time: 4.25am. I have to pick it up and stare at the luminous second hand to see if it's actually working. My eyes take time to adjust and the clock remains stilled for an impossibly elongated second before catching up with me and returning to normal speed. I press the clock to my ear, listen to its tiny ticking. I guess I hope it'll sound reassuring (everything will pass in time) but it just sounds reproachful (see how you've wasted your time?). With every gust of North Sea wind, rain's flung onto the window like a handful of carelessly scattered seeds. There are worse places to be than George Street on a night like this: the trawlers, the rigs. That's a comfort, isn't it? A couple of weeks ago, at New Year, at midnight, at the bells, I'd opened the window of my flat and listened with a kind of melancholic pleasure to the mournful sound of the ships' horns in the harbour. I imagined Ukrainians and Filipinos on the boats, bringing in the New Year even further from home, from family, than me.

The nursery school once called to say Georgie'd had a bad fall, might need stitches, could I come to collect her? Told my Perth boss what had happened, where I was going. He'd have excused me, I'm sure, but I didn't wait for permission, I was out the door before words could form in his mouth. They could've locked me in a room and I'd have walked through the walls. I was Superman. Nothing could stop me. I drove carefully – to be stopped would've held me up – but fast, mechanically, single-mindedly concentrating on every possible time-saving decision, planning ahead, choosing the best lanes, the right turns, the shortest, most efficient route to the nursery school. My car had a flashing light on the roof, a siren, wings if necessary, whatever it took. Was the school nurse's definition of a bad fall the same as mine? How bad?

How many stitches? I wouldn't know till I saw it myself.

The other kids were preoccupied measuring sand in different containers while Georgie sat crying, dripping blood onto her white shirt, pressing an ice pack onto her forehead. The school nurse held her hand but Georgie was inconsolable. I thanked the nurse for calling me, lifted Georgie up, took her out the school, telling her it'd be all right, it didn't look too bad, I'd had worse playing football. We'd just go up to the hospital, let the doctors have a wee look at it, they'd only want to clean it up – and she quietened down a lot to know it wasn't the worst ever, even though it was the worst ever for her, and the worst ever for me to see her.

The nurse at the hospital spoke soothingly of rabbits and teddy bears and good things to do at school as she cleaned Georgie's cut for the doctor. The doctor shone a light into Georgie's eyes, looked in her ears, up her nose, asked if she'd been sick, asked her how it happened, told her she was good, she was brave, passed her fit and gave me a leaflet on head knocks should any more serious symptoms develop. Finally another nurse came in, asked Georgie the same questions, spoke in the same soothing way, stuck five paper stitches over the wound, said they shouldn't be washed off for five days.

She'd fallen in the adventure playground. Nobody's fault, though I still felt a nagging guilt it should happen on a day when Helen was working out of town. I should've been there to catch her. I took the rest of the afternoon off: we went home via the newsagents, Georgie slept for a couple of hours, woke to fantastic treats of comics and sweets.

Aberdeen sleeps on oblivious. I get up, get dressed. Stare out the living room window, looking for Georgie's lighthouse silhouetted in black against the low, night sky. The watchtower looks less brutal to me now. I heard it's where Richard textiles used to hang fire hoses for lining with rubber. Not so threatening after all, then. It emanates no light. It's a darkhouse sending a beam of dark circling round the city but I've grown oddly attached to it. I'd sign a petition if they ever tried to knock it down.

I walk down the stairs, the wooden stairwell echoes with every step in the dark, waking my nameless neighbours the same as the nights they've woken me. I open the door of the close, stand a moment on the threshold. The wind slaps me once, rain stinging my face like a boxful of dressmaking pins. Pull my collar up, then I'm walking, just walking, don't care where.

CCTV cameras follow my progress through the empty streets. They must have thought they'd finished auditioning for tomorrow's Sheriff Court. If I could only throw a stone, score a direct hit, smash the lens of their prying eyes. They'd jump back in their seats. One of their screens blinking blind. I'd get some peace, some privacy, till I walked into range of the next one.

Union Street's lit brighter than daytime. Deserted, save for hundreds of mannequins staring fixedly from the clothes shop windows. Slaves to fashion. The Christmas lights are down now. There's flapping bunting strung across the road and adverts for a show at the theatre. Between occasional taxis and long-distance container lorries, the gulls reclaim the street, fighting over spilt take-away before the Council's street-cleaning truck polishes the kerbs. On and on a shop alarm rings out, ignored. I press the button at the traffic lights, what the hell, and the sound signal whines like a labrador puppy. I amble across the yellow grid at the crossroads where, midday, the traffic fumes would kill you if a Grampian Transport bus didn't get you first. I wander up towards the Castlegate. Look down Marischal Street to the harbour. Can't see the water from there. The ships look landlocked in granite. I sit on a bench below the Salvation Army citadel and look along the length of Union Street. The rain's soaked through my jeans and jacket, turned me a darker shade of blue. There's a rolling drunk in the distance. He looks no threat but it's better to keep moving, keep warm. Walking up King Street, I hear a baby squealing. It's unmistakable. Same as the first howling cry, first gulped breath at the maternity hospital. It's like a squeal of reproach that I missed Georgie's first cry. But it's just cats among the rubbish. Walk down Beach Boulevard where the boy racers cruise in the late evenings. I'm not thinking where I'm going. I have a vague idea I'll watch the sunrise at the beach. I start jogging to keep warm. A police car lies in wait. An officer on speedgun duty watches me run past. Calls in a description of my build, hair, clothes on police radio. I can't match any photo-fit for tonight because I'm left to keep on running.

Opposite the Beach Ballroom there are a few cars parked driver's side to driver's side even at this time of the night (maybe especially at this time of night). But I don't ask questions. They evil-eye me with suspicion but, really, I don't care. I've got that shield of indifference – invincibility, as a matter of fact – 'cause I've got nothing to lose. Nothing to lose worth more than I've already lost, I mean. I stop running when I'm near them to show I don't care.

Beyond the leisure centre, far beyond the last cars, I find a place away from other people. It's a luxury that's hard to find in the city even at this time. I sit there on the grass banking above the beach itself. The rain's eased off but it's a cold, harsh, penetrating wind that's whipping off the high tide as breakers smash onto the sand. I like the white noise of the waves and the wind and the gulls. I mean, it's not pleasant, it's not soothing, like those God-awful hippie tapes of whale noises and dolphins mating are supposed to be, but it stops me thinking, clears my head. Drowns out Gladys Knight and the Pips. I can taste the salt. Sense the all-engulfing, everlasting power of the sea for miles and miles and miles: corrosive, rusting and relentless. A ship's light blinks forlornly on the horizon, the sweeping beam from

Girdleness Lighthouse penetrates only so far before it's consumed by darkness.

Behind me the lights of Aberdeen, polluting the skies, making the clouds glow orange. Pittodrie stadium silent and deserted, as crowded with long-loved ghosts as the graveyard beside it. Crossed off, one by one, like numbers on a bingo card, the lights in the tower blocks go out each night, now they're few and far between, random lights behind multi-coloured curtains customising the uniform boxes. All those people. All those strangers. The Good People of Aberdeen. The Bad and the Ugly too. Muddling by, like me. I want elastic arms like Mr – fucken – Tickle. One arm stretched round Seaton, Bridge of Don, Bucksburn and Mastrick to meet the other stretched round Footdee, Torry, Kincorth, Mannofield and Summerhill. I'd clasp my hands together round about Lang Stracht and give the whole of Aberdeen a big squeeze. A big bosie.

There's no discernible moment when the dawn happens. The night fades out and day fades in on an imperceptibly slow dimmer switch. It's a gradual, grimy, industrial, North Sea sunrise with no sun and no daughter.

• • • • • • • • • • • • • • • • • •

Mrs Murray's late husband's Craven Mixture tobacco tin is so tightly packed with the apparatus of survival it hardly rattles. (Unlike Mr Murray, whose rattling, raking cough we'd heard through the wall as the original contents of my tin slowly killed the war hero in his carpet slippers.) As if this is the emergency I've been waiting for all my life, I fetch a sharp, no-nonsense knife from the kitchen. It seems a small-sized shame to open the survival kit now, I mean, after all this time, after everything that's happened since. A small-sized shame, like spearing and slicing through the perfect pink and white icing of a wedding cake with a shared knife. Seeing the sugar-sweet perfection crack and crumble only to reveal a dry, unpalatable base. Just an ordinary, everyday, small-sized shame, like the fall-out from a nuclear family's simple, tidy symmetry broken up. That sort of thing.

I slice through the seal on three sides of my survival kit. Prise open the air-tight container. The lid's hinged on the gummed-up glue of old insulation tape, like stringy cheese on a pizza. An invisible tinful of 1973 escapes into the air: Ziggy Stardust and the Spiders from Mars meet the World Wide Web. It's a pocket V&A, a matchbox Guggenheim, a little bit of juvenile history rolled neatly and tightly into a tin of Craven Mixture. Cotton wool packed hard into any spaces to reduce tell-tale rattle in case I was lost behind enemy lines. There's everything here I remembered. Everything I'd expected: needles and thread; six Disprin tablets; safety pins; fishing line; barbed hooks; tiny lead weights; matches soaked in candle wax to make them waterproof; birthday candles; the tiny magnifying glass for making fire from the rays of the sun; James' electric guitar strings for snares; a pencil stub; little sheets of paper, cut to fit the tin; a razor blade and some Elastoplasts.

These I remembered. These I expected. But there were things I'd forgotten. Sugar cubes wrapped in a paper envelope snaffled from the genteel surroundings of the former Atholl Coffee Shop, now the Pitlochry branch of a video rental chain, which could have given me that necessary extra boost of energy required to reach the Swiss border ahead of pursuing Nazis. Acronyms of survival tips – D.A.N.G.E.R., S.H.E.L.T.E.R., H.E.L.P! – I'd once faithfully memorized and written in leaning, lop-sided, microscopic capitals on tiny pieces of paper, only to read now, when they might actually be useful, and not be able to recall what they're short for. There's a tiny compass too, no bigger than a finger nail. And I'm transported to a bus double-decked out with streamers. Sunday School trip to Craigton Park, St Andrews. Kids running wild on the grass, later on the West Sands. A miniature railway, trampolines, crazy golf, Zoom and Fab lollipops, big five pence pieces into gobstopper machines, a piece of gum and a throwaway gift in every plastic capsule. A fair and happy swap: my silly, useless, frivolous bracelet for Mairi MacLeod's essential piece of survival equipment. The tiny compass perfect for my kit. Pointer swinging unreliably on its pivot, one way, then another, changing its mind. Finding magnetic North all too resistible. And now, somehow, rust has reached it. The pointer's stuck on south-west. No amount of shaking will budge it. And what else? A cardboard ID card, free from a cereal packet, emblazoned with 'The Man from U.N.C.L.E.' above a picture of me. A head and shoulders from the photo booth in Woolies. So naïve and self-assured for one with such a wonky fringe. But the look in my eyes! Such absolutes and certainties. I recognize that look. The school picture in my keycard wallet. Georgie, a couple of years younger than I was then. See? *Exactly* the same look in her eyes: Hey, Nixon! Brezhnev! Come ahead!

# 11|9 Publishing October 2000

The Wolfclaw Chronicles
Tom Bryan
A powerful debut novel bridging the cultures of Ireland,
Russia, Canada, Scotland and England.
ISBN 1-903238-10-2
Price £9.99

Rousseau Moon
David Cameron
Lyrical, intense, sensitive, foreboding – a remarkable first
collection.
ISBN 1-903238-15-3
Price £9.99

Life Drawing
Linda Cracknell
The eagerly awaited first collection from an award-winning
writer.
ISBN 1-903238-13-7
Price £9.99

Hi Bonnybrig & Other Greetings
Shug Hanlan
Strikingly original short stories and a very funny novella.
ISBN 1-903238-16-1
Price £9.99

The Tin Man
Martin Shannon
A debut novel from a new and exciting young writer.
ISBN 1-903238-11-0
Price £9.99

Occasional Demons
Raymond Soltysek
A dark, menacing and quite dazzling collection from one of
Scotland's most talented new writers.
ISBN 1-903238-12-9
Price £9.99

About 11:9

Who makes the decisions?

11:9 titles are selected by an editorial board of six people: Douglas Gifford, Professor and Head of Department of Scottish Literature, University of Glasgow; Donny O'Rourke, poet, lecturer and journalist; Paul Pender, screenwriter and independent film producer; Jan Rutherford, specialist in book marketing and promotion; Marion Sinclair, former editorial director of Polygon and lecturer in publishing and Neil Wilson, managing director of 11:9.

Our aims

Supported by the Scottish Arts Council National Lottery Fund and partnership funding, 11:9 publish the work of writers both unknown and established, living and working in Scotland or from a Scottish background.
11:9's brief is to publish contemporary literary novels, and is actively searching for new talent. If you wish to submit work send an introductory letter, a brief synopsis of your novel, a biographical note about yourself and two typed sample chapters to: Editorial Administrator, 11:9, Neil Wilson Publishing Ltd, Suite 303a, The Pentagon Centre, 36 Washington Street, Glasgow, G3 8AZ. Details are also available from our website at **www.11-9.co.uk.**

If you would like to be added to a mailing list about future publications, either register on our website or send your name and address to 11:9, Neil Wilson Publishing Ltd, Suite 303a, The Pentagon Centre, 36 Washington Street, Glasgow, G3 8AZ.

11:9 refers to 11 September 1997 when the Scottish people
voted to re-establish their parliament in Edinburgh